"Little Molly's all grown up,"

Dylan said in amazement.

Molly blushed. "I haven't been called that in a long time. I guess you're surprised to see me." She gave him a smile that didn't quite reach her eyes.

"I am. Pleasantly." He came the half step forward, and he embraced her. She was warm and cushioned, and holding her wasn't half bad.

"You're wondering why I'm here," Molly said. "I mean, I'm sure it's nice to see me and all, but what do I want?" She pulled out a gold wedding ring. "Do you remember this?"

"Of course. I bought this for your sister," he said.

"Then you gave it to me, the day she married another man." She drew a deep breath. "You said when I was ready for an adventure, I was to bring the ring to you." Color stained her cheeks and she ducked her head. "Well, I'm ready for that adventure, if you're still willing...."

Dear Reader,

The blissful days of summer may be drawing to a close, but love is just beginning to unfold for six special couples at Special Edition!

This month's THAT'S MY BABY! title is brought to you by reader-favorite Nikki Benjamin. *The Surprise Baby* is a heartfelt marriage of convenience story featuring an aloof CEO whose rigid rules about intimacy—and fatherhood—take a nosedive when an impulsive night of wedded bliss results in a surprise bundle of joy. You won't want to miss this tale about the wondrous power of love.

Fasten your seat belts! In these reunion romances, a trio of lovelorn ladies embark on the rocky road to true love. *The Wedding Ring Promise,* by bestselling author Susan Mallery, features a feisty heroine embarking on the adventure of a lifetime with the gorgeous rebel from her youth. Next, a willful spitfire succumbs to the charms of the tough-talkin' cowboy from her past in *A Family Kind of Guy* by Lisa Jackson—book one in her new FOREVER FAMILY miniseries. And in *Temporary Daddy,* by Jennifer Mikels, an orphaned baby draws an unlikely couple back together—for good!

Also don't miss *Warrior's Woman* by Laurie Paige—a seductive story about the healing force of a tender touch; and forbidden love was never more enticing than when a pair of star-crossed lovers fulfill their true destiny in *Meant To Be Married* by Ruth Wind.

I hope you enjoy each and every story to come!

Sincerely,

Karen Taylor Richman,
Senior Editor

Please address questions and book requests to:
Silhouette Reader Service
U.S.: 3010 Walden Ave., P.O. Box 1325, Buffalo, NY 14269
Canadian: P.O. Box 609, Fort Erie, Ont. L2A 5X3

SUSAN MALLERY

THE WEDDING RING PROMISE

Published by Silhouette Books
America's Publisher of Contemporary Romance

To those who face life's adversities
with grace, humor and courage

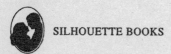

SILHOUETTE BOOKS

ISBN 0-373-24190-9

THE WEDDING RING PROMISE

Copyright © 1998 by Susan W. Macias

Printed in U.S.A.

SUSAN MALLERY

lives in sunny Southern California where the eccentricities of a writer are considered fairly normal. Her books are both reader favorites and bestsellers, with recent titles appearing on the Waldenbooks bestseller list and the *USA Today* bestseller list. Her 1995 Special Edition *Marriage on Demand* was awarded Best Special Edition by *Romantic Times* magazine.

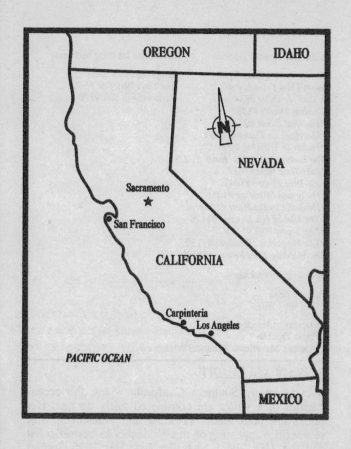

Prologue

"**D**early beloved, we are gathered here in the sight of God and this company..."

Molly Anderson tuned out the minister's words and sighed impatiently. She wasn't interested in the being gathered together or standing through what promised to be a long, boring ceremony. She didn't want to be here, and if the truth be told, her sister, the bride, didn't want her here, either. But their mother had insisted.

"Whatever will people think if little Molly isn't in the wedding?" her mother had asked. "Janet, make her one of your bridesmaids. You're going to have so many that she won't be in the way. If Molly is at the end of the line, she'll be up against the wall of the church. No one will even see her."

Molly raised her chin slightly and tightened her grip on her spray of peach roses. She knew she wasn't supposed to have heard that conversation. She hadn't *really* been eavesdropping. She'd just sorta been walking by the dining room. And it was her house, too, even if everyone seemed to forget that she lived there!

It didn't matter, she thought grimly. Janet hadn't wanted her to be in the wedding, and she, Molly, was only here because she'd been threatened with "severe punishment" if she didn't cooperate.

She shifted until she was able to lean against the wooden paneling of the church wall. The service continued. Molly watched without a whole lot of interest. This wasn't her idea of a romantic wedding at all. If nothing else, the bride and groom should be in love. But Janet was marrying Thomas because he was a successful lawyer and his family owned a huge law firm in San Francisco. Thomas was marrying Janet because she was beautiful. Janet got nearly everything because she was beautiful.

She made a stunning bride. Even Molly was willing to concede that. The silk-and-lace gown accentuated Janet's model-thin figure and sleek dark hair. She would look perfect in every picture. It wasn't fair, Molly thought as she tugged on the waist of her too-tight tea-length gown.

The style didn't suit her at all. For one thing, it was too sophisticated. At seventeen she was the youngest of the bridesmaids. She was also the shortest. Janet's friends were tall and willowy, like Janet herself. Molly didn't consider five foot four short, but compared with the rest of the family, she was practically a dwarf. Just one more reason she didn't fit in the family with—

The skin at the back of her neck prickled. Molly straightened, then turned to glance over her shoulder. A shadow moved into view at the rear of the church. The shadow became a man and her breath caught in her throat. Dylan! He was here!

She'd wondered if he would show up to see Janet marry

someone else. Was he tortured by the ceremony? Did he want to stalk up the center aisle and claim Janet as his own?

Molly was torn. Although she would have loved the drama of the event, she didn't want dumb old Janet marrying anyone as wonderful as Dylan. He was too…everything.

Knowing that her mother was going to kill her and figuring it would be worth it, Molly slipped down the side aisle toward the rear of the church. She moved quietly, and as far as she could tell, no one noticed her departure. As she stepped into the foyer, she saw Dylan had already walked out into the afternoon.

"Dylan," she called as she hurried after him. When she reached the stairs leading down to the sidewalk, she skidded to a stop.

His black motorcycle was parked at the curb. There were compartments on either side and a bundle tied onto the area behind his seat. Realization dawned, and with it a piercing pain in her chest.

"You're leaving." It wasn't a question.

He heard her and turned. "Hey, kid. What's up?"

She clutched her roses and stared at him. "You're leaving," she repeated. "Why?"

He shrugged. "There's nothing for me here. Not anymore."

It was one of those perfect spring days, the kind Southern California was known for. Bright blue sky, balmy temperature, a soft breeze. No doubt Janet had made arrangements for this weather well in advance. But all the loveliness of the day was nothing when compared with the beauty that was Dylan Black.

He was tall, just over six feet, with dark hair and eyes. His black leather jacket made his broad shoulders seem enormous. Jeans hugged his butt and thighs. He wore dark boots and an earring. Molly quivered just thinking about it all. He was her reason for living.

"You can't go," she said as she hurried down to stand next to him. "You just can't."

He gave her an easy smile, the one that made her forget to breathe. Dylan had first entered her life two years earlier, when Janet had started dating him. For the most part Molly hadn't paid much attention to her sister's boyfriends. They'd all been boring or stupid. But Dylan was different. Her diary was a testament to his virtues—as she saw them, anyway. The boys her own age had become insignificant by comparison. He actually noticed her and spoke to her. He teased her about being smart, seemed interested in her classes, and he treated her like a real person. If that wasn't heavenly enough, he never made fun of her braces, her bad skin or her baby fat. For the past two years, Molly had been praying Dylan would see what a dweeb Janet was and notice her instead.

She'd gotten the first part of her wish. Janet and Dylan had broken up, but her sister had been the one to end the relationship and Dylan hadn't turned to Molly for comfort.

"It's time for me to move on," he said now as he shoved his hands into his jeans pockets. "It's the way of the world, kid. But I'm gonna miss you."

"Really?" Her voice came out in a squeak.

"Sure. We're buddies." He gave her a sad smile that didn't reach his beautiful eyes.

Buddies? She bit back a sigh. Okay, she'd been hoping for more, but she could live with that.

"Where are you going to go?" she asked.

He shrugged. "Away from here. I thought I might try racing." He jerked his head toward his bike. "I'm pretty good on that thing."

"You're the best." She pressed her flowers to her chest.

If only she could ask him to take her with him. Molly exhaled. She might have a crush on Dylan, but she wasn't stupid. He was good to her, but he just saw her as Janet's little sister. If only she had a way of making him stay.

"You can't go," she said, remembering something important. "You promised me an adventure. With you. Remember? When I grow up."

This time the smile did reach his eyes. He stretched out his hand and touched her cheek. "Yeah, I remember. We're going away on my bike."

"Right. Well, I'm going to be grown up soon. If you're gone, how can I find you so we can take that trip? You wouldn't go back on your word, would you?"

"Come here," he said gruffly, and held out his arms.

In his worn leather jacket and scuffed boots, he looked like an outlaw. Molly had never been in love before, but she knew she would never feel this way about another man, ever.

She rushed toward him. He captured her and pulled her hard against him. The bouquet was crushed between them, but she didn't care. Nothing mattered but being close to Dylan.

She'd been hugged before, had even been kissed on a couple of very forgettable dates. But those had been boys and Dylan was very much a man. She tried to notice everything so she could remember it and think about it later. She had a bad feeling that he was going to leave her with little more than memories.

She laid her cheek against his shoulder and felt the cool smoothness of the leather. She inhaled the scent of him and absorbed the warmth of his body. He was strong and lean, and he held her as if she really mattered. Then he stepped back.

"I've gotta go," he said.

She nodded. "I understand. It's too hard to stay around here. You still love her."

One side of his mouth quirked up at the corner. "If this is love, it hurts like hell." He thought for a moment. "Tell you what, Molly. When you're all grown up and ready for that adventure, you come find me. Give me this. We'll go anywhere you want."

With that, he shoved his hand into his front pocket. When he pulled it out, he was holding a narrow, plain gold band. Molly sucked in a breath. It was, she knew, a wedding ring he must have bought for her sister.

"I didn't know," she whispered.

"There's nothing *to* know," he said. "I bought it, but then I never got around to asking her. Here, you take it. Bring me the ring when you're ready. Deal?"

He laid the ring in the palm of her hand. Molly closed her fingers around it and stared at him.

"Goodbye kid," he said, then settled onto his motorcycle.

Molly stood there and watched him drive off. It didn't matter that Dylan had bought the ring for Janet, that he'd actually wanted to marry her sister. It really didn't matter that Janet had been stupid enough to break up with him before he could propose. Molly had the ring now. As soon as she was finished growing up, she was going to find him and go away with him. She was going to make him fall in love with her and they were going to live happily ever after. She had his promise. A wedding ring promise.

Chapter One

Ten years later

"It's easier in the movies," Molly said as she leaned against the door frame and surveyed the mess that was her bedroom. In the movies or on television, when a character decided to escape from her life by packing up and leaving everything behind, there was an upswell of music, then the scene changed and she was on the road, or the plane or whatever. In real life, someone had to do the packing.

"As no one else seems to be volunteering, I guess that someone is me," Molly murmured.

She looked at the open suitcase on her bed, at the piles of clothing scattered around. There was a notepad on her dresser that listed the things she had to do before leaving. Stop the paper and the mail, check that her bills were paid. At least she didn't have a pet to worry about.

There was also the small issue of deciding where she wanted to go. Running away would be easier if she had a destination in mind. But right now, all she wanted was to go—to leave and never come back. Unfortunately, that wasn't an option.

She crossed to the bed and picked up a sweater. It was early May in Southern California, which meant warm days and cool nights. She tossed the sweater into the suitcase. Jeans were necessary, but did she need a dress? A dress or even a skirt and blouse meant panty hose and pumps, which were more than she wanted to deal with. Then there was the whole issue of the right purse and—

Molly swore under her breath. "None of this is important," she told herself. "Just *go*." She could feel the tears forming, tears that she'd promised herself she wouldn't be crying again. It wasn't supposed to keep hurting, but it did. If only she could forget. If only there were something she could do to fall asleep for the next couple of weeks until everything had been resolved.

She shook her head. It was going to take more than two weeks, she reminded herself. It could take months. So a year from now she would be fine, right?

She didn't have the answer. No one did. She sucked in a deep breath and blinked back the tears. She was strong and tough and she wasn't going to let the situation get her down. After squaring her shoulders, she crossed to her dresser and tugged out her lingerie drawer. She then returned to the bed and dumped the entire contents into her suitcase. If she couldn't decide what to take, she would take everything. That made life simpler.

She dropped the empty drawer onto the carpet and began quickly sorting through panties and bras. As she picked up a plain cotton sports bra, one of several she'd purchased recently, something caught her eye. A glint of light...a flash.

Molly fished around in the tangle of elastic and lace. As she pushed aside garments, the small object fell into a corner of the suitcase. She grabbed it and pulled it out.

For the first time in ten days, Molly smiled. She rubbed her thumb over the gold ring. Dylan's ring—the one he'd meant for her sister but had instead given her. It had been forever. Years. She sank onto the mattress. Whatever had happened to him? He'd ridden out of her life and disappeared, just like one of those western heroes she loved in the movies. Only instead of a trusty horse, Dylan had been astride his motorcycle.

She wondered where he was today. Did he still possess the same magic? There was a time when being close to Dylan had been enough to make her world right. She'd thought he was the most handsome, perfect male on the planet. She remembered how unattractive she'd been then, with her bad skin and braces, and winced. But Dylan had always had time for her. He'd made her feel special, and she would never forget him.

She slid the ring onto the third finger of her right hand. No doubt he was still breaking hearts at an alarming rate. Or maybe he'd grown up, like the rest of them, and was just some middle-aged guy with a wife, two kids and a mortgage. She tried to picture him driving a sensible sedan, but her imagination failed her. In her mind, Dylan would always be young and handsome, a dangerous rebel in black leather and boots.

Leaving the ring in place on her finger, she returned to her packing. She was folding a sensible long-sleeved cotton shirt when the phone rang. She knew who it was before she answered.

"I'm fine," she said as she picked up the receiver and cradled it between her shoulder and her neck.

"I could have been a salesperson," Janet said. "Then you would have felt really foolish."

"Nope, there was a definite 'Janet' sound to the ring. I knew it was you." She tossed the shirt into the suitcase, then sank onto the floor. "Seriously, I'm fine."

Janet sighed. The sound carried clearly down the length of the state. Janet and her husband, Thomas, lived in northern California, in Mill Valley, near San Francisco. "I don't believe you, Molly. And I'm worried. I know you tell me not to be, but I can't help it. You're my sister and I love you."

Molly pulled her knees to her chest. "I appreciate that and I love you, too. I couldn't have gotten through this without you. But you've gotta trust me. I'm doing okay." It was a small lie that shouldn't count at all.

"I considered coming down and spending a week or so with you. Until...you know."

Molly thought about Janet staying in her small condo and fussing over her. Actually, the idea had merit. She and her sister hadn't gotten along while they were growing up—a situation, they'd come to realize, that had been encouraged by their mother. But once Janet had married and moved away, the sisters had discovered they had more in common than they'd first thought and over the past ten years they'd developed a close, loving bond.

"As appealing as that sounds," Molly said, "you've got three kids and I know my nieces would never forgive me if I took their mom away from them, even for a short time. And to be completely honest, you miss Thomas when you're not with him. By day three, you're a whining mass of helpless jelly. You'd get on my nerves."

Molly said it lightly, partially because it was true and

partially because she was afraid she and Janet would do nothing but cry for the week. She needed a distraction more than she needed sympathy.

"Besides," she added, "I'm going away."

"You're right about the girls missing me, and how I get when I'm not with Thomas. Getting away is a good idea. Come see us. You know we'd love to have you."

"I want to," Molly said slowly. Oh, how she wanted to. Her sister and brother-in-law would pamper her, and the girls would help her forget. Family was healing. But… "I need a complete change of scene. I haven't decided where I'm going, but I'll let you know when I get there."

"I don't know whether I should push you into coming here or let you do what you want."

"You bossed me around enough when we were kids, so I think you should give me a break now."

Janet sighed again. "Fair enough. I'll trust you to know what's best. I'm just so frustrated. I want to *do* something."

"Tell me about it." Molly tucked a loose strand of hair behind her ear. As she brought her hand down, she noticed the ring on her finger. "Janet, do you remember Dylan Black?"

Her sister laughed. "There's a change in subject. Of course. He's the bad boy from my past. Dark and dangerous and so completely wrong for me. Thank goodness Thomas came along and rescued me from myself. I haven't thought of him in years. Why do you ask?"

"When I was packing, I found the ring he gave me. The wedding ring he bought you. I still have it, and finding it made me think of him."

"Let me see. He was at the ten-year high school reunion, although that was nearly five years ago. He has a custom motorcycle design firm in Riverside. Black something, I can't remember. The rumors were, he was doing well for himself."

"Interesting," Molly said, and changed the subject. They talked for a few more minutes, then Molly again promised she would think seriously about joining Janet and her family up north. If she didn't do that, she would at least let them know where she was going to be.

After the phone call, it took her another half hour to finish packing. Then Molly moved the suitcase into the living room, sat on her sofa and stared at the bag. Now what? Where did she go? She wanted to escape from her life for a week or two, to be in a place where she could forget what had happened, while trying to figure out what she wanted to do with her future.

A cruise? A train trip to New York? Maybe she could go to Acapulco and stay drunk for a week. Of course, one margarita made her silly, while two knocked her on her butt for the rest of the evening, so staying drunk would be virtually impossible. She needed a plan.

Her gaze fell on the ring. She turned her hand to make the gold glimmer. Even after all this time, she could still remember the thrill of that moment, when Dylan had given her the ring. Of course he hadn't meant it as a romantic gesture at all. It had been his way of letting her know that he hadn't forgotten his promise to her. That one day when she was grown up, the two of them would take off on an adventure. It seemed like a lifetime ago.

As Molly stared at the ring, an idea took hold. It was silly and foolish. She would be completely insane if she did it. After all, it had been ten years. He wouldn't even remember her...would he?

She rose to her feet. "It's a start," she whispered to herself. "A place to go in the morning." And she needed that more than anything. The rest of it didn't matter.

She would do this one crazy thing and visit Dylan Black, then she would go on from there. At least going to see him would give her journey a beginning. Maybe after that, she would head up north to stay with her sister. It didn't matter. All that she wanted was to run away so she could finally forget.

Dylan Black slammed down the phone and glared at it. Evie, his assistant, raised her dark eyebrows.

"Destroying the office equipment doesn't seem overly productive to me, but then, I'm just the hired help."

Dylan leaned back in his chair. "Tell me about it." He looked at her. "They're making the deal too hard to resist. I can't decide if I'm moving forward or selling my soul to the devil."

"If they're the devil, his prices have gone up. Most people I know would sell their souls for a lot less than several million dollars."

Dylan had to agree. But then, many people put much too low a price on their souls. He wasn't stupid. He knew exactly why they were tempting him—they wanted what he had. For them, this was a win-win situation. But what was it for him?

Evie shook her head. "You've got that pensive look about you. I hate it when you get like that, so I'm going to head back to the front office. If you need anything, buzz me."

"I will, thanks."

She closed the door behind her. Dylan turned his chair until he was staring out the window. The rugged, dry wilderness of the California desert stretched out behind the one-story complex. His critics said that establishing his custom motorcycle design firm, Black Lightning, out in the middle of Riverside had been a huge mistake. But the land had been cheap, there was a good labor pool and Dylan had wanted plenty of open space around him. It got hot as hell in the summer and he was nearly two hours from the Los Angeles International Airport, but all that was a small price to pay for autonomy. He'd poured everything he had into the company. In less than five years, he'd proved his critics wrong. Now he was touted as a visionary in the industry—the magician who set the trends. So why was he thinking of selling out?

He already knew the reason, and it had nothing to do with magic or even the devil. He was willing to sell his company because the deal on the table was too sweet to pass up. Not only was he being offered an obscene amount of money, but he had a guaranteed position in the new firm. He would finally have the resources to do all the research he wanted. He could design to his heart's content. All those projects that had been on the back burner could finally be explored. He would be a fool to pass up the offer.

Except for one detail. Along with the money and the new job offer came a boss to answer to. Dylan knew himself well enough to realize that would be a problem. The question was how big of one and could he live with the consequences? He would gain resources and lose control of Black Lightning. His lawyer had been on his back for weeks. After all, this was the chance of a lifetime. But his gut kept whispering that he had to wait and think this through. After all, he'd been the one to work twenty-hour days for all those years. The innovative designs were his. He'd taken the bikes on the racing circuit, sometimes giving them to riders so that new systems could be tested under the most grueling conditions. He'd poured himself into the company. How could he sell that? It would be like selling an arm or a leg.

Money versus principles. An age-old dilemma. Philosophers had been discussing that issue back when the earth's crust was still cooling. So which was it to be?

This would, he admitted, be a whole lot easier if he wasn't so much of a cynic. Years ago, when he'd still been a dreamer, he would have been insulted by the implication that he could be bought. If his then lawyer had even hinted at a buyout, Dylan would have shown him the door, then fired his corporate ass. When had life ceased to be so simple?

"The hell with it," he muttered, figuring he didn't have to decide right now. The interested company had given him two weeks to set up a preliminary meeting. If he still refused, they were withdrawing their offer. So he would wait until something changed, until he knew which side to fall on. In the meantime, there were reports to review.

He turned until he was facing his computer, then started tapping on keys. He'd just lost himself in the quarterly statements, when Evie buzzed him on the intercom.

"You have a visitor," she said. "Molly Anderson. She doesn't have an appointment, Dylan, but she says you'll remember her from several years ago."

It took him a second, then the memories clicked in place. Little Molly, Janet's baby sister. He *did* remember her, with her pale, curly hair and big eyes. She'd been a sweet kid—he recalled she'd had a crush on him. Usually that kind of stuff annoyed him, but in Molly's case he'd been flattered. Maybe because in her case he'd known exactly what she'd wanted from him. She'd been easy to read, and had had a basically good heart. He couldn't say that about many people these days.

"Send her in," he said.

He rose to his feet and crossed the room. By the time Evie opened his office door, he was there to welcome Molly. He had his arm extended and his smile ready. But the woman who stepped into the office wasn't the teenager he remembered.

She was still on the short side, maybe five foot four. Her curly hair had grown longer and she'd tamed it in a braid. Light makeup accentuated her large hazel brown eyes. He remembered she'd had bad skin as a kid, but time had changed that and now her cheeks glowed with natural color. Her smile was bright, her walk confident. A long-sleeved shirt and jeans accentuated a body that was generously curvy.

"Miss Anderson," Evie said, and left them alone.

"Little Molly's all grown up," he said, amazed she was here.

The woman in front of him nodded and blushed.

"I haven't been called that in a long time. I guess you're surprised to see me."

"I am. Pleasantly." He decided a handshake wasn't right for the situation. After all, this was Molly. He held out his arms. "For old times' sake?"

She came the half step forward and he embraced her. She was warm and cushioned, and holding her wasn't half-bad. But she seemed a little stiff and awkward, so he moved away and motioned for her to take a seat on the leather sofa placed in the corner of his office. Then he crossed to the wet bar by the bookcases.

"Soda? Wine?"

She shook her head. "No, thanks."

He settled next to her and rested one booted ankle on the opposite knee. He didn't have many unexpected visitors, and certainly not any blasts from his past. The intrusion didn't bother him; if anything, he was curious. "What brings you out here?"

She sat with her hands in her lap, her fingers twisting

together. "I'm not sure. I guess it was an impulse on my part. I hope you don't mind."

"Not at all. It's been years."

She nodded. "Ten. Not that I've been keeping track."

"You've grown up. You were always an adorable kid, but now you're a lovely woman." The line sounded smooth and sincere. Lines had always been easy for him.

She laughed. "And you're still as charming as ever. The truth is, I was homely, but I've improved some. I'll never be a cover model, but I'm okay with that."

He studied her. He couldn't remember the last time he'd thought about Molly, or even Janet, who at one time had been the love of his life, or so it had seemed when he was twenty-three.

She angled toward him. "I was talking with my sister and your name came up. I wondered how you were doing and I was heading out this way, so I thought I'd stop by. Is that too weird?"

"Not at all. I'm glad you did. So tell me about Molly Anderson. You're still using the same last name, so either you're not married or you're modern and independent, refusing to be shackled by society's expectations."

She gave him a smile that didn't seem to reach her eyes. "Not married. Let's see. I have a degree in accounting and I've been working as an accounts receivable supervisor for a telecommunications company in Los Angeles. I have the usual habits, both good and bad. I hear you're doing well."

He motioned to the office. "I design motorcycles. I didn't know I could make a living at something I love, so I'm generally happy."

Except for right now, he conceded, but he wasn't going to think about the decisions he had to make. Molly was an unexpected and surprisingly delightful distraction. He was suddenly pleased she'd looked him up.

He glanced at his watch. It was nearly noon. "If you have time," he said, "I'd love to take you to lunch. There's a great place about a mile down the road. Not much to look at, but they have the best hamburgers in the county." He grinned. "We can catch up with each other's lives, and I won't even make you ride on a motorcycle to get there."

"Sounds great," she said.

Thirty minutes later they were in a back booth of the restaurant. The waitress had already brought them drinks and taken their order. Molly was working her way through a margarita, while Dylan sipped his beer. He didn't usually drink in the middle of the day and he still had lots of work waiting for him back at the office, but he'd joined her when she'd ordered her drink.

As he watched Molly, he couldn't shake the feeling that something was wrong. She was more than nervous. Something about the way she kept glancing at him made him wonder why she'd come to see him. Her body was stiff, as if she were uncomfortable. She'd dodged all but his most basic questions, as though she didn't want to talk about her personal life.

He felt the attention of the other patrons. The town was small enough that everyone knew everyone else, if not by name then by sight. He didn't bring many women to this place, and those he did bring were nothing like Molly. He had a definite type—tall, leggy and brunette. He'd formed a fondness for that kind of woman when he'd dated Molly's sister, Janet.

"I know what you're thinking," Molly said.

Dylan shook his head. "I doubt that."

"You're wondering why I'm here. I mean, I'm sure it's nice to see me and all, but what do I want?"

Good guess on her part. Possibilities flashed through his mind. Money? A job? Sperm? The last thought almost made him smile. It didn't matter how many years had gone by; there was no way he could imagine little Molly asking anyone for sperm.

"Actually, I do want something," she said, and reached for her purse. She dug around inside and pulled out a small item, then tossed it on the table. "Sort of."

Dylan hadn't known what to except, but he was stunned when he saw a gold wedding band lying on the dark wood. "This is so sudden," he said, going for the joke because he wasn't sure what to say.

"It's not what you think," Molly told him.

"Good, because I don't know what to think."

"Do you remember the ring?"

He picked it up. "Of course." He'd only ever bought one wedding ring in his life. It had been for Janet, back when he'd known that if he had to try to go on without her, he would die. Obviously, he'd been wrong. Time was a great healer...so were life's lessons.

"I got this for your sister," he said.

"Then you gave it to me, the day she got married."

He nodded. Thinking that actually seeing part of the ceremony would heal the last of his wounds, he'd gone to the church. Molly had come out to tell him goodbye. He recalled tossing her the ring, but he couldn't remember why.

She drew in a deep breath. "I didn't want you to go. There were assorted reasons, but the only one I was willing to tell you was that you'd promised me an adventure when I grew up. So you handed me the ring and said that when I was ready for that adventure, I was to bring this to you." She cleared her throat. Color stained her cheeks, and she ducked her head so that she was staring at the table. "Well, I'm ready if you're still willing."

Chapter Two

Molly felt as though someone had installed a blender in her stomach. As if the almost violent sloshing and churning weren't enough, she had the horrible feeling she was going to throw up. Now, that would be a pleasant visual for Dylan to remember.

Nerves, she told herself. It was just nerves…that and tequila on a very empty stomach. Whatever had she been thinking? The problem was, of course, she hadn't been thinking. She hadn't allowed herself, because no normal, sane person would have asked Dylan what she'd just asked him. She wouldn't be surprised if he excused himself and called 911—asking that they bring those people in the white coats.

She forced herself to look at him, at the way his dark eyes had widened slightly. He didn't exactly look ready to bolt, which was very nice, considering. She doubted she would have been as polite in his position.

She cleared her throat. "If it makes you feel any better, I can't believe I said that."

"So we have something in common."

At least he hadn't lost his sense of humor. "Okay, it's crazy—I admit that. You probably think *I'm* crazy, too. Maybe I am, but don't worry, I'm not dangerous."

He rested the ring in the palm of his hand and stared at it. Molly found her gaze drawn to the row of calluses at the base of his fingers. He'd obviously spent a lot of time doing physical labor. She had a feeling that the first few years he was in business, he'd done most of the assembling himself. Probably late at night, alone in a warehouse somewhere. Dylan had always been determined and driven. She doubted that had changed. He wasn't the sort of man who gave in easily, nor did he get to be as successful as he obviously was by listening to harebrained schemes. He was going to tell her no.

She turned that thought over in her mind. She was surprisingly okay with it. It was enough that she'd asked. For once, she'd taken the initiative—she hadn't waited; she'd gone after something that was important to her. Maybe there was hope. A sense of pride filled her and she squared her shoulders. This was a tiny step toward the new life she wanted for herself.

"Here you go," the waitress said, placing huge platters with oversized burgers and a mountain of crisp, golden steak fries in front of each of them. She pulled bottles of catsup and mustard out of one apron pocket and a handful of extra paper napkins out of the other. "Enjoy." She gave them a broad smile and left.

The food smelled great. Molly's stomach growled in anticipation, but she wasn't sure she was going to be able to choke down a bite.

Dylan applied mustard to the inside of the top of the

bun, then settled the bread in place. But he made no move to pick up his burger. He raised his gaze to her face.

"Why?" he asked.

She knew she could pretend not to understand what he was asking, but that was too much like cheating. Why? A simple question. Unfortunately, she didn't have a simple answer. At least not one she was willing to share with him. It was too personal and too humiliating. But he did deserve an explanation of some kind.

She took the mustard and shook out a dollop, then smoothed it on the toasted top bun. "I've reached an impasse in my life. There are a lot of things I have to think about, some decisions that have to be made. I can't seem to focus on anything, so I decided to get away. I had no idea what to do or where to go."

"There's always the circus," he said.

She gave him a half smile. Her lips were still a little numb from the margarita. "I suppose, but I think I'm a bit old to run away to the circus. Besides, I've never been that fond of elephants. They scare me."

"I wouldn't want to get trapped underfoot," he agreed.

She picked up her burger, then set it back on the plate. "As I said, I hadn't decided where to go, but I figured inspiration would come to me, so I started packing. While I was going through my drawers, I found the ring. It gave me an idea, so here I am."

If the truth be told, she was a little sorry she'd given in to the impulse. As each minute passed, she was feeling more and more like a complete fool. What on earth had she been thinking? She supposed she actually hadn't been thinking at all. "I've already confessed that it was crazy. I don't usually give in to impulses, so I can't explain this one. I guess I shouldn't have come. I'm sorry, Dylan. Forget I ever said anything."

She pushed the plate away and wondered how she could make a graceful exit. After all, they'd driven to the restaurant in Dylan's sleek, expensive car. Even if it wasn't too far to walk back, she didn't have a clue where his office was.

He picked up a steak fry and ate it. "I haven't said no yet."

She felt her eyes widen. "You can't be considering what I'm asking."

"I might be." He grinned.

This smile was different from the one he'd given her when he'd first seen her. That one had been pleasant and welcoming, but more impersonal. This one was a thousand watts of male trouble in the making. She felt the heat clear down to her toes. She was sure that if she looked, she would see little puffs of smoke drifting out of her loafers.

"You realize if you even consider doing this you're crazy, too," she said.

"It won't be the first time someone has called me that."

He took a bite of his burger and chewed. Molly told herself to stop staring, but she couldn't seem to make her eyes behave. Some of her sadness and fear lifted. It was enough that he hadn't flat-out refused her. No matter what, she would remember this brief time, and when reality got too ugly, she would pull out this memory to make her smile.

Sunlight filtered into the restaurant, but it didn't quite reach their rear table. Overhead electric lanterns spilled a soft glow in their direction, illuminating Dylan like a spotlight on a movie set. He was handsome enough to be the leading man, she thought, pleased that although he'd matured, he still looked as wonderful and perfect as ever. There was something very pleasant about spending a few hours in the presence of a good-looking man. It didn't matter that they were physically mismatched or that she wasn't even close to being his type. This wasn't about wanting him in the way she had when she'd just been seventeen and deeply enamored with all things Dylan.

Aesthetically, he appealed to her. The dark hair, worn short—not even to his collar. Years before, it had touched his shoulders. She decided she liked the more conservative style better. His eyes were as she remembered, although there were a few faint lines in the corners. His mouth was firm, his jaw well shaped. The gold earring was gone. He'd filled out a little. From the hints of movement under his dress shirt and suit slacks, he was in the same great shape as before. He was still the most amazing man she'd ever met.

He had a confidence about him that spoke of his power. It was probably for the best that they didn't go away together. After all, she doubted her hormones were any more controllable than they had been ten years earlier. The last thing she needed in her life was to deal with having a crush on him. It would be silly.

A voice in her head whispered that right now she could use a little silliness, but she ignored the words.

Maybe they could skip the trip and simply fall into bed together. A night of great sex would clear her sinuses for a month.

Molly stiffened instantly, pressed her lips together and prayed with all her might that she'd simply thought that last bit—that she hadn't actually said it. She inhaled through her nose and watched Dylan take another bite of his burger. Nothing about his expression changed.

Okay, that was good. She hadn't spoken those words. He wouldn't get uncomfortable or, worse, laugh at her. Molly picked up her drink and took another sip. What was wrong with her? She knew better than to wish for the moon. Men like Dylan Black were interested in women like her sister. They wanted leggy, slender females with model-perfect faces. She was...not that.

Some people thought her wavy-curly hair was unusual, but she thought it was a pain, which is why she usually tied it back in a braid. Her hazel brown eyes were what she referred to as the color of "rain-washed mud." She had a decent smile, even though her mouth was too small. Her nose was too big, but her ears were cute. Her skin was clear now—adolescence had not been good for her skin. Then there was the matter of those twenty pounds she'd been trying to lose since she was born. In a world of size-eight beauties, she was a frumpy size twelve.

"You're looking fierce about something," Dylan said.

"It's not important."

His good humor faded. "Are you in trouble, Molly? Are you on the run from something?"

She was, but not in the way he meant the question. Besides, she wasn't about to explain about all that.

"If you're asking if I've committed a felony, the answer is no," she told him. "I *am* on the run, but only from myself. I haven't done anything wrong." And that was part of the problem, she thought. If only she had a few regrets about things she'd done, rather than wasting all her regret time on what she'd never gotten around to doing. "I just wanted to get away."

Which she was still going to do, regardless of what he said. She put down her margarita and leaned toward him. "Haven't you ever felt the world closing in on you? It's like no matter where you turn or what you do, there's no escape. It feels like nothing is changing or is ever going to, yet the reality is that nothing is the same." She shrugged. "I know I'm not making any sense."

Dylan stared at her. "You would be surprised at how much sense you *are* making."

"I just want to run away for a few days," she continued. "I want a chance to clear my head, to think things through." She gave him another half smile. "Maybe I'll get lucky and figure out a way to be someone else."

"Who would you want to be?"

"Anybody but me."

"Why is it so bad being Molly Anderson?"

Ah, more questions she would not answer. "You're going to have to trust me on that one, Dylan. It just is."

They sat in silence for a few minutes. Molly thought about eating a French fry, but she really wasn't hungry. It must be the nerves. Gee, if she kept this up for a few months, she might lose those twenty pounds.

"Your timing is interesting," Dylan said, and leaned back in the booth. He picked up his bottle of beer and took a sip.

Something flickered to life in Molly's chest. Until that moment, she hadn't really allowed herself to hope that he was being more than polite. Even when he'd told her he wasn't refusing her request outright, she hadn't allowed herself to believe this might be possible. She felt a quickening that was almost excitement. There were possibilities left in the world, and that thrilled her.

"In what way?" she asked.

"I'm wrestling with some difficult decisions myself. Mostly about my business." He made a dismissive gesture with his hand. "I won't bore you with the details, but for many reasons, I'm at a crossroads right now, too."

His dark gaze was intense. She felt as if he were staring into her soul. She wanted to look away because she knew he wouldn't find a whole lot there to impress him. She wished she were someone different, someone wonderful and interesting, so that a man like Dylan would want her. But she knew the truth. She was just Molly—bright but not brilliant, nice, sometimes funny. She wasn't wildly attractive, or witty, or charming, or any of those things that usually drew men like him.

If only she were beautiful, like Janet. Or skinny, again like Janet. She bit back a smile. If Janet were here, she would tease her sister about being way too annoying to love. Her humor faded as she thought about how wonderful her sister had been through all this. Molly was so grateful they'd finally come to terms with their relationship and that they were close.

"What did you have in mind for your adventure?" Dylan asked.

If Molly had been drinking at that moment, she would have spit across the table. As it was, she could only stare at him in wide-eyed shock. "Excuse me?"

"Your adventure." He picked up the ring and held it out. "That's why you're here. What did you want to do?"

Had she suddenly lost her hearing, or had Dylan really asked that question? Was he serious about this?

Molly opened her mouth, then closed it. Her mind stayed blank. "You're agreeing?"

"I'm considering. There's a difference. I want to know what you had in mind."

Molly shifted in her seat, torn between wild excitement and bone-numbing trepidation. It was one thing to think about an adventure with Dylan—fantasies were fun and safe. But this was real life. Was she actually willing to go away with him? After all, she hadn't seen him in ten years. He was a stranger. She would be insane—

She sucked in a deep breath. No, she wasn't insane. Dylan had been in his early twenties the last time she'd seen him. She knew about his basic character. She'd promised herself no more regrets. She already had too many to live with.

"I didn't have any place in mind," she told him honestly. "I don't care where I go or what I do. I just want to be away. My only stipulation is that I have access to a telephone. I'll need to check my answering machine every day."

"Let me guess. You're trying to make a boyfriend jealous."

If his statement hadn't been so painfully far from the truth, she might have laughed. "It's not that. I'm not currently seeing anyone, and even if I were, that's not my style. I've never been very good at those kind of games."

"Good. I didn't think so, but I had to ask." His gaze sharpened. "I'm trying to figure out how much of the Molly I remember is hiding in there."

"Enough. I've grown up, but I don't think I've changed that much." He still had the ability to make her heart pound, although she wasn't going to share that particular fact with him.

Dylan rubbed his jaw. He was so good-looking. Molly was momentarily impressed that she'd found the courage even to ask that he do this with her. Even if nothing came of it, she was pleased that she'd made it this far. So what if the tequila had given her the last little push over the edge—she was still willing to take most of the credit.

"Two weeks," he said without warning. "I could take off that much time. We can carry a cellular phone so that you'll be able to check messages. I'll choose the first place we go to, then you can pick activities once we're there. We'll negotiate for the destinations after that."

He paused expectantly. Molly could only look at him as she tried to absorb what he was saying. Had she really heard him correctly? Her heart pounded, but for the first time in weeks, it wasn't from fear but from excitement.

"Okay," she said cautiously, not sure if he was actually telling her he was agreeing or he was simply tossing ideas around.

Oh, but she wanted it to be true. Dylan had always been her fantasy. They had both changed and matured and she seriously doubted if she still had a crush on him. But she would really like the opportunity to find out how the grown man was different from the man-boy she remembered.

"We'll have separate rooms and split expenses fifty-fifty," he said. "Agreed?"

Molly had to resist the urge to roll her eyes. No doubt the poor guy was terrified she was going to come on to him the moment they were alone. She sighed. It made sense. After all, she *had* had a serious crush on him all those years ago and he was still incredibly gorgeous. However, she would do what she could to control her wayward self in his presence.

For a moment, she allowed herself to believe that his statement about separate rooms was made in order to make her feel safe. If only it were true. If only Dylan would look at her and find her attractive. But she knew about wishing after the moon. All it ever got anyone was a crick in the neck.

It wasn't just about her appearance, either, she reminded herself. If Dylan knew the truth about her, he would run so far and so fast he would leave skid marks on the road.

"That sounds fair," she agreed.

"Then I guess that's it," he said. "Do we have a deal?"

"You're willing to do it?" Molly asked, then felt instantly stupid. But she wanted to be sure. "We're really going to take an adventure together?"

"I'm game if you are."

Be careful what you wish for, a voice in her head whispered. She dismissed it and smiled. "I'm already packed."

"Great." He held out his hand. "Let's shake to seal the deal."

His long fingers engulfed hers. Heat flared between them, warming her from the inside out. She felt a faint tingling rippling through her body, and she didn't care that her reactions were the result of a drink on top of no food, or even remnants from her crush all those years ago. She didn't mind that she was the only one having all the reactions. It was enough that Dylan had agreed.

When he released his hand, he picked up his burger. "I'll need the rest of today and most of the morning to get my business affairs in order. We could take off just after noon tomorrow, if that's all right with you."

Molly was suddenly starved. She poured more mustard on her bun, then smoothed the bright yellow sauce in place. "That's great. I'm ready to go anytime. If you'll give me your phone number, I'll call and let you know where I'm staying tonight."

He swallowed his food. "Where do you live?"

"In L.A. I meant I would be getting a hotel room for the night out here."

"No problem. You can stay with me." He grinned. "I have a huge house up on one of the hills. I fell in love with the view, but the place is way too big for me. There are five bedrooms, and a couple are made up for guests."

Molly hesitated. "I wouldn't want to intrude." The truth was, she was uncomfortable at the thought of staying with him under any circumstances. Being at Dylan's house would be so intimate.

"I see. You're willing to go away with me, but you won't spend the night at my house? That makes sense."

"Oh." He had a point. She felt herself flushing. "I guess

you're right. Then thanks, I'd love to stay." If nothing else, she would enjoy getting a peek into his world. What would his house look like? Did he—

She was about to take a bite of her burger, but she stopped suddenly and set the food back on her plate. Her mouth got dry as realization flooded her. "I never thought to ask," she stammered. "You're not married or anything, are you? It doesn't matter as far as the travel, but I don't want to get in the way or cause trouble."

Actually, she was lying. If Dylan was married, she wouldn't want to go away with him, but saying that would sound too weird, as if she had some secret romantic agenda.

"If I was married, I wouldn't have agreed," he said. "I'm between women at the moment, so no explanations are required. You don't have to worry, kid—I live in a normal house. You won't find anything scary lurking in the closets."

His teasing smile was like a sucker punch to her belly. She nearly yelped in terror. She was *not* relieved that he wasn't married and she was *not* going to fall for him. Not Dylan, no way. She knew better. She currently had enough insanity in her life without adding more.

That out of the way, they finished eating. When they were done, Dylan snagged a clean paper napkin from the passing waitress and drew Molly a map.

"This is the shop," he said, motioning to a small box he'd made on the napkin. "The route to the house looks complicated, but once you're on the road it's pretty easy. Most of the time there's only one way to turn."

He explained the intricacies, then pulled his key chain out of his slacks pocket and took one key off the ring. "This is it," he said, handing it to her. "I'm trusting you not to run off with the family silver."

She closed her hand around the small bit of metal. It was

still warm from his body. "I appreciate this, Dylan," she said. "Both your willingness to come with me and the trust. I won't let you down."

He shrugged. "If I thought you were going to, I wouldn't give you the chance. Besides, I saw that little car you drive. I could hunt you down in a heartbeat."

"I'm sure you could."

She studied his broad shoulders, which nearly stretched out the seams of his dress shirt. He was powerfully built. What would it be like to be so strong that you never had to worry about being physically afraid? It was, she decided, something men took for granted.

"You ready to go?" he said, preparing to slide out of the booth.

She frowned. "We haven't paid the check."

"They automatically put it on my tab. I pay it monthly."

"What happened to splitting all expenses equally?"

He paused. "Young lady, you have a point. You also owe me ten bucks."

She laughed. "That's better." She extracted the bill from her wallet and handed it to him.

Outside, the sky was clear. Back in L.A. it had been hazy, with a combination of low clouds and smog. Beyond the restaurant, there were only open areas. The city of Riverside was a sprawling, mostly rural town, while the county itself stretched all the way to Arizona. She felt as if she were a thousand miles from home, instead of only sixty miles away.

"We'll go back to the office so you can collect your car," he said as he opened the passenger door of his Mercedes. "Then you can head up to the house and relax for the afternoon. If you're a typical female, we're going to have a talk about packing."

"I resent the implication," she said, trying not to think about the huge suitcase filling her trunk.

"I'm going to give you one duffel bag and that's all you get."

"You're not turning into a tyrant on me, are you?" she asked, not sure where he was going with this. Why on earth would it matter how many suitcases she brought and why would he want her to use one of his?

"I'm being practical." He touched the tip of her nose and grinned. "We're not taking a car on our adventure. We'll be riding on one of my bikes."

Her brain instantly provided a picture of a bicycle and she opened her mouth to protest. What on earth was he thinking? Then she remembered…this was Dylan. All bad boy and black leather—on a motorcycle.

Her eyes got wide, and the image was so powerful she couldn't speak. Then all she could do was laugh in sheer delight.

Dylan watched Molly drive away, then he turned back toward his building. As the sound of her car faded, he told himself to go inside, that a thousand things needed doing. Yet he stood there, staring at the brown hills and dry desert land.

He couldn't believe he'd given a strange woman the key to his house and blithely let her go there on her own. Even Molly had been surprised by his blind trust. What had he been thinking?

The truth was, he hadn't been thinking at all. His gut had said it was okay to trust Molly, and so he had. Weird, considering he never trusted anyone. What was it about her? Their past? Or maybe it was the vulnerability in her eyes. Something that called to him, begging for protection or comfort.

Slow down, guy, he told himself. He knew better than to create fantasies about women. They were only out for what they could get from a man, be it a good time in bed or a lifetime of financial support. Life had taught him that lesson well.

Which made his reasons for trusting Molly even more suspect. Except that he didn't believe she wanted anything from him. He couldn't say how or why this was true, but he'd acted as if it was. Maybe old age was making him senile. Reality was everybody wanted something, even Molly.

His admittedly cynical philosophy firmly back in place, he walked inside the building. Evie sat at her desk, her dark eyes wide with curiosity.

"Well?" she asked, making no pretense at being subtle. "Who is she and what did she want?"

Dylan leaned against her desk. "An old friend. I knew her years ago. I dated her older sister."

"Oh, that explains it." Evie wrinkled her nose. "I'm sure she's a nice person and all, but she's not your type. I mean the hair is curly and could be interesting, but she's real plain looking and kinda overweight."

Dylan straightened. "She's not plain," he said, irritation adding strength to his voice. "Janet was always the pretty one in the family, but Molly has a lot of nice features. And she's not overweight. Just curvy." He drew his eyebrows together and waited for Evie to contradict him. He didn't want to even think about why he felt the need to defend Molly. Maybe because she was one of those people who were good on the inside. So what if she wasn't traditionally beautiful—she had other qualities he admired.

"My mistake," Evie said, raising her hands in a gesture of surrender. "I was just a little surprised—that's all. You usually go for the model type. I think it's great you're looking for substance rather than flash.''

"I'm not looking for anything," he growled. "We're friends. Nothing more."

"I knew that," Evie said. She shifted uncomfortably. "I'm sorry if I said something I shouldn't have."

Dylan shook his head. "No, it's my fault. I'm—" What? What was wrong with him? Why did everything suddenly seem off?

"I'll be in my office," he told her, and headed for the back of the building.

He was getting soft. That must be it. Good thing he was going away. He would use the time to clear his head.

As he settled down to work, he noticed a faint sensation low in his gut. After a few minutes, he was able to identify it as anticipation. He, who normally hated anything that pulled him away from work, was actually looking forward to taking time off.

Chapter Three

There had been a mailbox with the house number at the bottom of the hill. As Molly shifted her car into first so it could climb the steep grade she wondered if she'd made a mistake. Did Dylan really live up here?

When she rounded the last bend and saw the house sprawling in front of her, she became more convinced that she must have made a wrong turn somewhere. The structure was huge. All wood and glass. Its back end blended into the hill rising behind the house. The front overlooked the city and desert beyond. From where she'd stopped she could see a four-car garage and what appeared to be part of a garden.

Molly sucked in a deep breath. This had to be the place. There had been only three other driveways on the street and none of the numbers had even been close. She knew property was cheaper out here, but sheesh, she hadn't expected a mansion. Looking at the impressive structure, she was glad she hadn't known about it before. Otherwise, she never would have found the courage to approach him.

She pulled her car to the side, in front of one of the garage's double doors, then turned off the engine. She decided to leave her suitcase in the trunk until she was absolutely sure this was the place. She moved up the walk to the wide front door and extracted the key Dylan had given her. Here goes nothing, she thought.

The key turned easily. He'd told her there wasn't an alarm to worry about, so she simply stepped inside.

The foyer ceiling stretched up at least twenty feet. Huge windows brought in the light from outside, illuminating dark wood beams, white stucco walls and many lush plants. The living room was in front of her, but to get to it, she had to cross over a cobblestone bridge and indoor stream. A stream?

Molly blinked several times, but the flowing water didn't go away. It continued to trickle down a rock formation on her right, then under the bridge to a shallow pool on her left. Several fish swam through the clear pond. What on earth had she gotten herself into?

She walked into the living room. The furniture was oversized. Dark blue leather sofas, glass-topped tables and more windows. The view was spectacular. She turned in a slow circle, taking in the attractive floor lamps, the displayed artwork, the dining room beyond. She figured her entire condo would fit comfortably into the space occupied by these two rooms alone. And there was still plenty of house for her to see.

Nearly eleven years ago, when Janet had first thought about breaking up with Dylan, Molly remembered listening at the door as her sister had talked to their mother, trying to decide what to do. Janet had been concerned about their differences in life-style and expectation. Dylan had grown up on the poor side of town, in a single-wide trailer. All he'd seemed to care about was his bike and Janet. She'd wanted a man with ambition. At the time Molly had thought her sister was incredibly stupid. Ambition was all well and good, but they were talking about Dylan Black. He was worth ten lawyers or doctors.

As Molly continued to study the impressive room, she realized she'd been right. A smile pulled at her mouth. He'd come a long way from that ratty old trailer. Maybe, while they were away together, she could ask him to tell her the story of what had happened to bring him here.

She returned to her car and collected her suitcase, then went back inside. Dylan had described the basic layout of the house, telling her to make herself at home. By nature, she wasn't much of a snoop, and even if she'd wanted to look around, this place was way too intimidating for her taste. So she didn't poke her head in all the open doors along the hallway. Instead, she headed for the last door on the left, and found it led to a guest room, just as he'd promised.

The four-poster queen-sized bed was attractive, as was the plain pine furniture. The comforter was a Laura Ashley print, with matching drapes at the windows. A few tasteful paintings decorated the cream-colored walls. Through a door on her left was a huge bathroom, complete with spa tub. Everything was perfectly clean. Dylan obviously had the use of a cleaning service. Or maybe someone came in a few days a week to tidy up.

She set her suitcase on the bed and opened it. Dylan had told her she would have to pack light for their adventure. After all, they were heading out on one of his motorcycles. A flicker of excitement tickled her tummy. She couldn't believe she was actually going to do this. She, little Molly Anderson, was going away with Dylan Black. It was, she thought, a miracle of sorts. And lately miracles had been in short supply in her life.

She sorted through clothing, deciding that casual would be best. She settled on jeans, shirts and a few toiletries. An oversized cotton T-shirt would work as a nightgown.

Fifteen minutes later she'd stacked the clothes she was taking neatly on the dresser and had secured the rest of her things in her suitcase. She stared at the ring Dylan had given back to her. She felt strange taking it with her, but she wasn't about to leave it behind, either. She shrugged, then grabbed a tissue from a ceramic container in the bathroom, wrapped the ring and tucked it in an inner pocket of her toiletry bag.

Molly glanced at her watch. She had a few hours before Dylan would be home. He'd told her about a library at the other end of the house. A good book would be a great distraction, but first she had to make a few phone calls. After fishing her calling card out of her wallet, she settled on the bed and put the phone on her lap. She dialed her home number, then entered her card number at the bong. When she heard the answering machine click on, she punched in the two-digit code that replayed any messages. The rapid beeping told her there weren't any.

It was really too soon to expect an answer, she told herself silently, willing away the disappointment. But it was so hard not to hope. So hard not to want a miracle—just one more. Was that asking too much?

When there wasn't an answer, she dialed in another number. The phone was picked up on the second ring.

"Hello?"

"Hi, it's me."

"Molly!" Janet's voice was warm and welcoming. "How are you? Or should I ask, Where are you? You've left already, haven't you?"

"Uh-huh. I'm—" Molly stared at the beautiful guest room and grinned. "You'll never guess where I am."

Her sister chuckled. "I hate playing guessing games. I'm lousy at them. You know that. Okay. You're in New York City."

"Nope. One more try, then I'll tell you. But I'll give you a hint. It's warm and there's a terrific view."

"Oh, that's easy. Hawaii. How great!"

Molly laughed. "Sorry, Janet, you're not even close. I'm in Dylan Black's guest room."

There was dead silence on the phone. Molly could picture her sister's mouth dropping open. She would form words without sound for at least thirty seconds.

A sputtering came over the phone, followed by a squawk. "You're *where?*"

"I know, I know. It's too strange. But remember the ring I was talking about?"

"Of course. It was actually *my* ring."

"You dumped him," Molly reminded her. "When I found it, I remembered what he'd said about promising me an adventure. I couldn't figure out where else to go, so here I am."

"Honey, are you all right?" Janet's voice was low with concern. "I know you had a crush on him and all, but this is very strange. It's been years. You don't know the man anymore. Are you sure this is safe?"

Molly thought about that for a second. "You're not saying anything I haven't already told myself. I know this sounds crazy, and in a way it is. But I didn't know what to do. If nothing else, Dylan is a fabulous distraction. And I need that right now."

"He's not a serial killer, is he? Not that he would tell you if he was."

Molly glanced around the room. "I don't think killing

pays this well," she told her sister. "His business is very successful. The house is great. Big and on the top of a hill. I—" A thought occurred to her. "Janet, are you mad because I'm here? Does it bother you?"

"If you're asking whether I'm over Dylan, please don't concern yourself. I've been over him for years. You know I love Thomas. It's been a decade, and the thrill is still there for us. Dylan was my first serious boyfriend and I'll always have fond memories of him, but it wouldn't have worked. We both knew that." Janet drew in a breath. "I'm sure he's doing well, but he hasn't changed, Molly. He's still a dangerous kind of man. I don't think he's ever married. Maybe he's not capable of that kind of commitment."

Molly stared at the phone. "We're taking an adventure, not getting involved."

"Things happen. I just want you to take care of yourself. You're in a vulnerable place right now. I don't want him to hurt you."

"You don't have to worry. He would have to be slightly interested in me to hurt me and we both know that's not going to happen."

"Don't," Janet pleaded. "You're adorable. Any man would be lucky to have you."

Molly tugged at her jeans, pulling the fabric away from her generous thighs. "Uh-huh. I do have that problem with all those men lining up outside the condo. It was so difficult to get away this morning, but I try to be gentle when I reject them."

"You're a brat."

"Just a minute ago you said I was adorable."

Janet laughed. "Molly, you make me crazy. Were there any messages?"

Molly's humor faded instantly. "No."

"It's really too soon to have heard."

"I know."

"Everything is fine."

"I know that, too." She knew it, but she didn't believe it.

"So where are you two off to?"

"I have no idea," Molly said. "Dylan is picking our destination."

"Are you sure about this?"

"I'm not sure about anything, Janet. But if you're asking me if I'm sure I want to go with Dylan, the answer is yes. There's nothing I want more. I need to escape and he's the perfect way to do that. So please try not to worry."

"I won't worry if you promise to stay in touch."

"I will—I swear."

Her sister sighed. "I love you, kid. Take care of yourself."

"I love you, too. Give Thomas and the girls a kiss for me. Bye."

She hung up the receiver. Without Janet's support, she wouldn't have gotten through the past week and a half. It was nice to have someone to worry about her. However, for the next few days she wasn't going to think about that, or about anything but having a wonderful time on her adventure.

Dylan automatically hit the button on the remote that controlled the garage door. As he slowed, he saw Molly's dark blue compact parked off to the side. That gave him pause. He wasn't used to coming home to find someone in his house. In the two years he'd lived there he'd had overnight company maybe three times. When he was involved with a woman, he generally stayed at her place. He preferred being able to leave when he liked and not having to ask her to go when he wanted to be alone.

He stared at the sensible American car. It was basic transportation, nothing fun, nothing flashy. But then, flashy wasn't Molly's style, or it hadn't been back when she was a teenager. He eased into his parking space and turned off the engine. After collecting his briefcase, he closed the garage door and entered the house.

"I'm home," he called, then frowned to wonder if he'd ever done that before. It was old television sitcom cliché—"Honey, I'm home."

"Hi," Molly answered. From the direction of her voice, he would guess she was in the library.

Dylan left his briefcase on the kitchen counter, collected a couple of beers from the refrigerator and went in search of his guest. He found her curled up in one of the leather recliners, reading. A floor lamp cast a warm circle of light over her and the book. Her feet were tucked under her and her shoes were neatly off to the side of the chair on the floor.

She hadn't noticed him and seemed engrossed in her book. For a moment Dylan simply watched her. He couldn't shake the odd feeling of knowing she'd been in the house while he was still at work. At the office he'd managed to focus on what he was doing and relegate their lunch to the back of his mind. But from time to time he'd found himself remembering something she'd said or picturing a quick movement of her hands. While he hadn't been excited about coming home to find her here, he hadn't dreaded it, either. The few occasions he'd let one of his women spend the night at his place he *had* felt trapped and awkward. Maybe the difference was he'd known Molly for a long time. More likely it was because they weren't involved, nor were they likely to be.

He moved toward her. "I probably should have asked if you like beer," he said, holding out one of the bottles.

"Except for water and coffee, it's about all I have. I don't do much entertaining."

She took the offered refreshment and smiled. "Thanks, it's fine. I confess I did take a peek in the refrigerator earlier. I had an apple. I could tell you don't spend a whole lot of time cooking."

"Never learned how." He took the seat across from hers and settled on the comfortable leather cushion. After a long swallow of beer, he loosened his tie, then pulled it free of his shirt.

"At the risk of sounding like a suburban wife, how was your day?" Her voice was teasing.

He liked that she was comfortable enough to kid him. Earlier, at the restaurant, he'd seen a lot of tension in her body. She'd downed her margarita as if it were a lifeline...or maybe the Dutch courage she'd needed to ask him about going away. Whatever it was, he was pleased that she'd finally relaxed a little.

"I've been busy. There's a lot to get through before I can leave." He leaned forward, resting his elbows on his knees and holding the bottle of beer in both hands. "I'm not going to be much of a host tonight," he said. "I have a briefcase full of work to finish up before morning. I figure—" He caught her smile. "What's so funny?"

She flicked her fingers toward him. "Nothing, it's just—" She shrugged. "Let's say you're not exactly what I expected. The Dylan I remember wore jeans and a black leather jacket. You're in a suit, with a tie. You're so respectable."

"Tell me about it," he grumbled. "I never thought it would come to this. I used to work in jeans all the time. Half my day was spent assembling bikes or fiddling with designs. Now I push around papers. I've become everything I hated when I was a kid. I wear a tie—something I swore

I'd never do. I drive a Mercedes. I have a cell phone. I get my clothes dry-cleaned.''

"You're a responsible citizen.''

"Worse. I'm old. Just last week I was in the video store and there were these three teenage boys making a lot of noise. Without thinking, I told them to quiet down. They walked off, but not before calling me 'an old man.' I realized they're right. I *am* old.''

Molly burst out laughing. "You're not even thirty-five. That's not old.''

"It is to a fifteen-year-old.''

"Do you really care what those boys think?''

"No, it's just—'' He couldn't explain it. Somehow everything had changed. He didn't know when or how that had happened, but it was one of the reasons he wanted to go away. He needed to clear his head and figure out what was important.

"I sold out,'' he said glumly, and wondered if he was about to do it again. Would he do what his lawyer and several other people had suggested and sell his company, or would he maintain his independence?

"You've become successful,'' Molly said. "There's a difference. You should be proud of yourself.''

Several strands of curly hair had escaped from her braid. They fluttered by her face and touched the top of her shoulder. Sometime in the afternoon she'd rolled up the sleeves of her shirt, exposing wrists and forearms. She had curves. Evie's assessment had been that she was overweight. Dylan wasn't sure what he thought of Molly. She wasn't what he was used to in a woman. Okay, so no one would ever call her beautiful, but in this light, gesturing as she talked and smiling, she was sort of pretty. She had a sincerity he liked. Molly was a real person—he didn't know many people he could say that about these days.

"Are you concerned the price is too high?" she asked. "Are you thinking that you've been forced to give up too much to get what you wanted?"

She saw way more than he was comfortable with. "Too much serious conversation," he said lightly, and rose to his feet. "If you looked in the refrigerator, you know I don't have food around. How do you feel about pizza for dinner?"

"Sounds fine."

"I know a great place that delivers. What would you like on it?"

"Anything." She stood up, as well. "Do you want me to call?"

"No, I have the number memorized. Single guy who lives alone—no surprise there, right? I'm going to put on jeans and call the pizza place. Then I need to get started on my work."

Molly held up her book. "Don't worry about entertaining me. I'll be fine."

"I appreciate that. I don't want this stuff hanging over me while we're away." He started for the door, then remembered something. "I'd like to leave about noon tomorrow. I thought we'd go to your place on our way out of town so you can drop off your car. Otherwise you'll have to come by here when we get back and that'll be nearly an hour out of your way."

"That's fine," she said. "So we're not heading east?"

If they were, leaving her car here would make more sense. "Nope, but that's all I'm going to say."

"I think I like the idea of a pleasant surprise," she told him.

They chatted for a couple more minutes, then he left the library and made his way to his bedroom. The guest room was at the other end of the hall. He'd forgotten to ask Molly if she'd found everything she needed. So much for being a good host. But when he returned to the library, she was gone. He ordered their pizza, collected his briefcase and started to work.

About a half hour later, there was a faint knock on the door. He called an absentminded "Come in" but didn't look up from the computer.

"Dinner's here," Molly told him. She placed a large plate with several slices of steaming pizza in front of him, along with a fresh beer. Before he could do more than thank her, she was gone.

Dylan stared at the closed door, torn between work and curiosity. Then he figured he'd better get back to his spreadsheet and turned his attention back to his papers.

It was nearly 1:30 p.m. the next afternoon when Molly closed the front door of her condo behind her. She could see through the courtyard to the street, where Dylan waited for her. She'd parked her car, taken in her big suitcase and checked her machine for messages. Now she was ready to begin.

Her stomach tightened with excitement and a little bit of nerves. For a second she thought about calling the whole thing off. After all, she barely knew the man. What on earth had she been thinking when she'd asked him to take her on an adventure?

"I'm not going to back out now," she said softly. "If I do, I'll be stuck on my own. I refuse to spend the next two weeks waiting for the phone to ring."

That resolved, she squared her shoulders and walked to the front of the building.

When Dylan saw her, he straightened and grabbed the extra helmet strapped on the seat behind him. He'd already loaded her small bag of clothes and toiletries. Molly eyed the helmet, then the motorcycle, and had another bout of second thoughts.

"I know what you're thinking," Dylan said, coming up to her and handing her the helmet. "My bike is perfectly safe. I've been driving it for years, so there's nothing to worry about."

"Oddly enough, my physical safety doesn't concern me," she said lightly. "I was questioning my mental stability. This is completely insane. Or haven't you figured that out?"

He pulled the helmet over her head and fastened the strap under her chin. "Then we're both crazy, because I agreed to this, right?"

"I suppose."

"Hey, that's supposed to make you feel better."

Barefoot, Dylan was a good eight or nine inches taller than her. In his boots, he towered over her. As she met his dark gaze, something shifted inside. A feeling, more a shot of heat than sizzle, but it certainly got her attention. Awareness, she thought. Of the man he was. At twenty-three Dylan had been a charmer. All grown up in his thirties, he was irresistible.

Talk about being silly, Molly thought. Finding Dylan attractive was about as useful as using a teaspoon to bale out a sinking ship. Still, it would be a distraction. As long as she didn't get carried away, she would be fine.

"You have everything?" he asked. "I didn't really expect you to fit all your stuff in that one bag, so I left a little room in mine."

"I can follow directions," she told him. "Don't worry about me. I have everything I need."

For reasons that still didn't make sense, she'd even repacked the ring. She wanted it close. Maybe as a talisman against all that was going to happen.

"Then let's get going," he said, and handed her a leather jacket. "This will be a little big, but you'll need it to stay warm. The breeze gets pretty stiff on the bike."

He helped her into the jacket, then fastened it. His ministrations made her feel like a child. It was probably how he thought of her, but she wasn't going to complain. For once, it was nice having someone take care of her.

When he was done, he touched her face. "There's still time to change your mind," he told her.

"I could say the same thing to you."

"Nope. I'm going."

"Then I'm going with you."

"Great." Dylan flashed her a quick smile that shocked her clear down to her thighs, then climbed onto the bike. He flipped down the clear plastic visor and motioned for her to get on behind him.

Molly swallowed hard. Ah, so she *hadn't* thought everything through. She hadn't really considered that being on a motorcycle with Dylan meant she would be riding behind him...touching him...touching him in an incredibly intimate way.

She didn't know whether to laugh or scream.

In the end she gave a strangled gargling sound, flipped down her visor and moved next to the bike. She had to maneuver her right leg over the seat, then sort of shift-slide into place. It wasn't graceful. She felt awkward and clumsy and incredibly large as she settled onto the seat. The machine bounced with her movements.

Dylan started the bike. "You're gonna have to hang on," he called over the rumble of the engine. "You can stick your hands in my jacket pockets or wrap your arms around me. Whichever is more comfortable."

"Sure," she said, as if it were no big deal. Right. She, like millions of American women, spent most of her day on a bike behind a guy, touching him, pressing up against him, feeling—

The bike moved forward. Molly yelped and grabbed for Dylan. He accelerated down the street, then headed into a turn. The three of them—him, her and the bike—tilted toward the ground. She shrieked again and held on with all her strength, wrapping her arms around his waist and squeezing.

"You've never been on a motorcycle before, have you?" Dylan called.

She shook her head, then realized he couldn't see the movement. "No," she said, speaking directly into his ear.

"Just relax. Don't fight me or the bike. You're going to be fine. I'll keep you safe."

Uh-huh. Sure. She believed that.

After a couple of minutes, she realized she was clenching her jaw. It was unlikely that keeping those muscles tight would do anything to prevent her immediate death, so she tried to relax that part of her body. They turned on Wilshire Boulevard and headed for the 405 freeway. Molly felt herself start to hyperventilate.

They were going on the freeway? Didn't he know the speed limit was sixty-five? They couldn't do that on a motorcycle. If nothing else, she would get bugs in her teeth.

The on-ramp was in front of them. Molly ducked her head behind Dylan's back and screamed as she felt them accelerate up the ramp. She closed her eyes tight, prayed really hard and waited.

Minutes ticked by. There was no fiery crash, no screech of brakes, no impending sense of death. Gradually she raised her head. The clear visor kept most of the rushing air off her face and out of her eyes. If she kept her mouth closed, the issue of bugs seemed manageable.

They were moving north. She didn't know how fast they

were going, but it felt like flying. The air was cool. Dylan and jacket both kept her warm. She'd traveled this freeway a thousand times before, yet everything looked different. It was as if she were seeing the world for the first time.

She straightened a little, easing her death grip on Dylan's midsection. The bike was more stable than she would have thought. She wouldn't want to drive it or anything, but it wasn't so bad being back here. The band of fear around her chest loosened just a little. For the first time in weeks, she was able to draw in a deep breath without feeling pain. The whole purpose of the journey was to live for the moment, she reminded herself. She couldn't change what was going to happen; she could only deal with the now.

After a while, Molly started reading road signs. She put her mouth close to his ear.

"San Francisco?" she asked.

He shook his head. "You're gonna have to wait."

"I hate that. Tell me now."

"No way."

She laughed. She settled her hands in his pockets and tried not to become so aware of his body pressing against hers. Or was she pressing against him? Not that it mattered. The reality was they were touching in a lot of places.

He's just a guy, she reminded herself. She was familiar with all the working parts and Dylan's couldn't be that different from everyone else's. There was no way he would ever be interested in her and she was just setting herself up for heartbreak if she imagined anything else. While it was perfectly all right to enjoy his fabulous body in these close quarters, she had better remember this was about transportation, not attraction.

Her wayward hormones didn't seem to be listening. She found it more and more difficult not to notice how her thighs pressed right up against his rather amazing butt.

Molly bit back a giggle. Oh, well, she would just have to endure the torture. There were many worse things in life. And if she ended up with another crush on him, so be it. She would deal with that just as she'd dealt with everything else recently. This time was for her, and if that meant she had fun being close to Dylan's hunky body, then she should just shut up and enjoy.

Chapter Four

The freeway slowed as it always did at the top of the Sepulveda Pass. Dylan moved into the right lane so he could make the transition. He didn't care what happened later, but he wanted to spend a couple of days by the ocean. He could only be a desert rat for so long before he needed to smell salt air.

The motorcycle engine hummed. Even though he hadn't had a chance to go for a ride in weeks, he always kept his bikes in perfect condition. It was a trait left over from his racing days. One he hadn't bothered changing. He liked the feel of the open road in front of him—well, clear except for the usual midafternoon traffic. It didn't seem to matter that it was the middle of the day in the middle of the week. L.A. always had traffic.

He bent into the curve of the transition road, then shot out onto the 101 freeway. Molly had grown used to the bike and now moved with him instead of fighting him on every turn. She was a fast learner, he thought, trying to ignore the feel of her hands lightly holding on to his waist.

To distract himself, he glanced at the cars around them and at the road signs. They should make good time. Maybe another hour or so to their first destination. They could pick up groceries, maybe cook on the beach and watch the sunset. He hadn't been gone a whole day yet, but already he felt lighter. As if he'd been able to leave his worries behind.

He'd been working too hard, he realized. He was long overdue for a vacation. But between the pressures of work, designing new bikes and trying to turn his company into a force in the industry, there hadn't been a whole lot of free time.

He also needed to get laid.

Dylan frowned, wishing he could shift position or something. This wasn't a problem he'd planned on. He swore under his breath and tried to figure out what was wrong. So he was on a motorcycle with a woman. He'd taken women on rides countless times and it wasn't a big deal. In this case, the woman was just little Molly, his first girlfriend's younger sister. Okay, so she'd grown up. That didn't mean anything. Why on earth couldn't he ignore the feel of her body pressed up against his? Apparently it had been way too long between women.

This wasn't about Molly, he told himself. She wasn't his type and he sure wasn't interested in her. She was way too round for his taste. He liked lean women with minimal curves. Evie had said she was overweight and he thought that was a little harsh, but naked Molly would be—

Lush.

The word came from nowhere and he wished it back there. But once it had formed in his brain, it sort of got lodged, as if it were not going to budge any time soon. He thought about how soft she would be. No angles or sharp hipbones, just smooth skin. Her breasts would spill over his hands. Without wanting to, he imagined cupping the generous curves, tracing the pale skin until she was writhing beneath him.

He could feel the heat of her right now. Dammit, obviously that was the problem. Their positions on the bike forced her right up against his butt. Was it his fault she was so warm? Even though he knew it was his imagination, he thought he could inhale the sweet scent of her body. They were both wearing jackets, so there was no way that her breasts could press against his back, yet he would swear he could feel their weight. Her hands—he just wanted her to move them a little lower. If only she would rub against him until—

"Until what?" he muttered, knowing she couldn't hear him. "Until you get so distracted you're a road hazard?"

But the images would not be denied. They flashed through his brain. Pictures of her under him, her thighs and belly a pillow for him. Of her above him, her breasts bouncing with each thrust. Of—

He swore again. Long and graphic, using words he'd nearly forgotten he knew. The solution was simple. When he got back home, he would call one of the women he dated on occasion and find a little relief. In the meantime, Molly was just a friend. He didn't do relationships and he doubted she'd ever played fast and loose in her life. Besides, this was pure speculation. The truth was, when faced with the reality of seeing her naked he doubted she would actually turn him on.

"You go to hell for lying same as stealing," he muttered to himself.

So he ignored the feel of her against him, ignored the heat and the imaginary scent. There was, he acknowledged, a certain pleasure in the wanting. It had been a long time since he'd actually wanted something he couldn't have. If nothing else, he was building a little character. Lately, life—and women—had gotten too easy. The kind he chose—those who weren't interested in anything but the game—were always available. They wanted something from him, and as long as he provided it, they would give him anything in return.

Miles later, he'd almost grown used to the discomfort of the wanting. In fact he found a perverse pleasure in it. Good thing Molly couldn't tell. Knowing he was turned on would probably scare her to death. Not that she was virgin. At least, he didn't think so. Dylan frowned as he realized he didn't know anything about Molly's personal life. She could be married with a half-dozen kids. Maybe he should have asked a few more questions. He shook his head. Right now, it didn't matter. They were going away, not starting anything together. When the two weeks were up, he would have made his decision about what to do with his company, and she, well, he hoped she would have solved her problems, too.

It was about an hour later when he drove down the off-ramp and circled under the freeway into the small town of Carpenteria. He pulled to the side of the road.

"We're here," he said. "What do you think?"

Molly looked around. "I thought we'd go farther north. We're, what, about twenty minutes south of Santa Barbara?"

"That's right. I rented a house on the beach for a couple of days. We can extend our stay here or head out. It's up to you. I've spent time here before. It's a nice little town. Off-season, like now, it's quiet. Just locals, with few tourists. We can head up to Santa Barbara for the day. There's plenty to do."

She nodded. "I like it."

"Good."

He drove down the street. He was familiar enough with the town to find the real estate office. Molly stayed on the bike while he filled out the two short forms and paid with a credit card. When he stepped back on the bike, she frowned.

"You're not going to get all macho on me, are you?" she asked. "I want to pay my half."

"That's what we agreed on." Dylan shoved the credit card receipt into his jacket pocket. "I figured we'd each pay for some stuff, then at the end of the two weeks, we'll total our expenses. Whoever paid the least writes the other a check for half the difference. I don't want to hassle with money every day. Agreed?"

She grinned at him.

"What's so funny?" he asked.

"I can't believe you're the same guy whose idea of a business transaction used to be illegally racing a quarter mile for beer money."

"We all have to grow up. Even me."

"I'd say you've more than grown up, Dylan."

She had, too, he thought as he slid back in the seat and felt the heat of her body. He'd managed to calm down some while in the real estate office, but after about thirty seconds of his butt nestling against her open thighs, he was ready again. If he hadn't already promised nothing would happen between them, and if he wasn't convinced it would be a bad idea for both of them, he might just want to find out how great it would be to make love with Molly. But he knew better.

Their house was small and old-fashioned, probably built in the midfifties. The sides were wood, the windows small. He doubted the whole thing was even nine hundred square feet. A far cry from his home up in the hills, but he liked it. The other houses on the street were also rentals and most of them were vacant. He and Molly would have peace and quiet. The best part was, their backyard was the beach and, beyond that, the Pacific Ocean.

"Home sweet home," he said as he turned off the engine. The cry of a seagull cut through the sudden silence.

Molly unstrapped her helmet and pulled it off. Her hair was a mess, all loose from her braid. The wild wavy curls blew around her face. She pushed them away impatiently.

"I can smell the ocean," she said. "It's nice."

He climbed off, then held out a hand to her. She hesitated before taking it, but when she swung her leg clear of the seat and tried to straighten, she grabbed hold more firmly.

"What happened?" she asked, taking a shaky step. "I feel like I've been at sea."

"You're stiff from the ride," he said. "You're not used to being on a bike, so you were pretty tense the whole way up. Plus you're using different muscles. Walk around. You'll stretch out."

She bent her knees a couple of times, then walked back and forth in front of the bike. He tried not to watch but found his attention drawn to the way she filled out her jeans. Her rear was nice and round. He figured he could get a good hold of her there, or maybe on her hips.

Dylan swore under his breath, then made himself concentrate on unpacking their few belongings. Let it go, he told himself. He had no business thinking about messing with her. Enjoying the ride up from L.A. was one thing, but it was time for some self-control.

The lecture helped…a little. He managed to avoid thinking about her curves, even when she unzipped her jacket, exposing the soft sweater she wore underneath. The swell of her breasts was only of passing interest. At least it would stay that way if he quickly averted his eyes.

"I've got the key," he said gruffly, then had to clear his throat. He led the way, mostly so she wouldn't see his arousal pressing against the fly of his jeans.

There were two steps up to the wooden porch. The front door looked flimsy, but Dylan figured they didn't have anything worth stealing, so it wasn't going to be a problem.

Inside, the house was a little musty. Molly went to the rear windows and opened the miniblinds. They had an instant view of the ocean. She caught her breath.

"It's so beautiful. The sky and the water are the perfect color of blue."

She smiled at him, an ingenuous smile that expected nothing in return. Oddly enough, he found himself wanting to give her something. He, who considered himself the last great cynic alive.

She wrinkled her nose. "I'll bet this place hasn't been lived in for months. Let's get it aired out." She pushed open the windows, then glanced around. "It's small but nice."

He followed her gaze. There was a blue-green floral print sofa and a wooden rocking chair, both facing the front wall. The television was nearly a Generation X-er it was so old, but Dylan didn't think they would be using it much. To his left was the eating area and the kitchen. On his right was a small open hallway with three doors right together. He would guess two of the doors led to the bedrooms, while the third was for the bathroom.

Molly headed in that direction. She opened the middle door.

"Oh, my," she said, and laughed. "I didn't know they made tile in this color. Dylan, come look."

He followed her, then had to peer over her shoulder. The bathroom was done in some god-awful yellow. The small vanity had been outlined in bright yellow tiles, while the inside was filled in with a lighter color. The flooring had once been yellow, as had the walls. Both had faded to nondescript beige. The fixtures were older than dirt. The only saving grace was the huge claw-footed tub with a shower head sticking out of the wall.

She looked back at him. "You take me to the nicest places."

"Hey, at least there's indoor plumbing. It's not as if we're camping."

"Oh, that's looking on the bright side." She grinned. "Now I'm scared to see the bedrooms."

"I'll bet they're not so bad."

He was right. The front room was small, with an extra-long twin bed and a single dresser. The rear bedroom had a queen-sized mattress, a dresser and two big windows overlooking the ocean.

Molly tilted her head. "Why don't you take this one," she said, pointing to the queen-sized bed. "It's bigger."

"And I need the bigger one because?"

She frowned. "I don't know. It seemed polite to offer."

Dylan wasn't surprised. In his experience, there were two kinds of women. Those who gave everything and those who expected everything. He'd already figured out which Molly was.

"You take it," he said, not sure why it was important to him, but suddenly it was.

"I don't need the extra space."

"I don't think either of us *needs* it, but that's not the point. Do you always sacrifice what you want for others?"

Her frown turned to a glare. "Yes. And your point would be what?"

"I don't have a point."

"Figures. So where exactly did you get your degree in

psychology, Dr. Black? You are a man of many talents, aren't you?"

"You're right," he said, walking in and setting her duffel bag on the bed in the larger room. "I crossed the line. But I would like you to have this one. At the next place, I'll take the room with the nicer view. Okay?"

She nodded. "Sorry I snapped at you. I guess..." Her voice trailed off.

"No problem. I can be a real grouch, too."

"I was not a grouch," she told him. "I was cranky."

"Oh, and there's a real difference?"

"Of course."

He caught the teasing glint in her eyes. "The subtleties escape me," he said. "You're going to have to explain them over dinner."

"I'll do my best. Although with you being a man and all, it might take a while."

He smiled. "So, we're going to play that game, are we? That women are superior?"

"Oh, you already know that. How nice. It will make things easier."

He gave her a mock glare. "Brat."

"Bully."

"Are we done with the *b* words?" he asked.

"I think so."

"Then I'll just take this to my room." He hefted his duffel bag. "Oh, before I forget, as requested." He unzipped the side pocket and pulled out his cellular phone. "It's charged, and I brought the charger. You said you only need to call out? I don't mind giving you the number if you want to receive calls."

She stared at the phone. There was something odd about the look in her eyes. He tried to read it and couldn't. Why did she want access to a phone? A fight with her boyfriend? A hot stock tip? What was so important?

But he didn't ask and she didn't answer. Instead, she gave him a quick smile that didn't come close to being sincere.

"Thanks," she said, motioning to the phone. "I won't be receiving any calls, but I would like to check my machine at home every day."

"No problem. I'll leave it on the kitchen counter." He started to leave the room, then turned back to her. "What would you like for dinner?"

Her pensiveness vanished instantly and the smile turned genuine. "I don't know. What do you like to cook?"

He found himself laughing with her. Molly was an odd combination of fearful child and confident woman. He liked that about her—in fact, he liked many things about her. Dylan knew he didn't like many people and it took a lot to earn his trust.

"I did the driving," he reminded her. "I agree that cooking duties should be shared most of the time, but I think tonight you owe me."

"Oh, do I?" She sighed dramatically. "I didn't realize you were the kind of man who liked to keep score. But if it's so important to you, I'll cook. Let's make it simple, though."

"There are grills down on the beach. We can pick up charcoal at the grocery store."

"It's going to have to be a small bag. We're riding a motorcycle."

"It'll fit."

"If you say so."

As she spoke, she pulled off the leather jacket he'd given her. The movement tightened her sweater across her breasts. He found himself mesmerized by her curves. He'd never really considered himself a breast man. As far as he was concerned, as long as the woman was happy with them he was, too. Maybe his attitude came from the fact that most of the women he'd been involved with were on the small side. But he was starting to see the appeal of more than a teaspoonful. Molly offered generous curves to tease and touch.

The fantasy grew, as did his reaction. He quickly dismissed the image of him slowly licking every inch of her pale curves.

He cleared his throat. "I'd like to unpack first. Will you be ready to go food shopping in about fifteen minutes?"

"Sure."

Dylan headed for the smaller bedroom. Obviously he hadn't thought the situation through. There were going to be complications on this trip—complications he hadn't bothered to consider.

She felt as if they were the last two people on earth. Molly leaned back against the big log next to their fire and stared up at the sky. It was only about nine in the evening, but it seemed later. Maybe because they were so alone. Several joggers had passed them around sunset, but since then she hadn't seen a soul.

It was a perfect night, she thought. The sound of the surf filled her ears. She liked the rush of the waves, even though she couldn't quite make out their shapes in the darkness. She inhaled the scent of the salt air and the water. There were few night creatures to disturb them, no birds, no scuttling of anything small.

She picked up the glass she held and took a sip. The Scotch was smooth. She'd never been much of a drinker, but she just might learn to like this, she thought lazily.

From across the fire, Dylan sighed. "Dinner was great," he told her.

"Yes, it was. Thanks for helping."

He motioned to the flames. "Open fire, raw meat, I couldn't help myself. I think it's genetic."

"If only we'd been eating the woolly mammoth," she said.

He gave her a lazy grin. "I've heard mammoth meat tastes a lot like chicken."

She chuckled. Dinner had been easy. They'd wrapped potatoes in foil and stuck them in the fire, then served a ready-made salad. Dylan had grilled the steaks. Back at the house was a half gallon of rocky road ice cream. Sometimes, Molly thought, life was very good.

Her gaze was drawn back to her companion. Dylan was so incredibly beautiful. She knew he would balk at her choice of words. Men were not supposed to be beautiful, but he was. Harsh planes and sculpted cheekbones blurred in the firelight. His jaw was strong, his mouth perfectly shaped. He wore jeans and a black sweatshirt and nearly disappeared into the shadows. For a second, she wondered if he was even there. Had she just imagined him?

Then she remembered the ride on his motorcycle. How his body had felt so close to hers. No, that had not been any fantasy, although the situation was bound to stir up a few. Oh, well, she told herself. There were worse fates than having a crush on Dylan. Yes, it was sort of embarrassing at her age, but if it distracted her and reminded her that she was alive, it would be worth it.

So she just might allow herself to fall for him...in a schoolgirl sort of way. And when the two weeks were over and she returned to her life already in progress— Molly sighed. She didn't know what she was going to do then. But for now, this was enough.

"You're looking serious about something," Dylan said. "Want to talk about it?"

"It's not that interesting."

His expression didn't change from polite interest, but she doubted he'd bought her disclaimer. His next question confirmed her suspicion.

"Want to tell me why you're here?" he asked.

She didn't pretend to misunderstand. There wasn't any point. Dylan wanted to know why, after all this time, she'd looked him up and invited him on an adventure. She had appeared without warning, so she probably did owe him an explanation.

"Would you believe me if I told you I'd had a really bad week?" she asked.

"If it's the truth."

"Surprisingly, it is. Obviously something has pushed me to want to escape from the world." She shifted, drawing her knees up toward her chest. She'd pulled off her shoes and socks and the sand was cold on her feet.

"I had the worst week of my life," she said. "Starting last Monday. The thing that really gets me is that I had no idea what was coming. I guess it's always like that. People go on doing the same thing day after day, then suddenly, it changes. With no warning."

"We do tend to overestimate our ability to control destiny," he said.

"Exactly." Molly tucked a loose strand of hair behind her right ear. "What really bugs me is that I've lived such a small life. I didn't realize it at the time, but I do now. I have a degree in business and I was an accounts receivable supervisor at a communications company. We were recently bought out by one of the really big firms. I found out last Monday that I'd been downsized."

She took another sip of the Scotch. The fiery liquid

burned down to her belly, where it warmed her from the inside. "The thing is," she continued, "they'd interviewed me. I was supposed to have a job. Then my new boss called me into his office and gave me the information." She thought about their conversation. "The creep wouldn't even look at me. He said they'd changed their minds and that they were letting me go. At least the compensation package was decent. I have six months' pay sitting in my savings account. What really frustrates me is that I'd turned down two other job offers when I thought the new company wanted to keep me. Of course both those other jobs are filled now."

"Sounds like a difficult situation. Do you think you'll have trouble finding another job?"

"Not especially. I mean there are no guarantees. It's just—" She shrugged. "That wasn't all that happened that week."

He stretched out his long legs in front of him and crossed them at the ankle. "Go on."

She felt like a character in a bad movie, with too many troubles and nowhere to go.

"On Tuesday my fiancé—" She shook her head. "Make that my *ex*-fiancé, called me from Mexico. It seems that he and his assistant had been working late hours in the past couple of months. One thing led to another and they ran off together to Mexico. Grant hoped I would understand."

Molly felt herself getting tense. Her chest was all tight and she found it hard to breathe. She had to force herself to consciously relax her muscles. "He said he wanted to let me know as soon as it happened, because he valued honesty in all his relationships. Oh, and he called me collect."

"The guy's obviously low-life scum."

"My thoughts exactly." She downed the last of her drink.

She was actually pretty proud of herself. She'd managed to get through all of it without even a hint of tears. Of course there was no way she was going to tell Dylan what had happened to her on Wednesday of that infamous week. She couldn't talk about it with someone like him. There was no way he would understand. He was just too perfect.

"There's more isn't there?"

He asked the question in a low, caring voice. His perception both startled and frightened her. She probably could have handled it all if he hadn't looked as if he were really worried. Her eyes began to burn and she blinked frantically.

"Isn't that enough?" she said, trying to make herself sound amused. "Or are you out for blood?"

"I'm not out for anything. I just sensed there was more. But you're right. That's plenty."

"Exactly," she lied. "So I decided to get away for a while. I wanted to regroup, think things through. Maybe come up with a plan. I've always played it safe in my life, made what I thought were sensible choices. In the end it doesn't matter. No matter what you do, how careful you are, life can still jump up and bite you in the butt when you least expect it. That's why I'm hiding away for a little while, so I can lick my wounds. I'm not brave like you."

Dylan rose to his feet, grabbed the bottle of Scotch and settled next to her. "I'm many things, Molly, but brave isn't one of them."

Suddenly he was too close and she could inhale the scent of him. She had to concentrate to get a complete sentence out. "Sure you are. Look at all you've done with your life. You weren't afraid. You saw what you wanted and you went after it. I admire you a lot."

"Don't bother. It's easy to be brave when you don't have anything to lose."

He didn't touch her, which was both good and bad. In a way she wanted him to take her in his arms and swear that he would always love her. The thought nearly made her giggle. Like that was going to happen.

Her humor restored, she decided her crush on Dylan was going to be a good thing for her.

They sat in silence for a while. After Dylan poured her more Scotch, she continued to sip the dark liquid. She didn't feel the need to talk or to explain herself. That freedom was a pleasant change. With Grant, silences had made her nervous.

The night continued to close around them. Maybe the rest of the world *had* disappeared and they were the only ones left. The thought gave her the courage to voice something she'd been wondering about ever since she first saw him.

"I have a question," she said.

"I might have an answer. Fire away."

"It's about Janet. Are you sorry things didn't work out?"

Dylan stretched his arms above his head, then sank back against the log. "If you'd asked me that the day of her wedding, I would have told you yes. I really thought I loved her. It nearly killed me to watch her get married."

Molly told herself it was no more than she expected, but it still hurt to hear his confession. "I see."

He glanced at her. "The thing is, six weeks after I left town, I was on my knees thanking God for my escape. I guess I should have been more grateful that Janet had had the good sense to let me go. We were kids. It was fun then, but we didn't belong together. I see that now."

"You don't miss her?"

"Not really. I took off determined to show her I could

be somebody. That quickly turned into proving the idea to myself. Janet was the catalyst for my leaving town, and I'm glad. But I wouldn't change the past. With the hindsight of an adult, I don't think Janet and I really loved each other. It was a kid thing."

That made her feel a little better. Better that he'd gotten over her sister. After all, Janet was happily married. Besides, it would really annoy her, Molly, if Dylan was still in love with her sister.

"When you left, you started racing motorcycles, right?" she asked.

"I was just a fool on a bike. More heart and courage than talent. After a while I figured out I was better at designing than racing."

"Did you win with your bike or just with the women?" she asked, teasing him.

He grinned. "I did do a little better with the ladies. That checkered flag was always elusive. To be honest, the women hurt a lot more than the crashes."

That sobered her. "You were hurt?"

"A couple times." He shrugged. "It comes with the business." He leaned close. "Tell you what, Molly. I'll show you my scars if you'll show me yours."

She knew in her head he couldn't understand what his words would mean to her, but she still felt as if he'd slapped her across the face. An unexpected sob burst from her. She covered her mouth as she stumbled to her feet. She had to get away. Now! How had he known? she wondered.

She didn't bother to ask. She just turned toward the darkness and ran.

Chapter Five

Dylan stared after Molly until she disappeared into the night. What had just happened? What had he said? Then he figured it really didn't matter. It was dark on the beach and she was alone. He hadn't meant to say anything to upset her and the tight knot in his gut told him he would make damn sure not to do it again.

He scrambled to his feet and headed after her. There was just enough light from the moon to make out her shape. She'd stopped by the surf and was crouching. To disappear, he wondered, or just to hold in the pain?

The sound of her sobs was muffled by the crash of the waves on the shore, but he could still hear the heart-wrenching cries. His gut tightened a little more. He cursed himself. Obviously she'd misunderstood his crack about sharing scars. She probably thought he was making light of her being dumped by her fiancé. The man was a bastard, he thought grimly. Any guy who would do something that incredibly low was the worst kind of scum. She was better off without him, although he doubted she would believe that today. In time she would see that she was lucky to have escaped—but for now, she was in pain and he was the reason.

"Molly, I'm sorry," he said, coming up behind her and touching her shoulder.

She flinched. "I'm fine. Go away."

"You're not fine and I'm not going away. I didn't mean anything by what I said. I was teasing, but I can see how you'd take it wrong. I didn't mean to be a jerk."

She shook her head. He didn't know what that meant. Was she dismissing his apology, or telling him it didn't matter? Not knowing what else to do, he pulled her to her feet and drew her close.

She stood still, not relaxing against him but not resisting, either. He wrapped his arms around her. Another sob shook her.

"Hush," he murmured. "It's okay."

"It's not. That's the whole point. I just don't think I can get through this."

He wasn't sure what the "this" was. Her job? Grant?

"We'll get through tonight together," he told her. "Don't worry about tomorrow, okay? Let that take care of itself. Just deal with tonight."

He placed one hand on the back of her head and urged her to rest her cheek against his shoulder. She was a little thing. He was used to tall women who came close to looking him in the eye. He sort of liked how Molly was smaller.

She was soft, too. As he rubbed her back, he felt pliant skin and muscle, not ribs. Both their jackets were open and her breasts pressed against his chest. They were as he'd imagined them when he'd been thinking about her riding with him on the bike. Warm and soft, full curves that seemed to burn into him.

The need swept through him, a wanting he could only endure as heat and blood rushed into his groin. But he didn't press himself into her, didn't want her to know that his thoughts had turned passionate. Mostly because through it all, he could still feel the waves of pain rolling off her. She needed so much more than he had to offer.

"I'm sorry," he said again, because he couldn't think of any other words.

"Don't be," she told him, and sniffed. "You didn't do anything wrong."

"But I—"

She raised her head and stared at him. In the soft light of the moon her face was pretty, he realized with some surprise. Light glinted off the tracks of her tears.

"It's okay, Dylan," she told him. "You were just teasing. I overreacted." She wiped her face with the back of her hand. "I'll make you a deal. You stop feeling bad and apologizing and I'll stop crying. How's that?"

Her eyes were large, a hazel brown that in the night were simply dark and mysterious. He had the oddest sensation that he could get lost in those eyes, drown a happy man in those depths. He wanted—no, he *needed*—to be close to her. In her, not in the sense of making love, although that would be nice, too, but inside the person, a part of who she was.

The longing was as strong as it was unexpected. He didn't understand it and that should have scared the daylights out of him. But oddly enough, it didn't. When he couldn't figure out a way to crawl inside and be one with her, he did the next best thing. He kissed her.

Molly had plenty of warning. At least she would have if she'd really thought he was going to do what it looked like he wanted to do. One minute Dylan had been hugging her, comforting her as one comforts a hurt child. The next thing she knew, his hands were cupping her face and he was moving close. In that heartbeat she could have pulled back or protested. But she hadn't really thought he was going to kiss her. After all, this was Dylan and she was just, well, Molly.

His mouth touched hers. She half expected the world to jerk to a halt as the rotation of the plant burped in shock. When that didn't happen, she waited for Dylan to realize who she was and what he was doing. Once he figured that out, he would jump back in disgust. But he didn't. Instead he kept his lips pressed against hers. The warm, firm contact jolted her clear down to her feet where her toes curled into the cold sand.

She swallowed, not sure what to do. A scream built up inside, but she suppressed it. This was not the time for screaming. She felt a little awkward standing there like that with her hands trapped between their bodies. Had he really meant to kiss her?

He must have, she told herself. He was still cupping her face, his touch all tender, as if she were someone who really mattered to him. She realized her eyes were closed, so she opened them and was stunned to see *his* eyes were closed. Oddly enough, that made the kiss even more intimate, although she wasn't exactly sure why.

His mouth moved. For a panicked heartbeat, she was afraid he was going to pull away. He didn't. Instead he moved his lips back and forth before gently pressing the tip of his tongue against her bottom lip.

Molly's heart lurched. She actually felt the organ give a giant jump-shudder in her chest. Flames ignited all over her body as heat flooded her. She felt herself begin to tremble and she had to move her hands to hold on to his waist so she wouldn't fall. It was magic—no, better than magic because it was real. This was actually happening to her. Here on the beach, Dylan was kissing her.

He buried one of his hands in her hair. The action caused her head to tilt slightly. He adjusted himself so they were still kissing, then his mouth opened against hers.

She responded without thinking, parting her lips, then telling herself she was a fool. He wouldn't want to kiss her *that* way. Would he?

Apparently he would.

She felt the first caress of his tongue against the inside of her lower lip. Her breath caught. Then he delved into her mouth. He tasted of Scotch and sin, flavored with some unique sweetness that had to be the essence of him. She allowed herself to sag against him, to let him support her while he worked his exquisite perfection in her mouth.

All of her body reacted to the kiss. Her breasts swelled, then ached for his tender touch. Between her thighs, her woman's place dampened to ready itself for all he had to offer. Her skin felt sensitized to even the slightest brush of cloth or air. Low in her belly, the wanting began like a steady hum of need.

This was not the brief kiss he'd given her all those years ago. This wasn't a kiss between friends. This was a kiss from a man to a woman, a kiss of passion and promise. The only question was why.

He pulled back enough to whisper her name, then trailed kisses down to her jaw. From there he traced a damp line to her ear. She quivered as he nibbled, taking her lobe in his mouth and tickling it with his tongue. Involuntary shivers rippled through her. She pressed closer to him, wanting more, wanting him never to stop. What did the whys matter? For this moment, it was enough that she was alive and could feel.

She pressed against him. As she did, he shifted a little. In the back of her mind, reality intruded. Thoughts formed, and though she tried to ignore them, they persisted.

They were not touching below the waist. She moved closer again and he stepped back. Again. There was something he didn't want her to lean against. Why?

And then she knew. The truth was cold and brutal and it nearly ripped out her heart. None of this mattered to him. He didn't want her to press against him only to find out he wasn't the least bit turned on by what they were doing.

The pain was so intense it took her breath away. Still, pride was stronger. She had to get out of this situation so she could be alone. Once in her room, she would figure out how to survive the humiliation and find the courage to face Dylan again. Or maybe she would just pack up her stuff and run.

It wasn't even his fault, she thought sadly. He was just trying to be a good guy and offer comfort. If wishes were horses and all that... But they weren't. They were just wishes.

She straightened, then moved away. Dylan let her go, but when she looked at him, he seemed dazed.

"Molly?"

He sounded confused and slightly overwhelmed. If she hadn't known about the lack of physical evidence of his desire, she would have sworn he had been as caught up in the moment as she had been.

"You don't have to do this," she said, and was pleased when her voice sounded normal. "I asked you for an adventure, but mercy kisses are not part of the deal. Compassion is fine. I can handle that, but pity really annoys me. So let's just forget this ever happened, okay?"

For the second time that evening, she disappeared into the night. Dylan stared after her, wondering what had gone wrong. One minute he'd been kissing Molly and thinking that he might just explode right then and there, and the next she was pushing him away and talking about mercy kisses.

"Dammit, Molly, I kissed you because I wanted to, not out of some twisted sense of pity," he called after her, but it was too late. She'd already gone into the house.

He cursed under his breath, then returned to the fire to collect their belongings. He wished it *had* been pity. Then he wouldn't be so uncomfortable right now, with need pumping through his groin. He started stacking plates. Why would she think he was just pretending? What would be the point?

He couldn't come up with any answers, not for her behavior or his. He told himself it was no big deal. But it was. Why would he want Molly? She wasn't his type, at least not physically. She was Janet's little sister. Nothing more.

But she hadn't felt like anyone's little sister in his arms. There she'd been all woman and he'd wanted her. He had agreed to come away with her because he needed the break and he thought they might have a few laughs together. But it was already turning out to be more complicated than that. Molly wasn't the woman he'd imagined her to be, or maybe he was the one who had changed.

His arms full of their belongings, he headed back for the house. One thing was sure, he told himself, he wasn't going to apologize. First, he hadn't broken any rules. Second, he'd liked kissing her way too much to want to forget it had ever happened.

Molly was still awake at midnight. She had heard Dylan come in a couple hours ago after making several trips to pick up their things from the beach. She'd felt badly about him doing all the work, but there was no way she could have faced him. She wasn't sure she would ever be able to do that. Maybe it would be better for everyone if she just left.

Except…she didn't want to go. She didn't want to have to find another place to hide out and she didn't want to leave Dylan. Which meant she had to make peace with what had happened between them.

Was it really so terrible? she asked herself. When she thought about it logically, or tried to, she could almost convince herself it was no big deal. They'd talked about her life and how everything had fallen apart. He'd tried to tease her and she'd overreacted. He'd come after her to make sure she was all right, then when he'd seen she wasn't, he'd offered comfort.

That was really the extent of his crimes. He hadn't been turned on when he'd kissed her, but that was hardly against the law. It wasn't his fault that her crush had returned in full force, leaving her no way to save face after what had been—for her, at least—an incredibly passionate experience. He'd done nothing wrong. That's what she had to focus on, because it was the truth. Dylan had actually been very sweet. Running away now would be cowardly, not to mention incredibly stupid. She liked being with him. For the next couple of weeks she was going to need a distraction and he was the best one she could think of. Besides, she liked *him*.

Molly crossed to the window and stared out into the darkness. So what if her foolish pride had been a little battered? She'd survived worse. Pray God she would live to survive worse again. The trick was to get over it and move on. Because in her heart of hearts, she knew she didn't want to leave. Not now.

"I promised myself no regrets," she whispered into the darkness. "No what-ifs, no second guessing. I promised myself that I was going to live my life, instead of always taking the safe route.''

The words hung in the air like an accusation. She hadn't really forgotten her promise to herself; she'd just misplaced the message. Well, she'd remembered now, and she was going to keep that promise, no matter what.

In the morning she would make peace with Dylan, apologize for her behavior and put the whole thing behind her. She would continue to enjoy her crush on him in the privacy of her own mind and she would stop expecting him to participate in any way. No regrets, she promised herself. Just living.

When Dylan stepped out of the shower, he smelled cooking. His stomach growled, which didn't make sense. He normally made do with some coffee and maybe a donut if Evie brought them into the office. But suddenly, breakfast sounded great.

He hurried through dressing and shaving, then combed his damp hair and made his way to the kitchen. He paused in the doorway and watched Molly.

She was stirring something in a large bowl. A pot of coffee was already sitting on their small table and bacon sizzled on the stove. The domestic scene should have made him want to run for cover. After all, if any of his bed partners dared to start the day this way, he was usually out the door before they could manage a quick ''Good morning.'' Of course he rarely spent the night with them, thereby avoiding the whole issue.

With Molly he didn't want to run. Instead he found himself thinking about walking up behind her and wrapping his arms around her waist. He wanted to inhale the scent of her soft skin, brush his lips against her nape, then trail kisses down her spine until her skin broke out in gooseflesh.

He thought about taking the bowl from her and setting it down, then turning her toward him and kissing her. The counter looked a little high, but he would bet the table was the right height. He imaged her sitting in just a shirt, her legs spread, welcoming him as he—

"Good morning."

He heard the words, then had to consciously drag himself back from his very pleasant daydream. He swallowed, then shifted, hoping she wouldn't notice the sudden change taking place in the front of his jeans.

"Uh, hi," he managed, his voice sounding slightly thick and husky.

Molly wore a long-sleeved white shirt rolled up to her elbows. The tails hung to about midthigh. Her feet were bare, as was her face. Her hair had been pulled back into a braid that hung down her back. She had to be about twenty-seven or twenty-eight, but she looked the way she had at seventeen. He thought about how she'd been then, with braces and bad skin. Okay, he amended, maybe she looked a little different now, but not much.

She gave him a quick smile, then nodded at the bowl. "I'm making pancakes. I hope you like them."

"They're my favorite and I'm suddenly starved."

"Good. Have a seat."

He moved into the kitchen. "Can I help?"

"No, I've got everything under control." She bit on her lower lip. "Dylan, about last night—"

He held up a hand to stop her. "You don't have to explain."

"Good, because I'm not going to, but I *am* going to apologize. I can't take away my overreaction, but I can try to make amends." She held out the bowl. "Hence the pancakes. They're supposed to fix everything."

He didn't mind that she was keeping a few secrets from

him. Lord knows he had a bunch of his own. But he liked that she was willing to admit she'd acted a little strange.

"Apology pancakes, huh?" he said as he settled into one of the metal chairs at the small table. "I don't know if that's a good idea. You're putting them under a lot of pressure. You think they'll be able to perform now? I would guess you've scarred those little suckers for life. They're going to be in pancake therapy for a long time."

She stared at him for a full two seconds, then she started to laugh. "If we eat them, the problem is solved, right?" she said.

"I hadn't thought of that. It seems extreme, but it would probably work."

"And here I worried that I was the crazy one," she told him as she set to work, pouring the batter into a frying pan.

A few minutes later, she set a stack of pancakes in front of him, then brought over a plate of bacon, as well. After pouring coffee, she joined him.

"These look great," he said.

"Let's hope they taste great, too."

"They will."

He said the words easily, but he knew in his heart it didn't matter. Right now he couldn't taste anything. He could only look at her and remember what it had been like last night to hold her in his arms and kiss her. He wanted her—again. That was getting to be a common problem. The thing was, he wasn't going to do anything about it.

He filled a plate for her, then took food for himself. "Thanks, Molly. You didn't have to do this, but I appreciate it. Tell you what. Let's start over and be friends. I like you. I think we could have a lot of fun together."

Her smile made her pretty. Funny how all those years ago, he'd never noticed she had a great smile. Maybe he'd been too young and to into himself and appearances. Maybe he'd never taken the time to look.

"I'd like that," she told him. "I like you, too, Dylan. We always had fun together before. There's no reason to think that's changed."

"My thoughts exactly." He was a grown-up. There was no reason he couldn't keep his libido under control. Or he would just start wearing looser jeans.

She chewed on her pancakes for a minute, then swallowed. "But I'm still sorry about last night. I completely lost it. I've been under a lot of pressure lately what with my job and Grant."

"Hey, thanks for the apology, but it's time to let it go. Anyone would have reacted to all that. Bad enough to have a company turn on you, but when you're also dealing with an incredible jerk like that, what can you do but get annoyed?"

She stared at him. There was a faint flush on her face, probably from the cooking. He liked the color in her cheeks.

"Grant isn't really a jerk," she said.

Dylan set down his fork. "Explain that to me. Women always do that. Some guy treats them like dirt, then when someone calls him a name the woman defends him."

Molly opened her mouth, then closed it, then shook her head. "You're right. I can't believe it. Women do that. Why? Training, maybe? I don't know why I said that. He *is* a jerk. At times I've wished I could find him and just beat him up. I plan to forget him as soon as I can, but that doesn't mean I don't have the right to be furious."

"Good. Because if you really had anything decent to say about him, I would lose all respect for you."

"If you catch me defending him again, tell me, okay?"

"Sure." He leaned forward and rested his elbows on the

table. "I mean that, Molly. I will say something. I don't think people should stay in a relationship if they're not happy, but there are plenty of less cowardly ways to leave. What Grant did was pure slime. You're lucky to be rid of him. I'm sure it doesn't feel that way now, but it's true."

"I appreciate what you're telling me. Oddly enough, you'd be surprised by how little I miss him. Which just goes to show I should never have agreed to marry him. It's just that I thought..." Her voice trailed off. Some of the light faded from her eyes.

"What did you think?" he prompted.

"That he was safe. He's a lawyer with a well-respected firm. Just the kind of guy my mother would have picked. I don't know. I keep coming up against my choices and not liking what I see."

"Better that you found out now. Guys like him spend their lives being slime. If he ran around with some woman before the wedding, imagine what he would have done afterward."

"Is that anger I hear in your voice?" she asked. "This is something you feel strongly about?"

"Absolutely. I'm a firm believer in monogamy. I might not be able to sustain a relationship for very long, but while I'm in it, I'm there. Okay, as a kid in my late teens I was more interested in quantity, but everybody grows up. Grant's a loser and you're better off without him. If it would make you feel better, I'd be happy to beat him up for you."

She burst out laughing. "Dylan, you say the sweetest things, but no, thanks. I believe that fate or whatever you want to call it will catch up with Grant in time." She tilted her head. "I wouldn't have guessed that about you. The monogamy thing."

"Because I'm the type who runs around?"

"No." She frowned. "How strange. I wouldn't think of you as running around, but I haven't thought of you as faithful, either."

"It pretty much has to be one or the other." He kept his tone light, not wanting her to know how her good opinion of him had suddenly become very important.

"I guess I figured you were so attractive to women that you were constantly tempted. But I don't think I'm saying it wouldn't be your fault. This is complicated. I suppose the bottom line is, I'm impressed."

He took a sip of coffee. "I don't know that I've said anything that special."

"Philosophy over pancakes," she said, and smiled. "Whatever will I get if I make waffles?"

"French poetry," he teased.

"Really?" She made a show of looking around the kitchen. "I must check to see if we have a waffle iron."

Chapter Six

The small Dutch town of Solvang was designed for tourists. In the summer and on weekends it was crowded, but midweek and off-season, like now, there were only a handful of people looking in shop windows and going into the many restaurants. Molly raised her face toward the warm sunshine and smiled. Life was very nice. She'd thought she might have a good time with Dylan, but she hadn't expected to enjoy herself as much as she was. The past four days had been filled with fun and pleasant conversation. He was someone she found she liked spending time with, and not just because he was so easy to look at.

They were taking their vacation one day at a time. This morning, they'd decided to drive about an hour north of their beach house, to Solvang. This afternoon, they were going to explore the local wine country.

"They've got a real windmill thing going on here," Dy-

Ian said as they paused in front of a shop window. Several ceramic blue-and-white windmills gleamed in the light.

"That's part of the appeal," Molly said. "But they also have one-of-a-kind art, lace, pretty things for the home. And food. Great food."

He checked his watch. "So we'll be stopping for lunch?"

"I'd like to. The pastries are heaven."

"You've been here before?"

She nodded. "But not since I was a kid. I came over one weekend with a girlfriend and her family. It was a lot of fun."

As they turned from the window to start down the street, Dylan's arm brushed against hers. She'd grown used to the casual touches that were a part of their day. Used to, but not unmindful of. It didn't matter what she was thinking about. If Dylan touched her in any way, her entire body went on alert. At times it was a very nice distraction. If she could get him to touch her whenever she was worried or feeling anxious, she would never have to deal with personal trauma again.

They moved to the next shop. This one sold crystal. It was filled with tiny fantasy pieces of dragons and griffins, stunning pitchers, vases and glasses.

"Don't fall in love with anything," Dylan warned. "Whatever you buy still has to fit in your duffel bag. The motorcycle doesn't have any extra storage."

"I could always have it shipped back," she reminded him.

"Good point."

She thought about his bike. She'd grown to like riding it. While she would prefer to keep her car for everyday transportation, she wouldn't mind having a motorcycle around for weekends.

"How'd you get into racing?" she asked as they strolled down the street. On their left was a large park, on their right more shops. At the end of the street was a restaurant she remembered as being excellent. Maybe they would have lunch there.

"Through the back door," Dylan said. "When I left town I had about twenty bucks in my pocket. I rode east for a couple of days, until the money ran out, then got a job at a bike repair shop. I was pretty good, especially at modifications. One of my regular customers, Bill Jensen, raced a string of bikes. He offered to let me ride for him on weekends."

"How'd you do?"

He shrugged. "Regionally I did okay, but when I went national, I struggled. I was great at making changes on my bikes, but the actual racing got to be more of a job."

Molly tried to picture what it must have been like. "I've never even been to a motorcycle race."

"Then we'll have to educate you."

"I'd like that."

He looked down at her as she glanced up, and their gazes locked. Dark hair, dark eyes, handsome features. He was walking, breathing temptation, she thought. And nice. She had to bite down on her lower lip to keep from smiling, aware Dylan would want to know what was so funny and that he would hate being called nice.

"You never came back," she said to change the subject. "Once you left town, you were gone."

"There was nothing to come back to." He shoved his hands into his jeans pockets. He wore a long-sleeved burgundy shirt, with the sleeves rolled up to his elbows. "I thought about it. Coming home, I mean. But to what? I doubt my folks even noticed I was gone. The road was a nice distraction."

"I know exactly what you mean."

"Yeah?" He gave her a quick smile. "I remember my first win. Some Podunk town in West Texas. There were twenty of us and I was in the lead from the start. I nearly lost it on the first curve, what with all the excitement, but I hung on and won."

"And then there were a billion women hanging on you."

Dark eyebrows raised. "That's a slight exaggeration. There might have been one or two."

"I think there are always one or two hanging around wherever you go."

"It's not what you think, Molly." He started down the sidewalk. "They aren't interested in a relationship. They want to spend the night with a winner. Names aren't always exchanged. It gets old real fast. That was the toughest part of the road. Traveling all the time, not being able to keep in touch with friends. I was never successful enough to have a crew. I moved around with Bill's guys sometimes, but a lot of the time, I was on my own."

"It sounds a little lonely."

"It was."

Molly mulled that over. She wouldn't have thought Dylan would ever have cause to be lonely. He was the kind of man who naturally drew people to him. Of course, he spent a lot of time shutting people out, as well, so she supposed it made sense that he didn't have a lot of hangers-on. So they had something in common. In fact, they had more in common than she ever would have guessed.

"Tell me how you got from racing to designing bikes."

He looked at her. "Why all the questions?"

"I'm interested. We're friends, right? Friends want to know about each other's lives. Or am I treading on something personal?"

"I think I can share a few of my secrets with you, but you have to promise not to tell."

His voice was light and teasing. It seemed to skitter down her spine and made her shiver in the most delightful way. "I swear." She made an X over her heart. "I will take your design secrets to my grave."

She shivered again, but this time it wasn't from delight. That had been a poor choice of words. She pushed the thought aside and concentrated on Dylan. "So there you were," she said, "a young studmuffin on the trail to victory. One night you heard a voice saying, 'If you build the motorcycles, they will come.'"

He stopped in the middle of the sidewalk and glared at her. "Studmuffin?"

"It's a term of endearment."

"Studmuffin? I'm not some male bimbo."

"By using the word 'male' to differentiate, are you saying the term 'bimbo' is female by definition?"

He groaned. "You're the one calling me a studmuffin, so why am I the one in trouble?"

"Just luck."

He pulled his hands from his pockets and held them up in a gesture of surrender. "Okay, I'll let the studmuffin crack go if you'll ignore the gender issue of bimbo. Deal?"

"Yes. Now, tell me about designing."

"Only if we can go get some lunch. I'm starved. What about that place?" He pointed to the restaurant at the end of the street.

"It's fine."

They started walking toward it. Once they were inside and seated, they scanned the menus, then ordered.

"I was just helping out a buddy at first," Dylan said, leaning back in the booth. "He knew what I'd done to my bike. He was having some trouble with his, so I took a look at it, made a couple of modifications. Then he won the next three races. Word got out. I made more changes, then I worked up my first design."

"Sounds like a labor of love."

"It was. Things were slow at first. I didn't have any money, no savings. That would have been sensible." He grinned and she smiled in return.

She liked hearing about his past, learning how things had changed for him.

"Seven years ago my bikes started winning regionally. Five years ago, we took the national championship. I opened the business with less than no money. Just a lot of sweat and a couple of orders. It was tough at first, but I loved it. I built the first dozen bikes on my own. I was next door to a machine shop and would use their equipment to make some of the parts. It was crazy."

"But fun." She could see the remembered pleasure in his expression.

"Yeah. Those were good times."

"You showed them all."

The waitress appeared with their sodas. They thanked her and she left.

"I would guess most everyone back home is surprised," he said. "No one thought I would amount to much. Not even me."

"You have come a long way," she agreed. "Look at your house. It's amazing."

He peeled the paper off his straw and shrugged, looking a little self-conscious. "I know it's kinda big for one person."

"Kinda! You could house a small army in it. Dylan, you have an indoor stream and pond. That house belongs on a movie set, not in someone's life."

"I know. It happened to be for sale when I was looking.

I got a really good deal." He looked like a kid explaining why he'd eaten cookies before dinner. It hadn't been *his* fault they'd just been there, calling to him.

"Uh-huh. Like I believe that. But that's not the point. You don't have to justify your house to me. You earned it."

His expression turned serious. "I think that's why I bought it. Because I could. It's a long way from that ugly, dark trailer I grew up in. I hated that place. All I wanted was to get away. When I was a kid, that meant being gone all the time."

"But you didn't leave after you graduated from high school."

"I couldn't. When my dad died, I didn't want to leave my mom. She was drinking so much I knew she wouldn't last long." He took a long swallow of his soda. "She didn't. Then I stuck around for Janet. Once that ended, there was nothing to keep me in town."

Molly had heard the stories—everyone in town had. That both Dylan's parents drank. That his father beat both mother and child. That visits to the emergency room for treatment of lacerations and broken bones were not uncommon.

She wanted to reach out to him but didn't know how. What was she supposed to say? That she understood? She didn't. Even though her past had been less than perfect, it was nothing compared with his childhood.

"I'm sorry," she managed at last.

"Me, too, but there's nothing I can do about it. I think about the drinking. They say it can be genetic, so I watch it. I partied some when I was younger, but now I have a couple of beers a week. That bottle of Scotch we've been sharing is the first hard liquor I've had in two or three years. I don't worry about it, but I also know not to tempt fate."

"I'm glad," she said. "I would hate for anything to happen to you."

"Thanks, kid."

He looked at her. Something flickered in his eyes. For that second Molly wanted to know what he was thinking. But then she dismissed the idea. She only wanted to know if he was secretly lusting after her person. And that was so incredibly unlikely that she had to smile to herself. Probably Dylan had simply spotted the waitress with their orders.

As if the fates wanted to prove her point, the woman appeared at the side of the table and set plates in front of them. "Eat up," she said. "But save room for dessert. We've got some very special pastries, freshly made this morning."

"Sounds great," Dylan said, picking up his sandwich.

Molly stared after the waitress. "Maybe I'll just watch you eat yours."

"Don't you want dessert?" he asked.

"Of course. It's just…" Her voice trailed off. "There is the issue of these extra twenty pounds."

"Is one dessert going to make that much difference?"

Rather than answer, she took a bite of her sandwich. It was crazy, she told herself. What had she expected? That he would deny she needed to lose weight? But if the knot of disappointment in her chest was anything to go by, that was exactly what she'd hoped for. As if Dylan wouldn't notice the extra pounds on her frame. Compared with his usual women, she was a toad. A large toad. Maybe a cow. She could moo at him and see if he reacted.

Stop it! she told herself. She wasn't going to get all weird about his reaction and she wasn't going to risk wallowing in self-pity. She knew the danger of that. The reality was, she needed to lose some weight. Of course Dylan noticed, but so what? What did it matter? They were still friends. He still liked her. Even if she suddenly lost the twenty pounds, she wouldn't be the kind of woman to make him lose control. She had to remember that she was the one with the crush, not he.

They chatted about different things during lunch. When the waitress returned, Molly went ahead and ordered dessert. Dylan ordered a different one and announced that they would share. Molly nodded her agreement.

This was enough, she thought. These bits of happiness were the entire point of life. That's what she had to keep remembering.

Molly leaned back against the counter in the winery and took another sip of her glass. "You know," she told him, "we're on a motorcycle. There's no way we can actually buy any wine, even if we fall in love with it. Where on earth would we put it?"

There was color in her cheeks and her smile was as easy as he'd seen it. Dylan wanted to believe it was more than the fact that they'd been sampling wine for nearly an hour. He wanted to believe that their time together had helped her deal with her life. But he didn't think he would be able to take all the credit. It was definitely the wine.

"We can buy a couple of bottles," he said. "You're right. There's no room to take them back with us. But we can drink them while we're away."

Molly frowned. "I don't want to create any trouble."

It took him a couple of minutes to figure out what she was talking about and then he realized she meant the history of alcoholism in his family. "I think I can handle sharing wine with you for a few days."

She finished the sample in her glass and set it on the counter. "The Merlot is very nice," she said.

He nodded at the woman who'd been serving them. "We'll take two bottles of that and three of the Chardonnay."

"Hmm, you read my mind," Molly said, then pressed a hand to her forehead. "I feel a bit wobbly. It's barely four in the afternoon and I'm drunk. Talk about a lightweight."

"It's not the time of day that's the problem," he told her. "It's the fact that you've had the equivalent of less than two glasses of wine. At least you're a cheap date."

"Everyone needs a skill," she said. "So I guess that's mine." She blinked as if to clear her vision.

"Okay, let's walk this off," he said, then took her arm and glanced at the salesperson. "We'll be back in a few minutes."

"I'll wrap up the wine," she said.

"Thanks."

Dylan led Molly outside. There were several trees by the gravel parking lot, along with wooden picnic tables.

"Let's go sit in the shade," he said, guiding her toward the benches.

"We can sing camp songs. I'm not sure how many I remember, but we can make up words."

"At least you're a happy drunk."

"I'm not drunk." She glared at him, obviously indignant. "If I were drunk, I'd be throwing myself at you."

He thought about the motorcycle ride over, how Molly had felt behind him on the bike, her body all pressed up against his. "I wonder if there's a liquor store in town and if they carry tequila," he muttered.

"What?" she asked.

"Nothing. Sit." He held her arm until she'd lowered herself to the bench, then he took a seat on the bench across from hers, using the table as a back rest.

"I'm really not drunk," she said.

"I know. You're just happy."

She thought about that one, then nodded. "You're right. I'm happy and I haven't been happy for a long time." She leaned back and rested her elbows on the table behind her. "You'd think if I was engaged that Grant would have made me happy, but he didn't." She paused. "What a slug. A slime. A slithery snake of a scorpion. A slippery, smelly, s—"

"Molly?"

"Huh?" She stared at him. "I was using *s* words."

"I got that. We all understand that Grant is not a nice man."

"He's a complete toad."

Dylan chuckled, then waited to see if they were going to go through *t* words next, but Molly didn't offer any more. Instead she stared up at the sky. Her position—arms spread, elbows nearly at shoulder level—thrust out her breasts in his general direction. He tried not to look, but it was way too tempting. She wore a sweatshirt. The garment was loose enough to hide the curves, but he knew they were there. That they were and he couldn't see them was driving him crazy. Everything about her was driving him crazy. But he liked it. He liked the wanting and not having. He liked being with her. He just liked her. The truth was, he didn't have many friends in his life and he was glad to count Molly as one of the few.

He looked at her face and caught her studying him. "What?" he asked.

"I was just wondering. A few days ago you asked me why I wanted to go away for a couple of weeks. What's your reason, Dylan? Why did you leave everything in your world to come away with me?"

"That's easy. I have some decisions to make and I'm

not sure what to do. I thought time away would help me decide.''

"What's the problem?"

"Black Lightning."

"Your company? I thought it was doing really well."

"It is. We've got more work than we can handle. We're turning customers away every week. We'll be expanding pretty soon, but I don't want to do it too quickly because I'm concerned about quality control. That's number one with me. I'm trapped in the office more than I would like, so I don't get to spend much time on the floor. I haven't been doing much designing lately, either. The problem is, a big motorcycle company wants to buy me out. They've promised me a place in the corporation, my own design staff and lots of money. I would get to do what I love, but I would lose control. That's what it comes down to, really. Money versus freedom. If I take the offer, am I being smart or selling out?''

"Good question. What does your gut tell you?"

"Right now it's keeping quiet."

"Bummer." She stretched her arms over her head, then let her hands fall into her lap. "Want to know what I think?"

Surprisingly, he did. Suddenly her opinion was very important to him. "Yes, I do."

"Does the money matter? I've seen your house. You're not exactly poor."

He laughed. "Agreed. Personally, I'm doing well. Some of the appeal of their offer is that I would get to expand right now. I'll get the capital and have the time to keep everybody honest. If I wait, who knows how long it will be until I can find the time and money to grow like that."

"Will it still work for you when you're doing it for someone else?" she asked. "You're not exactly a team player, Dylan. You've always gone your own way. Do you think you would survive in corporate America?''

He'd wondered about that himself. "Good question, and I don't have an answer. I feel as if I'm being tempted by the devil."

"Maybe you are. I would guess the devil has a way of making his offers look very enticing. After all, that's his job. My advice is to listen to your gut and your heart. Until you know what Black Lightning means to you, you won't know what you'll lose by giving it up."

Her words made a lot of sense. "I appreciate your input."

"My pleasure. Sounds like we both have a lot to think about."

Her more than him, he told himself. The other company was threatening to withdraw their offer if he didn't respond, but he knew they would be back. He had time on his side. But Molly—she had some tough decisions to make. Grant, her job. Considering all that was going on, she was amazingly together and calm about the whole thing.

"What are *you* going to do?" he asked.

A strand of hair worked free of her braid and fluttered around her face. She tucked it behind her ear. "I don't know. Right now, I'm not sure I even care. I have money in the bank, so nothing is immediately pressing. I suppose I'm fortunate that way. Although I sure don't feel lucky." She sighed.

"Would you want to go into the same line of work?"

"Maybe. I liked it, but I didn't love it. I'll miss the people more than the job."

"What do you love? Maybe that's a place to start."

She got very still, then sadness filled her face. For a moment Dylan thought she was going to cry and he fought against panic. What had he said?

But she didn't cry. She just shrugged. "At one time I would have told you I loved Grant, but now I wonder if that was ever true." She sighed again. "I don't even want to call him names anymore, so the wine must be wearing off. Darn. I liked being happy, even if it was just for the moment. To answer your question, I don't know what I love. Maybe that's what I have to find out."

"There are career-counseling centers available," he said. "You could take some tests to find out what you're good at. Maybe the same line of work in a different field."

She rose to her feet. "Maybe. I don't want to talk about this right now."

"You can't wait forever. You're going to have to do something about a job."

Her gaze was steady. "I know, but not today. All right? If you don't mind, I'd like to head back to the house now."

"Molly—"

She raised her hand. "I know you mean well. It's that guy thing about wanting to fix everything. But I can't be fixed. Not yet, anyway. Just let it go, Dylan. Trust me when I tell you there are things you don't understand."

He wanted to say more, but she walked off before he got the chance. He collected their wine, then followed her to the bike.

For once, when they rode back to the house, she didn't lean against him. He figured she was holding on to the bar under the seat, and he found himself missing the feel of her body pressing against his.

Molly had been gone for too long. Dylan stared out the back window of their tiny house and wondered if he should go after her. When they'd returned from the winery, she'd told him she wanted to take a walk and clear away the last of the wine. That had been nearly an hour ago. It was near sunset and he was getting concerned.

Even as he told himself it was none of his business, he grabbed his coat and headed for the front door. He knew what was wrong. He'd pressed her too much when he'd mentioned her job. It wasn't any of his business. She'd come away so she could escape what was bothering her, not so he could throw it in her face. While he hated the generalization, he knew it was true: as a man, he liked to fix things.

A few clouds lingered on the horizon. They were pale yellow and gold from the setting sun. The sea was restless. He could see whitecaps in the distance. The surf was loud tonight, thundering against the sand as it rolled endlessly onto the shore.

He turned north because that was the direction they always took when they strolled along the beach. Cold wind snapped at his jacket and blew through his hair. As he walked, he searched the beach, looking for a trace of her and trying to ignore the voice in the back of his head that whispered there was something she wasn't telling him.

His gut might be silent on the subject of what to do about selling his company, but it had plenty to say about Molly Anderson. For one thing, it was extremely vocal on the issue of wanting her. For now, he pushed that aside. There was also the question of what else was going on. More than once he'd had the sense that she was keeping secrets. After all, she checked her answering machine every night. He couldn't imagine what her secrets were, but maybe they were the reason she'd reacted so strongly earlier. Or maybe he was battling ghosts as a way to excuse his own probing.

There was a play area up ahead, with several benches. At this time of day, with the weather on the cool side, no children were around. He saw an old man sitting on a bench, with a large dog next to him. Someone else was a little ways in front, on the sand. As he got closer, he realized the second person was Molly. Around her, climbing over her, licking her face and chewing on her fingers, were a half-dozen black Labrador puppies.

The old man looked up as he approached, then motioned to Molly.

"She your wife?"

For an instant, Dylan wanted to say yes. He didn't know why, yet the need to claim her was strong. "A friend," he said, instead.

"Puppies are good for what ails you."

At the old man's words, Dylan looked more closely, and realized Molly was crying. Even as she petted and played with the dogs, tears trailed down her cheeks.

She hadn't seen him and he didn't do anything to call attention to himself. When the old man moved to make room on the bench, he shook his head. No, he would go back to the house and give Molly her privacy. But he ached for her. Why was she crying? Was it because of their conversation? Did it have something to do with those damn phone calls she made every night? He wanted to ask but didn't.

The wind caught her hair and tore most of it free from her braid. The long strands blew around her face. One of the dark puppies yapped and lunged for a curl. She laughed and gently pushed the animal away.

The setting sun caught her then, the pale blond of her hair, the glistening moisture on her cheek. She was, he realized, incredibly beautiful and so terribly sad. He wasn't sure why he hadn't seen either before. He wanted to do something or say something, but he had no right to intrude on this very private moment. So he turned back the way he'd come and returned to the house to wait.

Chapter Seven

The day was perfect. Blue sky, warm temperatures, slight breeze. Molly leaned back against the waterproof cushions in the cockpit of the sailboat and struggled to keep her eyes open. The urge to drift, the way the boat did, was strong.

"Do you want me to do anything?" she asked Dylan.

He sat by the tiller, also relaxed, although he looked way more alert than she felt. They were both in jeans, T-shirts and athletic shoes.

"I thought you hadn't been sailing before," he said.

"I haven't."

"Then how would you know what to do?"

She closed her eyes and smiled. "I figured you'd tell me. I don't actually want to do anything. I'm being polite."

"Don't bother. You look relaxed sitting there. Just enjoy the sail."

"If you insist."

She did as he requested, sinking lower into the cushions.

The salt air was a tangy perfume and the gentle rocking of the boat made her feel surprisingly safe.

"I thought I'd be scared," she said, keeping her eyes closed. "What with being out on the water and all. But it's nice."

"We have plenty of life jackets. I checked before we cast off."

"You're very organized. I think I like that." Her mind meandered from topic to topic. She'd had trouble sleeping the past couple of nights so it was pleasant to fade into that half awake, half asleep place.

Images from their various outings flitted through her brain. She smiled at the memory of them trying to grill fish for dinner the previous night. As it had cooked, the fillets had started getting flaky. The grill's wires were nearly an inch apart and bit by bit their dinner had fallen into the fire. Molly had noticed it first. She'd burst into laughter and hadn't been able to get herself together enough to rescue their food. By the time Dylan figured out what she'd found so funny, hardly anything was left. They'd been forced to go out for dinner.

"What's so funny?" he asked.

She looked at him. "I was thinking about dinner last night."

He groaned. "I can't believe we lost that piece of fish. It looked great. We're going to have to get a different grill. Maybe one more like a screen."

She shifted so she was lying on her back, facing him. She tucked one arm under her head. The mainsail, as Dylan had called it, held steady in the breeze.

"Tell me something," she said. "How did a motorcycle racer and designer like you get to know so much about sailing?"

He grinned. "A woman I dated was obsessed with the

sport. We went out every weekend. She came from a long line of sailors. The whole family was into racing and everything. She taught me. The relationship didn't work, but I found I liked sailing. I go out when I can. Over the past couple of years that hasn't been as much as I would like. If I lived closer to the ocean, I'd buy a boat. Maybe in the future."

"Must have been a ton of them," she said.

"Boats?"

"No, women."

"I haven't been a saint, but I haven't been a complete jerk, either."

There had been at least three serious girlfriends before he'd dated Janet. Make that three she knew about. There could have been others. He'd spent part of the past ten years on the racing circuit. She would bet that the women had been plentiful, especially for a man like him. It wasn't just that he was the cliché of tall, dark and dangerous. He was also smart and funny. An irresistible combination and she had the crush to prove it.

"How many?" she asked.

"Molly! I can't believe you'd ask me that."

She couldn't, either, but now that she had, she wanted to know. "Come on, Dylan, what does it matter if you tell me the truth? We're friends, right? Friends share information."

"Not that kind of information."

She sat up and leaned toward him. "Oh, please! How many?"

"I am not discussing my past with you."

He looked serious, but she saw the twinkle in his eyes.

"Fifty? A hundred?"

"Less than a hundred," he told her.

"Oh, that's narrowing it down. Thank you so very much. What does that mean? Ninety-nine or ninety-eight?"

"I'm not going to tell you. A gentleman does not kiss and tell."

"I'm not asking for names or even a brief rundown on their likes and dislikes," she said. "Although that would be interesting. Just a idea of how many different women have done the wild thing with you."

He looked at her. "The wild thing?"

She nodded. "Yup. You *know* you want to tell me."

"Actually, I don't. How would you feel if I asked you the same question? I'm sure you wouldn't want to explain your love life to me."

Molly thought about that for a second. "If anything," she said, "I would feel depressed."

"Why?"

Because I'm not like you, she thought, but she couldn't say that to him. He wouldn't understand and she didn't want the humiliation of having to explain it. Her life was so small. Sometimes just thinking about it made her want to weep. But she was going to change that, she promised herself. Actually, she *was* changing it. Right now, just being with him was different from anything she'd allowed herself before.

"Molly?"

His voice was low and concerned, as if he actually cared about her. She supposed he did...in his way. After all, they were friends. She sighed at the thought. Friends. Great. He still thought of her as Janet's little sister, while she was forced to lie awake at nights imagining how wonderful it would be to make love with him.

"Two," she said at last, because she couldn't think of anything funny to say. "There have been two men in my life. Including Grant. And the fact that I slept with that loser is just too depressing for words.''

"You're kidding.''

His mouth wasn't exactly hanging open, but it was pretty close. "What did you expect?'' she asked. "Life is different for the rest of us. We can't all be beautiful people, you know. Some of us are just mere mortals.''

"We're all mere mortals. I don't understand why you're putting yourself down like that. You're very attractive.''

Now it was her turn to have her mouth drop open. "Me?'' She made a great show of looking around, as if checking to see who else was on the boat. "Dylan, get real.''

"I am being real, and honest. You don't think you're pretty?''

Why was he making her say this? "No, I don't. I'll admit that I'm not hideous, but I'm not anyone's idea of attractive.''

"That's crazy.''

He sounded sincere, which was nice. He even looked concerned, as if he were searching for a way to convince her he was telling the truth. How could she not like him for that?

"I think you're attractive,'' he said. "Grant must have agreed with me, or he wouldn't have wanted to date you. That's two against one.''

Despite the dark cloud threatening her mood, she had to smile. "Well, two against one. Okay, then. That makes all the difference in the world.'' She leaned back against the cushions. "I don't suppose it matters much anymore. About Grant, I mean, or even what he thinks of me. That's over.''

"Do you miss him?''

"Not as much as I would have thought. Isn't that sad? We dated for over a year before he proposed. I would have thought that I'd miss him horribly. Of course, I've had a lot of other things on my mind.''

"Like your job," he said.

She nodded, knowing losing her job was the least of her troubles right now. "I'm beginning to wonder if I ever loved him. Actually, I'm really wondering if I even believe in love anymore. I can't find any proof it exists. I think parents love their kids and vice versa. I believe in different kinds of love. Just not romantic love. Maybe it's all a plot made up by the media so we'll send flowers and greeting cards.''

"You're too young to be that cynical," he told her.

"Age has nothing to do with it. Sometimes I feel a million years old.''

"You look good for a million.''

She had to smile at that. "Just when I get ready to start my pity party, you come along and make me laugh. I should hate you for that.''

"But you don't.''

"No, I don't. I wish it were different, though. I wish I could go back and believe. I would like men and women to love each other and to actually want to be together. I want them to want to make love, instead of just to get off physically.''

"Is that what you think?" he asked. "It's about physical release, not emotional bonding?''

"Yes." She shrugged. "Maybe. I don't know. You're the expert. What do you think?''

"I'm still surprised to find a cynic lurking inside you.''

She told herself that if he knew the truth about her, he would be less surprised, but she wasn't going to share that with him. Better for him to be a little startled than to pity her. She couldn't stand that one.

"You didn't answer my question," she reminded him. "What do you believe about love?"

He was quiet for a long time. Molly raised her head toward the sun and absorbed the heat. It was nice being out here. Most of the time, she didn't mind if she and Dylan didn't talk. It was comfortable just to be in the same room. But this time, she really wanted to know what he thought.

"We need to head back," he said, moving to the other side of the tiller, then releasing the sail so they could come about. "Watch your head."

Molly ducked under the boom and shifted to the other side of the cockpit. When they were under way, heading toward the shore and the marina, Dylan cleared his throat.

"I haven't forgotten your question," he said. "I'm not sure how to answer it."

"You don't have to. We can change the subject."

"I don't mind. It's just not something I spend a lot of time thinking about. Do I believe in love?"

She found herself surprisingly eager to hear his answer. As if it would somehow affect her situation. Which was insane, she reminded herself.

"I don't know that I've ever been in love," he said at last, his voice low and thoughtful. "I've cared, but that's not love. I had a lot of feelings for your sister, but Janet and I had more hormones than genuine caring going for us."

"I'll tell her you said that," she teased.

"Gee, thanks."

His quick smile faded. With their shift in position, the wind had changed. It blew a lock of hair onto his forehead. She liked the casual disarray.

"I don't know that I'm capable of loving anyone, because I've never seen love in action," he said. "My parents never cared about me or each other. Maybe I have a missing gene or something.''

"What about the women who have loved you?" she asked.

"There haven't been any."

She stared at him. "Women? Of course there have. We just talked about them."

He smiled sadly. "None of them loved me, Molly."

"Not one out of all ninety-nine?"

"Not one."

"I don't believe that."

He smoothed his hair back. "Some of them cared about me, but most of them wanted something that I could provide. Sex, excitement, a good dance partner.''

"You dance?"

He laughed and this time the humor was genuine. "No, I was making a point.''

"Too bad. I always wanted to learn to dance."

"Someday we'll learn together," he promised.

She wanted to believe him. She wanted to think they were going to have a "someday," but she knew they weren't. Their relationship, if she could even call it that, was strictly temporary.

"What I was pointing out," he continued, "is that everyone wants something.''

"Now who's being the cynic?" she asked.

"Agreed, but if someone like you won't believe in love, what chance does a guy like me have?''

"You're saying it's my fault?"

"No, I'm saying I wish you still believed. If I ever get the chance, I'm going to beat Grant into a pile of broken bones.''

She liked that image. "Thanks for the offer, but I was

questioning everything long before Grant took off with his secretary."

"Don't give up, Molly," he told her. "My life is a series of monogamous relationships, but you can have more."

"So you see one woman, then you break up and start seeing someone else?"

"Something like that."

She pulled one knee up to her chest and wrapped her arms around her leg. "Do you ever miss them when they're gone?"

"Some, but always less than I should."

None of this shocked her, but she had hoped Dylan would have the answers to all her questions. Obviously they were both still searching for the truth. Life was not an easy journey.

Will you miss me?

She thought the question but didn't actually speak it. She was too afraid. She didn't want to know that he was going to let her go easily. She knew that she would remember him. Long after their adventure was over, she would look back and savor each day they'd spent together. Whatever the outcome, she would be grateful that he'd helped her get through this difficult time.

"I don't connect with people that well," he said. "I never have. I learned early to keep my emotional distance. Look what happened with Janet. I thought I wanted to marry her, but six weeks later, I was grateful I'd escaped." He glanced at her. "How's she doing?"

"Very well. When she married Thomas, I thought she was doing it for the money and the position, but it's been ten years and she's still crazy about him." She hesitated, not sure what all she should tell him.

"Go on," he said. "I'd like to hear about her. Don't worry, you're not opening scars."

"If you're sure."

He nodded. "Tell me everything."

"They have three kids. All girls, and just as pretty as my sister. Janet is a stay-at-home mom and she loves it. They live in a great house, up by San Francisco. Thomas's law firm is very successful. I go up and visit whenever I can. I love being an aunt."

She pressed her lips together. There was a time when she'd thought about having kids of her own. Now she wasn't so sure. And not just because Grant had turned out to be a jerk.

"I'll bet you spoil those three girls."

"I try as often as I can." She looked at him, at the emotions flashing through his eyes. She couldn't read them all. "Are you all right with this, Dylan?"

"Sure. I have regrets about my life, but they don't include Janet."

Molly had her own set of regrets. She wondered if she was going to have a lot more in the next few weeks. But if everything worked out the way she hoped, she would never have another regret as long as she lived. She was learning how to be in the moment and not worry about anything else.

But those thoughts weren't for today, she reminded herself. For today there was the ocean and the sky and the magic that was Dylan.

"Was there anyone else you came close to marrying?" she asked.

"Nope, just Janet. Since then I've been a lot more cautious." He reached down and opened the small cooler they'd brought with them. After pulling out a soda, he offered her one. She took it.

"I don't know how someone *knows* that he's met the person he wants to be with for the rest of his life," he said.

"What does love look like or feel like? How are we supposed to know when it's real?"

Molly sat up straight. "Exactly! That's what I've been thinking. It's a crazy way to run a life. What if both people are wrong? I know a lot of marriages end in divorce, but I hate that. I would want to be sure that it was forever. And I don't think that's possible."

She opened her soda. "That's what I hate about Grant. Even more than the fact that he left me for another woman, I really resent that I don't miss him more. How could I have been so wrong? Maybe I'm in shock or something."

"Sorry, but I think you'd be feeling the pain if there was any to feel."

"Then how are we supposed to know when it's real? Lightning bolts from the sky?"

He glanced up at the large white sail. "The mast is metal. Maybe we should ask for a different sign."

"Okay, then a voice from the heavens."

"That would get my attention," he agreed.

He was smiling. She shook her head. "Fine, laugh at me, but I'm serious. Next time I want to be sure."

"I agree with you. I don't plan to tell someone I love her until I can answer all the questions we've been discussing."

"Me, too. It's too hard otherwise."

She didn't hate Grant for what he'd done, but she was angry about it. The sad part was, her regrets weren't about losing him but about losing her dream of a family and children.

Dylan read her mind. "You want kids, Molly?"

With all her heart, but would they be in her future? That question could bring her to tears. "I'm not sure," she lied.

"I can see you as a mom," he said. "I think you'd be great."

"Thanks." She sipped her soda, hoping the physical action would be a distraction. "First I'd have to have a husband. I don't think I could be a single mom. They're amazing women and I'm pretty average. Seeing as we've both just sworn off love, I don't think I'm going to be getting married any time soon, so talking about kids seems a little premature."

Dylan reached out his hand toward her. She stared at him for a second, then placed her fingers on his palm. He squeezed gently.

"I'm having a really good time," he told her. "Thanks for coming away with me."

She didn't know what to say, or even if she could talk. Her throat was suddenly tight, and it wasn't all because of the electricity shooting up her arm.

"Thank you," she said. She knew that she wouldn't have survived this time without him. "I can't begin to tell you how much this has meant to me. I owe you."

"No way. I needed to get away and I wouldn't have done it without you." He chuckled. "Tell you what. When we hit shore, we'll arm-wrestle to figure out who owes whom more."

"Deal."

He squeezed her fingers once more, then released her. Molly leaned back in her seat and smiled. This was, she thought, the most perfect day. If she were given one wish, it would be that this time never ended.

"I'll be right back," Molly said as she picked up his cellular phone and disappeared into her bedroom.

Dylan watched her go, wondering, as he did every night, who she was hoping had left a message on her machine and why. The calls never lasted long, just a couple of minutes, and she hadn't missed one night in the past week.

He still didn't have any answers. Was she checking her machine, hoping to hear from Grant?

Dylan stretched out on the sofa. He couldn't believe that, especially after the conversation they'd had that afternoon on the boat. There was no way she would want Grant back in her life. Of course, that was his opinion, and Lord knows women had shocked him many times in the past. Maybe she'd been on some job interviews and was waiting to hear the results. Maybe—

"Hell, this is getting me nowhere. If I want to know so badly, I should just ask."

But he knew he wouldn't. It was against the rules. Just as he wouldn't touch her or hold her, even though he wanted to.

The wanting hadn't gone away. He'd thought it would. After all, he rarely maintained interest in a woman for very long. But with Molly, he found himself thinking about her more and more. Spending time with her didn't alleviate the symptoms. If anything, they got worse. Maybe it was because he liked her so much.

He rose to his feet, crossed to the window and stared out into the darkness. He hated that she went into another room and closed herself off from him. He hated that she had secrets. He wanted there to be something special between them. When he was willing to be honest, like now, he would admit, if only to himself, that he was really enjoying his time away. But specifically because he was with her. She was a lot of fun, someone he could talk to. He liked that they laughed together. They had similar tastes in food and music. They liked to read the same books.

He couldn't remember the last time he'd allowed anyone to be his friend, especially a woman. Molly had started out as Janet's little sister, but now she was so much more. He cared about her. He worried about her future, which was one of the reasons her nightly phone calls frustrated him. And he wanted her. Still.

Sometimes he was amazed by how much he thought about being with her. It wasn't just about sex, either. He didn't agree with her that people didn't make love, that they "got off," instead. He was willing to admit he'd had sex a lot more times than he'd made love, but he knew it would be the latter with Molly. He could sense that it would be different and very special. When he thought about being with her, he didn't just long for the physical release; he wanted the actual intimacy of holding her close, touching her, tasting her. He wanted to watch her expression change; he wanted to please her and to remember being together for a long time afterward. Then he wanted her to tell him what was wrong so he could fix it for her.

She was different from the other women he'd had in his life. With them it had been easy. He'd been out for the good time and they'd been out for what they could get. He wasn't sure that Molly wanted anything from him. What he wanted with Molly was to care.

It wasn't love, he told himself. Like her, he wasn't sure love existed. He wasn't worth loving—he'd known that for a long time. Oddly, it hurt to think that someone like Molly couldn't ever love him.

The bedroom door opened and she stepped out into the light. He couldn't read her expression. Normally he didn't comment, but tonight he couldn't help asking, "Is everything all right?"

She nodded. "It's fine. No messages at home."

He wanted to ask if that was good or bad, but he didn't have the right and he didn't want to upset her. He wished he could go to her and hold her tightly in his arms. That might make them both feel better.

Before he could figure out if she would appreciate the

gesture, she crossed to the small kitchen table. "You ready to continue our card game?" she asked. "I know I was winning."

She gave him a quick smile as she spoke. Then he saw it—the sadness in her eyes. The pain. The fear.

He walked over to her and touched her shoulder. "Molly, let me help."

She shook her head. "You can't do anything. I wish you could, but I have to get through this on my own."

"Is it about Grant or your job?"

She wouldn't meet his gaze. "Let's just play cards," she whispered. "The best thing you can do for me is let me forget. That's really what I want. To pretend none of this is actually happening to me."

He knew she wasn't talking about their time together but about whatever was bothering her. He wanted to insist that she tell him everything. The not knowing was driving him crazy. But he didn't. Instead he held out the chair for her, then took the seat opposite.

If playing cards helped her to forget, then that's what he would do with her. He would do anything. Even not ask again what was wrong.

Chapter Eight

"It was an old sedan. Not much power, a real sleeper," Dylan said, and grinned at the memory. "First, I redid the exhaust system—opened it up so the engine could breathe. You could hear that baby coming from three blocks away. Then I tinkered with the engine a little. Gave it more power."

"Why?" Molly asked. "I thought you liked Mrs. Carson."

"I did. That's why I worked on her car. She didn't have any money, so I did it free. Even paid for the parts myself." His smile faded. "When my folks were too drunk to feed me or even give as damn whether I came home, Mrs. Carson cared. She used to watch for me, and if I stayed out too late, she tore into me. One time she got so mad I thought she was going to hit me." He shrugged. "Of course, she wasn't even five feet, and I doubt she weighed ninety pounds. Still, the sight of her with her fists planted on her hips as she lectured me from the top step of her trailer was enough to put the fear of God into me.''

"I'm glad someone was looking out for you," Molly said.

He glanced at her. She walked next to him on the beach. They'd just finished an early dinner and were watching the sunset.

"I was nearly seventeen. I could take care of myself."

"That's not the point," she told him. "We can all take care of ourselves. We just shouldn't have to manage everything alone. It's nice that she was there for you. And that you cared about her, too. Even if you did destroy her car."

"I didn't destroy it. I improved it." He raised his hands in a gesture of protest. "I'll admit I souped up the engine a little, but I fixed an oil leak and gave her a complete tune-up. I also replaced her shock absorbers and rotated the tires. The truth is, when I was done that car could practically fly. She loved it. I warned her, but she didn't listen. Two days later, she came home all proud and excited. At the ripe old age of sixty-four she'd finally gotten her first speeding ticket. You'd have thought she'd won first prize in a beauty contest."

"Are you trying to tell me she was *happy* about the speeding ticket?"

"She was grinning from ear to ear."

Molly rolled her eyes. "The worst part of all this is that I actually want to believe you."

"I'll admit I was a wild kid," Dylan said, "but I wasn't bad. I didn't get into much trouble. At least not as much as everyone thought."

"You were the hottest thing around." Molly paused and motioned to the sand. "Is this all right?"

"Sure."

She sank down and he took a seat next to her. They faced the ocean. She pulled her knees up to her chest and wrapped her arms around her legs. "You were something," she said, picking up the thread of conversation. "Do you remember that movie *Dirty Dancing*?"

"I think so. A family spends a few weeks at a mountain resort and one of the daughters falls for a dancer."

"Exactly." She sighed. "That's what I think about when I remember you back then. The bad boy who tempted all the nice girls. Everyone had a crush on you. Even me."

She made the statement casually. Dylan waited to see if she would notice what she'd just admitted. She did. She stiffened, then squared her shoulders.

"What I meant is…" Her voice trailed off.

"Yes?" He couldn't keep the pleasure from his voice. A crush? Molly? He'd known that she liked him a lot, but crush was different. That implied a certain romantic interest.

"Well, you know," she finished lamely.

"Not really. I'd like to hear the details."

She looked at him. "Oh, I'll just bet. How thrilling for you to hear about my infatuation. If you'd known at the time, you would have hurt yourself laughing."

Without thinking, he touched her cheek. "Don't say that. It's not true. I would have been flattered. I always liked you, Molly."

"Yeah, but I was just Janet's little sister."

"You were bright and funny, someone I enjoyed spending time with."

She had left her long hair loose tonight and it blew gently in the wind. He wanted to touch the strands to see if they were as soft as they looked. He wanted to let his fingers get tangled in the curls as he pulled her close for a kiss.

"You were never interested in me," she said.

"I thought we were friends. Besides, you were only seventeen. I believe the slang expression is 'jailbait.'"

She rested her chin on her knees. "You're being kind. Not that I don't appreciate it, but the truth is you never saw me as anyone special. I don't blame you," she said quickly, before he could interrupt. "I didn't blossom in high school. I was the typical teenage ugly duckling."

"Now you're a beautiful swan."

She raised her eyebrows. "Nice comeback. Not true, but nice. I know my limitations. I'm a decent duck. Not ugly, but not a swan, either." She patted her hips. "A well-rounded duck, but I can make my way through the pond."

He hadn't been lying when he'd told her she was a beautiful swan, but he sensed she wouldn't believe him. He also wanted to tell her that he liked her curves. Yes, they were different from what he was used to, but the truth was he couldn't stop thinking about them, about touching all of her, including her curves. There was something very welcoming about her body, a womanly essence that drew him.

"But you," she said. "You were gorgeous in high school."

"That's a little strong."

"Not at all. I remember the first time I saw you drive up on your motorcycle. You wore a black leather jacket. I thought I was going to die right there in the living room. I thought my mother was going to have a fit, but that's another story." She shifted, straightening her legs and leaning back on her elbows. "It's interesting. Some people peak in high school, but most of us get better with age. You seem to be doing as well now as you were then."

"If that's a compliment, then thank you," he said. "I would like to think I'm a lot smarter. Some of the things that mattered to me then don't matter now."

"Like what?"

He grinned. "I'm less concerned about how fast I can get my date into bed. I've learned that waiting really does make it better. I would like to think my best years are still ahead of me."

"I hope I can say the same about myself."

Molly sounded relaxed as she spoke, but Dylan sensed the tension in her body. Her jaw was tight and her smile had a forced quality.

He almost asked. He opened his mouth and started to form the words, but he couldn't. Not only because he didn't want to pry, but because he was suddenly afraid. Not of Molly, but of her secret. So he returned to a topic guaranteed to distract them both.

"Tell me more about your crush on me," he said.

She laughed and the tension faded. "What would you like to know?"

"Everything. Start at the beginning and talk slowly. Did you keep a diary, recording every conversation? Did you go around the house after I'd been there and pick up a used napkin or a piece of a cookie I'd left behind? Did you try to cut off a lock of my hair?"

She stared at him. "I had a crush, I wasn't looking to put a curse on you. Jeez. None of that. I guess I was doing the crush thing all wrong."

He pretended disappointment. "Not even one little curl?"

"No. I did other things. I hung around when you came to pick up Janet."

He thought about those days so very long ago. "I remember that. We used to talk."

"Exactly."

She looked out toward the ocean. He turned his gaze in that direction and saw that the sun was close to the horizon.

The sky was alive with color. Pinks, yellows, orange. The water was dark and mysterious.

"Janet was always late getting ready," Molly said. "I liked that about my sister. Back then, that was about all I did like about her. I used to spend part of the day thinking up witty things to say to you. Or I'd go to the library, read joke books and memorize them."

"You didn't."

She nodded. "Pretty humiliating, huh?"

"Not at all." He wouldn't admit it for the world, but he liked that she'd gone to all that trouble.

"I had this fantasy," she said. "I used to tell myself that one day I was going to get you to realize Janet was a complete loser and make you fall in love with me, instead. We would run off together." She wrinkled her nose. "I could never figure out where. College was important to me, but I wasn't sure you'd want me to go. That was a logistical problem I couldn't quite work out."

"I would have supported your schooling."

"Really?" She laughed. "If only I'd known that back then, I would have tried harder."

What would it have been like? he wondered. If he'd fallen for Molly instead of her sister. He shook his head. It wouldn't have happened. Molly had been too young, although the age difference wasn't an issue today. And she'd been right about improving with the passing years. She was an attractive woman now, but she *had* been an ugly duckling back in high school. In his early twenties that sort of thing had still mattered to him.

She stared at the sunset, but her expression told him that she was actually seeing the past. "It wasn't just the black leather jacket or your good looks," she said. "I liked how you always took the time to be nice to me. I knew you were smart, too. Mother kept telling Janet you weren't going to amount to much, but I thought you had a lot of potential. I'm glad I was right. Despite the motorcycle and the attitude, you weren't just a typical bad boy.''

He was surprised she'd seen past the facade. Surprised and pleased. ''I appreciate the confidence you had in me.''

''Sometimes I think teenage affections are the most honest. At least for that microsecond while they exist. For the most part, they're pretty fickle.''

Had hers been? He wondered, but he didn't ask. He would like to think that she'd hung on to at least a hint of what she'd felt. Not likely, he told himself. Wishing didn't make it so. Nevertheless, it was nice to think that at one time he'd mattered to her. Not that it cleared up their present situation. He still didn't know what was going on between them. He didn't have a clue how she felt. As for his feelings, the only thing he knew for sure was that he wanted her. Telling himself he preferred flash to substance didn't seem to be helping.

He stretched out on his elbows, mimicking her posture. ''I'm glad you came looking for me,'' he told her. ''I'm having a great time.''

''Me, too.'' She hesitated. ''I'd like it if we could stay friends.''

Her cheeks darkened with color. *He* liked that he made her a little nervous, almost as much as he liked that she didn't want to lose touch with him. ''I think it's a great idea.''

He'd never chosen well when it came to women, but he knew he'd made the right decision with Molly. Even if it was just friendship, she was someone he could be proud to have in his life. Still, when she rolled toward him and gave him that sweet smile of hers, he found it hard to remember that their goal was to just be friends. He found himself wanting to brush his fingers against her cheek, maybe outline her mouth. It was against the rules and it would mess up everything, but damn, she was hard to resist.

Speaking of which... He sat up straight and shifted so she wouldn't be able to see the physical manifestation of his thoughts. So much for being subtle.

"Is everything okay?" she asked. "You've gotten quiet."

He focused his attention on the last rays of sunlight. "I'm fine. Just thinking about things."

"Like?"

He thought of a couple dozen vaguely humorous comebacks. A quip about the value of the American dollar compared with the Japanese yen. Or something about wanting to try parasailing. But in the end he couldn't lie to her. He also couldn't tell her exactly what he'd been thinking. Instead, he decided to show her.

He rolled onto one hip, braced himself on his elbow and leaned toward her. He didn't actually touch her, but he moved slowly, giving her plenty of cues about his intentions, wanting her to have the time and room to pull back if she needed to. But she didn't. She stayed exactly in place, her hazel brown eyes getting bigger and bigger until they were all he saw. Then, right before his lips touched her, he closed his eyes so he could feel what was happening between them.

She was as sweet and warm as he remembered. Her lips yielded to him, as if they, too, felt the homecoming. He pressed his mouth against hers, then parted slightly. When she followed his lead, a small sound escaped from deep in her throat. Half moan, half cry. Of pleasure? Of shock? Did she welcome him or want to run?

Even though he ached to take her in his arms, he hesitated, still wanting to give her time to change her mind. Then she did the most amazing thing. She shifted so she

PLAY TIC-TAC-TOE

OR FREE BOOKS AND A GREAT FREE GIFT!

Use this sticker to **PLAY TIC-TAC-TOE.** See instructions inside!

THERE'S NO COST*NO OBLIGATION!

Get **2** books and a fabulous mystery gift! **ABSOLUTELY FREE!**

Turn the page to play!

Play TIC-TAC-TOE and get FREE GIFTS!

HOW TO PLAY:

1. Play the tic-tac-toe scratch-off game at the right for your FREE BOOKS and FREE GIFT!

2. Send back this card and you'll receive TWO brand-new Silhouette Special Edition® novels. These books have a cover price of $4.75 each, but they are yours to keep absolutely free.

3. There's no catch. You're under no obligation to buy anything. We charge nothing — ZERO — for your first shipment. And you don't have to make any minimum number of purchases — not even one!

4. The fact is, thousands of readers enjoy receiving books by mail from the Silhouette Reader Service™ months before they're available in stores. They like the convenience of home delivery, and they love our discount prices!

5. We hope that after receiving your free books you'll want to remain a subscriber. But the choice is yours — to continue or cancel, any time at all! So why not take us up on our invitation, with no risk of any kind. You'll be glad you did!

YOURS **FREE** A FABULOUS **MYSTERY GIFT!**

We can't tell you what it is…
but we're sure you'll like it!

A FREE GIFT —
just for playing
TIC-TAC-TOE!

DETACH AND MAIL CARD TODAY!

First, scratch the gold boxes on the tic-tac-toe board. Then remove the "X" sticker from the front and affix it so that you get three X's in a row. This means you can get TWO FREE Silhouette Special Edition® novels and a **FREE MYSTERY GIFT!**

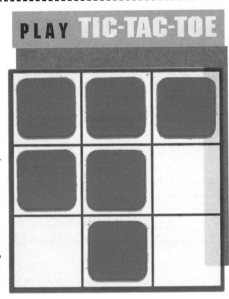

PLAY TIC-TAC-TOE

YES! Please send me all the gifts for which I qualify. I understand that I am under no obligation to purchase any books, as explained on the back of this card.

(C-SIL-SE-08/98)

335 SDL CH62

Name
(PLEASE PRINT CLEARLY)

Address   Apt.#

City   Prov.   Postal Code

The Silhouette Reader Service™ — Here's how it works:

Accepting free books places you under no obligation to buy anything. You may keep the books and gift and return the shipping statement marked "cancel." If you do not cancel, about a month later we'll send you 6 additional novels, and bill you just $3.96 each, plus 25¢ delivery per book and GST. * That's the complete price — and compared to cover prices of $4.75 each — quite a bargain! You may cancel at any time, but if you choose to continue, every month we'll send you 6 more books, which you may either purchase at the discount price...or return to us and cancel your subscription.

*Terms and prices subject to change without notice.
Canadian residents will be charged applicable provincial taxes and GST.

If offer card is missing, write to: Silhouette Reader Service, P.O. Box 609, Fort Erie, Ontario L2A 5X3

0195619199-L2A5X3-BR01

SILHOUETTE READER SERVICE
PO BOX 609
FORT ERIE ONT
L2A 9Z9

MAIL▶POSTE
Canada Post Corporation/ Société canadienne des postes

Postage paid   Port payé
If mailed in Canada   si posté au Canada

Business   Réponse
Reply   d'affaires

0195619199   01

was on her side, facing him. She placed her hand on his cheek. With a muffled groan of his own, he wrapped his arms around her and pulled her against him.

Molly heard as well as felt Dylan's rumble. His chest vibrated with the sound and she was torn between the wonder of him kissing her and the urge to shout with the joy of it all. She hadn't done anything to get him to kiss her. He'd started it all on his own. Surely a man like him wouldn't provide mercy kisses more than once. Maybe, just maybe, he wanted her.

Wanting her even a little would be enough, she told herself as she melted against him. He was so strong. The powerful length of his legs, the breadth of his chest. Now he pulled her so that she lay partially across him. Her hip was against his belly. Close, but not close enough to know if he was as aroused as she was.

Then his tongue touched her lower lip and nothing mattered anymore. Nothing but the feel of him against her. The moist heat, the pleasure he stirred. He didn't attack her. Instead he entered gently, teasing her, circling her tongue with his. He explored her mouth, finding places that made her gasp, then whimper with delight. He retreated and she followed, discovering him, feeling the passion flaring between them.

In the back of her mind, she was aware that they were on the beach and it wasn't dark yet. When she'd last glanced around, they'd been alone. She wondered if they still were. Not that it mattered. Dylan wouldn't take this any further. Not only because they were on a public beach but also because he wasn't interested in her that way. Still, this was enough.

He broke away from her mouth and kissed a damp trail along her jaw, then spent several minutes by her ear. After making her shiver and whisper his name, he moved her hair and nibbled along her nape. She thought she might die right then and there. It would be, she told herself, the perfect way to go.

While one hand held her hair away from her neck, the other traced a line from her shoulder down her back to her hip. From here, he cupped her rear. He squeezed the full curve. Molly had never been pleased with her generous build, but when Dylan was touching her, she didn't really care about anything but how he made her feel.

She arched against him, urging him to continue, wanting more. Wanting everything. She moved her hands up and down his back, reveling in the feel of his muscles bunching and releasing. It didn't matter why he was doing this. It didn't matter that this was huge mistake. So what if they weren't a couple and this wasn't going to end with them in bed together—it was lovely, and that was enough. She deserved a little time off from the trauma that was her life. They weren't hurting anyone. It would be better, she admitted, if Dylan actually cared about her. But she wasn't a fool; she wasn't going to go wishing for the moon. He was strong and he liked her. She believed that. They were friends. For a little while she would borrow his strength. When this was over, she would have the memories to get her through the dark times.

"Molly." He whispered her name like a prayer. "I want you."

The words were magic—an incantation designed to melt the last of her reserves. She pulled back a little and stared at him. "Really?"

He chuckled, a gasping sound that held a hint of pain. "What did you think? Don't give me that mercy kiss stuff again. You can't believe that."

"No," she said, not sure what she believed.

He swore under his breath. "I'm making out with you

like a teenager, right in the middle of the beach. If that's not carried away, you need to tell me what is."

She smiled and touched his lower lip. The skin was damp from their kisses. "Thank you."

"No thanks expected or wanted."

He squeezed the back of her neck and drew her close. As his mouth moved against hers, he shifted so that she was nearly lying on top of him. Her leg slipped between his. That's when she felt it. His arousal pressed against the top of her thigh.

She'd hoped, she'd wanted, but she hadn't been sure. Without stopping to think, she brought her hand down and laid her palm against him. Through the layer of his jeans, she felt him jump. His breath hissed through his teeth.

He deepened their kiss. He angled his head so he could go deeper. The passion grew. Her hips arched toward him. She could feel herself swelling to accept him. She was already wet. His hand moved from her hip to her waist, then up to her breast. Her nipples were hard. She could feel them pressing against the confines of her cotton sports bra. She ached for him to touch her there, even as she dreaded it.

His hand closed over her right breast. She froze. He moved his fingers against her, teasing the hard tip, sending shards of pleasure shooting through her. It was wonderful...and hideous. She had to make him stop.

"No!" she said loudly, and jerked free. "No. Stop. I can't."

The world blurred and she realized she'd started to cry.

"Molly? What's wrong?"

It was all too humiliating. She stumbled to her feet, trying to push against the ground but instead encountering warm flesh. She stumbled, and staggered, then finally found her balance. It had grown dark. For a moment she was

confused about where she was, but then she heard the surf.
As always, the ocean provided a point of reference.

With the sobs choking her and the tears making it impossible to see, she turned from him and started to run.

Dylan stayed by the water for a long time. He waited
until Molly finally returned to the house. The moon had
long since risen and most of the stars were out when he
finally headed home.

There were too many questions, and he didn't have a
single answer. What he knew for sure was that he'd broken
the rules. Somehow something great between them had
been shattered and he only had himself to blame. He had
to apologize to her. The problem was, he wasn't sorry about
what had happened. Actually, he was sorry she'd run off,
but until then, he'd been extremely happy with the turn of
events.

The thing was, he'd promised not to come on to her. No
doubt she'd thought she could trust him. Twice now he'd
proved her wrong. It didn't matter that she hadn't protested
or even that she'd responded as if she'd wanted him as
much as he wanted her. He'd betrayed a friend and that
was eating him up inside.

He sucked in a breath and wished it were colder out here
on the sand. There was a cool breeze, but it wasn't enough
to take the edge off his desire. He was fourteen different
kinds of a bastard, he told himself. Despite the fact that
she'd run off in tears, he still wanted her. He wanted to
carry her into his bed and show her that there really was
more than just getting off. That the phrase "making love"
was true. He wanted to love her, every part of her. With
his mouth, his hands, with all his body. He wanted to make
her forget where she was—hell, *who* she was. He wanted

to take her so high that she lost her breath. He wanted to listen to her panting and feel her shaking as she recovered.

Instead, he was going to tell her he was sorry. Not for kissing her. He could never regret that. He'd kissed plenty of women in his time, but there was something special about Molly. Something wonderful that made him forget himself. No, he would apologize because he'd obviously hurt her. After all, she'd run off in tears. He didn't want to hurt her and he didn't want her to regret anything about their relationship. He would tell her that.

He headed for the house. His steps were slow and steady. A faint sense of dread skittered across the back of his neck, almost as if he wasn't going to like what he found inside. As he entered, he glanced at the kitchen table. The keys to the bike were still there, as were the duffel bags in the corner. She hadn't left.

Faint light spilled out of her open bedroom door. He crossed the small living room and knocked. She sat on the bed with her legs pulled up to her chest. Her hair was in disarray around her shoulders, her face pale, her eyes huge. She looked up at him.

She wasn't crying anymore, but the expression of pain and sadness on her face nearly ripped out his heart. He had to hang on to the door frame to keep from going to his knees.

"Molly."

"Hey, Dylan. I thought you might be spending the night on the beach." Her attempted smile was all the more tragic for the effort and its failure.

"Nah. I was just thinking."

"I know what about," she said. "I'm sorry. I didn't mean to run off like that."

"Hey, stop it." He moved into the room. There wasn't anywhere to sit but the bed and he didn't want to settle there. It was too much like invading her personal space. He shoved his hands into his jeans pockets and leaned against the wall. "*I'm* here to apologize, not you."

"You have nothing to apologize for."

"Yeah, I do. I scared you. I didn't mean to. I guess—" He shrugged. "Things got a little out of hand, and I'm sorry about that. We had a deal and I forgot." This was harder than he'd thought. He swallowed. "I really care about you, Molly. I respect you. Bed partners are easy to come by but not friends, and that's what I consider you. I don't want to mess things up between us. You're too important. I hope you'll forgive me for getting out of line. I swear, it won't happen again."

He was serious, Molly thought. What an amazing turn of events. He'd kissed her and touched her in a way that had made her feel so incredibly special. He'd been aroused, and in return she'd run off with no explanation. Now he was the one apologizing.

"It's not what you think," she said slowly, not sure what she was going to tell him. Not the truth. He wouldn't want to hear it and she didn't think she had the strength to tell him.

"I know what it is," he said. "I don't want you to think I didn't like what we were doing, because I did. The kissing, the touching—they were great. But our friendship means more to me than that."

He was an unexpected and lovely gift in her life. He really cared about her, and she hadn't known if anyone could ever care about her again. It wasn't love, but she didn't trust in love anymore. This was better. They could be friends for a long time. She could depend on him—he was the kind of man she could trust. A good man. He was also funny, smart, sexy and gorgeous. Talk about an irresistible package.

She could feel the tears forming again. She fought them because she was tired of crying, tired of being scared and alone.

"You're important to me, Molly. Please give me another chance."

She squeezed her eyes closed and held out her hand. He was at her side in an instant. His warm fingers engulfed hers.

She drew in a deep breath and struggled for control. "You've got it all wrong," she said at last. "I'm not sorry that we kissed or touched. It was lovely. More than that. So special—you'll never know how much that meant to me."

She looked at him, at his familiar face. They'd both changed, yet it felt as if she'd always known him. The crush was still there, a little different because she was different, but just as powerful as ever.

Then she knew. It was time to tell him the truth. Not only because he deserved to know why she was acting so crazy, but also because she needed him. Selfishly, she knew there would come a time when his strength might be all that kept her going. Even if just for another minute. Until their time was up. After that, she would find another way to be strong.

"I liked it," she said, urging him to sit on the bed. He settled next to her, close enough for her to feel the heat of him. "Maybe too much."

"Molly?" Questions darkened his eyes. "What are you saying?"

"That wasn't a hint," she said. "Okay, I'll admit it might have been a little one, but don't act on it. I'm trying to distract myself, but it's not working."

Oh, this was so hard. Telling Janet had been tough, but this was worse. Probably because she didn't know how he was going to react. Would he recoil? She braced herself for that or worse. If he couldn't handle it, then she would deal with it on her own. The past couple of weeks had taught her she was strong, too.

"You're confusing me," he said. "And scaring me. What's wrong?"

"Nothing. Everything." She released his hand so he would be free to leave if he wanted to. She drew in a deep breath. "I did like what we were doing on the beach. I liked the kissing and touching, but froze because you touched my breast."

"Did I hurt you?"

"No."

He studied her face. She could read the questions there. He swore. "Did someone attack you?"

If only it were that simple. "No. Do you remember when you asked me why I'd run away from my life and I told you about that bad week?"

He nodded.

"There was more to it." She found it easier to talk now. She didn't have to think about the words; they just came on their own. She focused on his perfect face and made her mind blank.

"On Monday I lost my job and on Tuesday Grant called me from Mexico. On Wednesday morning, while I was in the shower, I found a lump in my left breast."

Chapter Nine

She was shaking, but not so much that she couldn't talk. Molly drew in a breath. There, she'd said it. So far Dylan hadn't run, but that was probably because he was still in shock. Once he got over it, he might take off for parts unknown. Until then, though, she was going to keep talking.

"I was doing my monthly breast self-exam," she said. "It's so strange, because I do one every month. A lot of women do. When I first started doing them I was scared because I didn't want to find anything. I know that sounds weird, because if I'm checking my breasts, then I'm sort of accepting the fact that there could be a lump. But after a few months, it's like you forget."

She shook her head. "Sorry. I'm getting off the point."

"It's okay," he said, his voice low and quiet. "Tell the story however you see fit."

When she'd first come in the bedroom, she'd clicked on

the lamp on her nightstand. The light spilled across most of the bed and the floor, but much of Dylan was in shadow, including his face. She was having trouble reading his expression, but part of that could be because she didn't really want to know what he was thinking. She'd done a lot of reading on the subject and she knew that many men couldn't handle the thought of a woman in their lives being sick. She braced herself for that kind of reaction.

"I was moving my fingers around my breast when I felt something," she said. She had to will herself to stay calm. Just talking about it brought the fear back. She remembered the horror that had filled her when she'd found the lump. She'd been so scared she'd thought she was going to throw up. Even now it was difficult not to curl up in a ball and give in to the panic.

"I called my doctor and they got me in that day. She examined me. At first she thought it might be a cyst." She looked at him expectantly.

He shook his head. "I don't know what that is."

"It's generally harmless. Cysts grow in the breast. They're sacs that fill up with fluid. They're painful, but not a big problem. Usually the doctor can use a needle to aspirate them—you know, remove the fluid. But my lump wasn't a cyst. There wasn't any fluid. The next step was a mammogram."

She didn't want to think about it. She didn't want to remember the cold terror of that day or the pressure of the mammography equipment pressing down on her. She'd cried during the procedure. Not because it hurt but because she was so afraid and so alone.

"Afterward my doctor still wasn't sure, so she suggested a procedure to remove the lump. It would be examined right then and she would let me know what it was. That was scheduled for Friday of that week."

Molly wrapped her arms around her chest and tried to force a smile. She didn't know how it looked, but she had a feeling it failed completely. She wanted to run away. Leave behind all the fear and the questions. The problem was, there wasn't anywhere else to go. She *had* run away and the problem had come with her. There was nothing to do but endure.

"What did they find?" he asked.

"They're not sure. The cells were atypical. I think it's a fancy way of saying they don't know what they've got. My doctor sent it out to a lab for analysis. The day I decided to come looking for you, her office had called. They'd heard back from the first lab, but they were sending the sample out again. They wanted a second opinion."

She'd been doing so well explaining all this to him that the tears were unexpected. She caught her breath as they burned her eyes. Then a single tear escaped and rolled down her cheek. She quickly wiped it away.

"The d-doctor says it's just quality control," she continued, her voice thickening. "That she wants to be sure and not to worry. But I can't help it. I keep thinking that it's so horrible they're insisting on a second opinion. She's told me to be patient, to try to fill my days with things that can help me forget, but it's h-hard."

More tears. They were falling faster now.

"That's why I use the cell phone every night. The doctor is going to let me know when she gets the results back from th-the lab. I'm waiting to hear about the lump."

She couldn't look at Dylan. She didn't want to know what he was thinking. Was he horrified? Probably. Even as she tried to get control of herself and tell herself everything was fine, she waited to feel the bed shift as he stood up.

The preparation didn't help. When the mattress moved, she thought she was going to throw up. Then two warm, strong arms enveloped her, pulling her close. The comfort was so unexpected, so wonderful, she lost it completely and started to sob.

Dylan held Molly tightly against his chest. Not knowing what else to do, he kept quiet, letting her deal with her pain in her own way. For himself, he didn't know what he felt. Shock, certainly. Actually, stunned was more like it. He couldn't remember all that he'd imagined when she'd disappeared each evening to make her phone call. He'd wondered if she was checking for a message from Grant, or maybe to hear about a job interview. He'd never thought it could be something like this.

He rested his cheek against her hair. "Molly," he murmured. "Sweet Molly. I can't believe all you've had to deal with. No wonder you wanted to run away."

"It's hard sometimes," she said, her words muffled against his chest. "Janet has been really supportive. After I told her about the lump, she wanted to come down when they took it out. But she's got her daughters and Thomas. Then she wanted me to come up and stay with her. She promised the girls would be a huge distraction. I think that if you hadn't been willing to come away with me, I would have gone there."

She raised her head. There were tears on her face and her eyes were red. He didn't care. She was beautiful.

"Thank you," she said. "Thank you for not running off or backing away. Whatever it is, it's not contagious."

He wiped away her tears. "It never occurred to me it was. I'm not afraid of you. I'm—" He shrugged. "Taking it all in, I guess."

"Maybe I shouldn't have dumped this on you."

"No. Don't say that. We're friends, and friends share information with each other."

She nodded, then pressed her face into his chest once

more. He stroked her hair and her back. He understood her fear that he would run. Actually, the thought had never occurred to him. He didn't think an 8.5 earthquake would have been enough to dislodge him from the bed. Even now, he was too shocked to do anything but hold her.

He swore silently. Talk about having to deal with a difficult situation. If nothing else, hearing about Molly's life certainly put his petty problems in perspective. All this time he'd been worried about whether to sell his company, while she was wrestling with a potentially life-threatening situation.

A cold knot formed in his stomach as he repeated his last thought. Two words stood out. Life-threatening. Panic seized him.

Molly could die.

He resisted the need to squeeze her tighter in his arms, as if holding her closer would keep her safe. Dear God, he didn't want to lose her. Not now, not when he'd just found her. Not ever. Molly was special, one of the good guys. She didn't deserve this.

He grimaced as he realized no one deserved it.

"What are you thinking?" she asked.

"Nothing."

"Liar. You just stiffened up. If you need to walk away from me, I'll understand."

"No way, kid. You're stuck with me." He brushed his cheek against her hair and inhaled the sweet scent of her body. "I was just thinking that it's not fair."

"You've got to let that one go," she told him. "I've been over it and over it and there's no good answer. You're right. It's not fair. So what?"

She sounded strong and sure of herself. "I'm a guy," he said. "I want to fix it."

"You can't."

"I know."

That was the hell of it. He did know.

"Don't make yourself crazy, Dylan," she said. "That's not why I told you. I just wanted you to understand the situation. Considering everything, I'm doing really well. This time with you has been terrific for me. I've actually been able to forget and just have fun. I needed that."

"You've handled everything very well. I'm impressed."

"Don't be. I'm putting one foot in front of the other. There's no courage in that."

"You're wrong."

She chuckled. "Your favorite words."

"I have other words I like just as much."

"I don't think so." She smiled up at him. There were still tears on her face, but the pain and darkness had faded from her eyes. He hugged her and she hugged him back.

He liked the feel of her arms around his waist. Her hands rubbed against his back. Of course he still wanted her. His arousal pressed painfully against his jeans. But that didn't matter anymore. He would never do anything to hurt her or...

He grabbed her arms and pushed her away so that he could look at her. "Did I hurt you?" he asked, suddenly frantic. She'd had a lump removed. Isn't that what she'd said? That meant surgery. Even if it was an outpatient procedure, they'd cut her. "When I touched your breast, did I rub against the incision? Is that why you ran off?"

Color stained her cheeks, but she didn't turn away. "No. You touched my right breast and the lump was in the other one."

He sagged with relief. "Jeez, Molly, I was afraid I'd grabbed you there." He winced at the thought. "Talk about insensitive."

"No. Don't do that." She shrugged off his grip, then

took his hands in hers. "Don't treat me like I'm going to break. I couldn't stand that. Yes, I'm a little sore and bruised, but it's no big deal. Don't treat me any differently. Please. That's the whole point of coming away—to forget. You need to promise me that nothing will be different. I told you only because of how I acted. I didn't want you thinking I was crazy."

How could he make that promise? Of course it was going to be different. He knew that her life might be in danger. He wanted to find a way to protect her or even heal her. Neither option was available to him and he didn't know how he was supposed to survive that.

Then he got it. This wasn't about him at all; it was about Molly. Her feelings were what mattered. She'd spent the past couple of weeks living with a fear he couldn't begin to imagine. If she needed him to treat her the way he always had, then he would find a way to do that. It was the least he could do for her.

"Promise," he said, and made an X over his heart.

She smiled. "Thank you."

He shifted so that he was leaning up against the headboard, then he pulled her close. She resisted.

"You don't have to do this," she told him.

"Thanks for the feedback, but if it's not too much trouble, I'd like a little human contact." He looked at her. "Sorry, Molly. I'm making you uncomfortable, aren't I?" He started to get off the bed.

She threw herself across him. "No, don't go, Dylan. I thought you were feeling sorry for me. Actually, I'd like a little physical contact, too."

He found himself stretched out on her bed. She lay next to him, her head on his shoulder, her hand resting on his chest. He stroked her hair.

There was a comfortable silence between them. Dylan

continued to think about all that she'd told him and tried to absorb the information. It was still impossible to believe. Molly? His Molly? He hated that she'd gone through all of it alone.

"You should have called Janet to be with you," he said. "She's your sister. She cares."

"I know. I didn't want to be a bother."

Translation—she didn't think she was worth it. He recognized the feeling because he felt the same way about himself. It was fine for someone like him, but Molly deserved more.

"You couldn't be a bother," he said. "You're very special."

She groaned. "Don't get weird on me. You promised not to treat me differently."

"I thought you were special yesterday. I just didn't get around to telling you."

"I'm not sure I believe that."

He rolled toward her and touched her face. "You are the proud owner of that problem, not me. I wouldn't lie to you. I think you're very special." He traced a line from her forehead to her nose, then down to her mouth. "I'm glad you told me. I will try very hard not to treat you any differently. We'll continue to have fun together so you're distracted. Agreed?"

She nodded. A single tear spilled out of her eye.

"What's wrong?" he asked.

"Nothing. You're just being so sweet to me."

"I know it's after the fact, but I'm here. You're not alone anymore."

"I know. That feels very nice. Thank you."

She leaned forward and kissed him gently on the mouth. He waited, but she didn't deepen the kiss. Despite everything, he still wanted her. The passion still burned inside, but it was different now. The heat was tempered with tenderness. While that didn't take away the wanting, it changed it into something even more powerful. He had a fierce desire to bring her pleasure, to wipe out all the bad memories. He couldn't fix her, but he would very much like to help her forget.

She cuddled against him. After a while, her breathing deepened and he realized she'd fallen asleep. Moving slowly so as not to awaken her, he stretched up and turned out the light. He wasn't sure if he was going to sleep tonight, but that didn't matter. He only wanted to be here, in Molly's bed, with her in his arms.

He didn't understand all that he was feeling. Of course he was scared for her, and maybe a little for himself. Molly wasn't model perfect or even his type, yet he couldn't imagine spending this time with anyone else.

She was also incredibly lovely. Not just in her physical appearance, which he had been slow to recognize, but she was filled with an inner grace—part courage, part acceptance. Part determination to go on, no matter what. In three short days, life had dealt her some hard blows. A lesser person might have caved under even one of them. But Molly was determined to continue on. He was proud to know her.

He closed his eyes against the darkness and concentrated on the sound of her steady breathing. He was so afraid of losing her. The world in general and his life in particular would be smaller and meaner without her bright smile and gentle spirit.

The truth hit him with all the subtlety of a blow from a baseball bat. Somehow in the past week and a half, she'd gotten under his skin. He'd let her inside, and now there was no way to force her out. It was too late to not care.

* * *

Molly woke up slowly. Her body clock told her it was sometime in the middle of the night. At first she wasn't sure where she was. The shadows in the room were familiar, but her mind wouldn't focus on them. Then she realized the reason for her confusion. There was a man in her bed.

The heat of Dylan's body kept her warm, despite the fact that she was on top of the covers instead of underneath. She was curled up against him, her legs between his, his chin resting on her head. She didn't remember going to sleep, but she did recall the details of their conversation. How he'd listened to her tell about finding the lump. The sadness and concern on his face. And, most important of all, the way he'd held her.

She'd been terrified that he would run when he learned the truth. That he would consider her deformed or a monster. Instead he'd pulled her close and offered comfort. She would never be able to find the words to thank him. No matter what happened between them or when she finally heard from her doctor, she would always have that memory to carry with her. It was a precious gift.

"Why aren't you asleep?" he asked, his voice low and husky.

The intimacy of the moment made her shiver—but not with concern. Desire flooded her, a liquid need that dampened the secret place between her thighs.

"I could ask you the same question."

"I was asleep," he said. "You woke me up."

"Sorry. I won't be so noisy next time."

He chuckled. The sound vibrated in his chest. She loved being here with him like this. She never wanted to move.

He murmured her name, then wrapped his arms around her. "Thanks for not making me sleep alone," he said.

"What are you talking about? You're doing this for me."

"I'm not that altruistic. I confess to completely selfish motives."

"Like I believe that."

He raised his head and looked at her. Stubble darkened his jaw, giving him a slightly sinister appearance. Yet she wasn't afraid. She saw the affection lurking in his eyes.

"If you're going to nag me about that pity thing again, I'll be forced to take stern measures with you," he said.

That confused her. "What are you saying?"

"That our conversation was upsetting to me. I care about you. I don't want anything happening to you. I appreciate the fact that we're together tonight. If I can hold you, I can sleep. Otherwise I'd just be lying awake, staring at the ceiling."

"Really?" Oh, how she wanted to believe him. She wanted to think that she mattered that much to him.

"Guys don't lie about anything that makes them look weak. Trust me on this. We love to be heroes, not wimps."

She had to smile at that one. "You could never be wimpy."

"I have my moments."

She liked this, talking in the dark. She could make out some of his features, but not clearly. He was all colors of black and gray, blending with the night, making her think of some mysterious creature who only appears after sundown.

He relaxed back on the bed and drew her up so her head rested on his chest. "Is this okay?" he asked. "I mean, is the position comfortable? You're not putting weight on your incision are you?"

"I'm fine." She raised herself up on one elbow. "Look, Dylan, you promised me you'd treat me like nothing had changed. That means you can't go around asking how I feel every fifteen minutes. It will make me crazy."

"Okay. I'll try. If it will help, you can start doing all the cooking."

She grinned. "I think that's taking it a little too far. I like that we share that particular chore."

"If you insist. You can wash the bike tomorrow."

"Gee, thanks."

He tucked one hand behind his head. "I do what I can."

She rested her chin on his shoulder. They were quiet for a while. Because of the silence and darkness outside, there was the illusion that they were the only two people around. If only that were true. Then she might have a chance with him.

Otherwise Dylan was off-limits to her. It didn't matter that he liked her or even that he was worried about her. In his eyes they were friends, nothing more. She knew better than to wish for what she could never have. But it was hard to not think about being with him. About him touching her.

She'd liked his kissing and the way he held her so close. She'd liked the feel of his hands on her. Even when he'd touched her breast, she'd been so incredibly aroused. She raised her head. He *had* touched her breast. On his own. Which meant what, exactly?

"Why did you touch my breast?" she blurted out without thinking. The words seem to echo in the silence of the room. Color flamed on her cheeks, burning clear down to the bone. She wanted to die.

She had to clear her throat before she could speak again. "What I meant is—" Her voice trailed off. What did she mean?

"I'm waiting," he said.

She knew he was looking at her. She could feel his interested gaze. Why had she blurted that out?

"Nothing," she managed at last.

"Don't say that. The conversation was just getting interesting. That was quite a question. Why did I touch your breast? I suppose the simple answer is that I wanted to. I thought it would feel good to both of us."

She let that one drift in her mind for a little while. "Because we were kissing?" she asked cautiously.

"Yes."

She remembered feeling his hardness. So he'd been aroused by the situation. Did that mean he'd wanted to make love with her? It was an amazing thought. Making love meant being naked together. She didn't think she could handle that. Before it would have been difficult enough, what with the extra twenty pounds she carried, but now, with the still-healing incision on her breast, it was impossible. He would be disgusted.

If only Dylan were someone else. Someone less perfect. But then she wouldn't want him as much. Not that his perfection mattered, but she admired all of him. Changing one or two things would make him a different person and then her feeling would change.

"What are you thinking?" he asked.

"That you're too perfect."

He laughed. "Now I know you're sleep deprived. I'm so far from perfect I wouldn't know which way to go to get close. Go back to sleep, Molly. Unless you want to explore the whole breast-touching issue some more."

She knew he was teasing her about that, and it was very nice. There was no way that he wanted her. Still, the pretense was a pleasure.

She did as he requested, resting her head back on his shoulder and listening to the steady beat of his heart. Slow and strong. That's what she needed in her life—a little strength. She would bet that he wouldn't mind if she borrowed some of his. Just to get her through all this.

He tightened his arms around her and the last thing she remembered was heat of his body surrounding her like a warm, sensual blanket.

Chapter Ten

The next time Molly woke up it was morning. Sunlight poured in through open blinds. She rolled onto her side and found herself alone in the bed. The only indication that Dylan had been there were the rumpled covers and pillow and the warm feeling that lingered in her stomach.

The fear was still there, she thought, probing her emotions. She still desperately wanted the doctor to call and say that she was all right. But she was also stronger than she'd been. Telling Dylan everything had helped her determination to get through this, no matter what.

She heard him moving around in the other room. She supposed she should get up and start her day, but she didn't want to. She enjoyed lying here, remembering what it had been like when he'd held her in his arms. She couldn't remember ever falling asleep that way before. She and Grant had rarely spent the night together, and even when they had, they hadn't cuddled while falling asleep.

In addition to recalling all that had happened the previous night, she felt safe. Probably for the first time in a couple of weeks. It didn't matter that there wasn't any reason for her change of heart. Dylan couldn't actually protect her from what the lab would find. Yet some part of her thought that he could. She smiled. If only that were true.

"You're looking cheerful about something," he said.

She glanced up and saw Dylan standing in the doorway. He held a mug of coffee in each hand. She pushed her hair out of her face, suddenly a little self-conscious about her rumpled appearance, then shifted so that she was sitting up against the headboard.

"'Morning," she said. "How'd you sleep?"

"Great. And you?"

"The same."

He walked into the room and sank down on the mattress. He'd obviously already showered and shaved. His jaw was smooth, his dark hair damp. He wore a short-sleeved polo shirt tucked into jeans. As usual, he was too good-looking for comfort.

"Before you say it," he began, handing her a mug, "I didn't do this because of what you told me last night. I generally get up first to make coffee the morning after I spend the night in a woman's bed."

She wasn't sure how to take that. "But we didn't..." Her voice trailed off.

"A mere technicality. We have slept together and that's what matters."

She smiled. "Hey, if it gets the coffee delivered to my bedside, I'm not going to complain."

"You might after you taste it."

She took a cautious sip, but the steaming liquid was great. "Not to worry. I like it."

His gaze was steady, his body language open. Yet something had fundamentally shifted between them. She sensed it. "It's not going to be the same as it was, is it?"

"No. It can't be. I know too much. Guess you're gonna have to kill me now."

His teasing brightened her spirits. "Oh, I think you can be trusted."

His humor faded. "I hope so, Molly. That's important to me. I want you to trust me and depend on me. I want—" He shrugged. "I don't know what I want. To fix it, I guess, and I can't. I need to know what I can talk about and what I can't. What questions are going to bother you? Should I really try to pretend nothing is different? Would you rather not even have this conversation?"

"I don't mind talking about it," she said slowly. "As for what you can ask, ask anything. I don't have very many secrets left."

"I don't want to pry."

"I know." His concern touched her. "I have a lot of questions, too. Unfortunately until they've figured out what it is there aren't going to be many answers."

"I think you're very brave."

That made her laugh. "I'm not. I'm scared almost all the time."

"You don't act like it."

"I'm good at faking it."

Dylan took her free hand in his. "Sometimes that's enough. What's the expression? 'Fake it until you make it.'"

"That's how I get through the day. I feel like I'm on an emotional roller coaster. Sometimes I'm strong and I know I'm going to be fine. Other times I worry about dying. I think about what I'll do if they find that the lump is malignant. I worry about losing my breast, and then I tell myself

I'm stupid to be concerned about something that insignificant.''

''Molly, don't,'' he said, and set his coffee on the nightstand. He shifted so he was holding her hand in both of his. ''You feel how you feel. There's no right or wrong. You're under tremendous stress. Give yourself a break. If you end up having surgery to remove the breast, you'll need to mourn the loss, but please believe it's not going to change who you are.''

She wanted to believe him. She could see that he was being sincere. But they were from different worlds. ''What is it like being so physically perfect?'' she asked.

''What?''

''Look at you. You're like my sister. Tall, good-looking, physically fit. What is that like?''

His mouth pulled into a straight line. ''Why are you asking me that? You're a very attractive woman.''

''I'm not perfect.''

''Neither am I.''

''Let's just say you're within whispering distance of the goal and I don't know where they keep the playing field.''

''Stop it,'' he commanded. ''You're vibrant, smart, fun and pretty. Any man would be lucky to have you.''

She wished she could believe what he was saying, but he was being kind. ''Grant managed not to feel particularly blessed.''

''Grant is a jerk and he doesn't get a vote.''

''You're very sweet,'' she said. ''I appreciate that. I suppose the good news about Grant is that he ran off before I found the lump. I would have foolishly expected him to give me a little emotional support and hand-holding. The situation would have been even more difficult if he'd disappeared after that.''

"If he'd taken off after you'd told him about the lump, I would now be hunting him down like a rabid dog."

She didn't think Dylan would actually head to Mexico to protect and defend her, but she liked that he'd said he would. No one had ever done that before. She also liked how he was touching her. His fingers were warm and strong against her own. While she knew he meant the contact as comfort, a part of her was responding at a very physical level. Arousal was actually a nice way to start the day.

She leaned toward him. "You're very special to me. I want you to know how much I appreciate all this."

"Don't get any ideas," he said. "I'm not being altruistic. I'm here because I want to be here."

She actually believed him, which made it even nicer. "Thanks."

He released her hand and picked up his coffee. "Ready for a subject change?"

"Sure."

"What would you like to do today?"

She thought about that for a second and then laughed.

"Why do I feel like I'm about to be asked to spend the day at an outlet mall?" he asked.

"Don't worry," she told him. "It's not that at all. Actually, I laughed for two reasons. First, it's been what, ten days? I thought we were going to be moving on."

"Do you want to leave?"

"No. I like it here. I just think it's funny that we ran less than a hundred miles from Los Angeles. If I'd known it was going to be so easy to escape, I would have done it a lot sooner."

"What's the second thing that made you laugh?"

"Where I would like to go. Don't get all weird on me. I'm suggesting it because it's beautiful, not because it's morbid."

He frowned. "Where?"

"The Santa Barbara Mission."

He tapped the tip of her nose. "Your wish is my command."

"Really? Then I want to go to Paris for lunch."

"At one time I think people could walk from one end of California to the other, staying at missions," Molly said as they left the main church building. "They're supposed to be only a day's ride apart. Or is it a day's walk? No, that would put them too close together. I guess my point is that there are a bunch of them."

She paused on the steps and looked up at the old building. Dylan followed her gaze. The stone and wood structure had lasted for more than a hundred years. "It's beautiful," he said. "Just like you promised."

"We don't have many old things still standing. Between the earthquakes, the Santa Ana winds, the fires and some not-so-natural disasters, our style seems to be to make way for the new. If you liked the sanctuary, wait until you see the grounds. They're lovely, too."

Dylan followed her around to the side of the church. Here there were old gnarled trees and neatly trimmed bushes. Sections of the graveyard had been walled off from each other, creating smaller areas used by large families. Everywhere flowers bloomed. Southern California winters were mild, so most plants kept their leaves. Come spring they burst into bloom, and they retained their color well into fall.

She led the way into an older section. There were ornate statues of small angels, large tombstones, a profusion of flowers, and benches scattered around. Molly sank onto a stone seat, then patted the space next to her.

"I like this part," she said. "There are graves dating

back to the early 1800s. I think a few of the original Spanish families are buried here.'' She glanced at him and smiled. "What do you think?"

"I've never been to the mission before."

"I already figured that out. Do you hate it?"

"Not at all.''

He took a seat next to her. The afternoon was warm. They were both in short sleeves. Molly's T-shirt did nothing to disguise her curves. Dylan found himself trying not to notice her breasts, as if it wasn't right to look at them now. That confused him. They were the same size and shape they'd been this time yesterday. But then it had been safe to think about touching them and tasting them. He wasn't sure how those rules had changed. Molly had told him he could ask her whatever he liked, but he didn't think that was one of those questions. After all, how was she supposed to answer him?

The truth was, knowing about her lump had changed everything, even though it wasn't supposed to. He was worried about her in ways he hadn't been before. However, one thing was still the same—he still wanted her. Even as he told himself he had no right to be thinking that way, he kept picturing her in his bed, naked, her hair spread across the pillow, her thighs open and welcoming. He could probably be arrested for his thoughts.

He tried to force the images away. Molly didn't help. She leaned back and rested her elbows on the bench, thrusting her chest forward. He wondered about the surgery to remove the lump. She would have maybe a couple stitches or some bruising. Did that mean her breasts were any less sensitive? As long as he avoided the tender area in her left breast, wouldn't they both find pleasure in him caressing her?

Let it go, he ordered himself. He glanced around, hoping

to find something to talk about. All he saw were plants and graves. Despite the perfect weather, it was midday, mid-week, and they were the only tourists around.

"It's quiet here," he said, knowing it was a feeble effort at best.

"I know. That's why I like it. I try to make it up here every time I come to Santa Barbara. That's my favorite," she said, pointing to a group of tombstones laid out in rows in front of a statue of Jesus. "It's a family and they're all still together. Five generations."

He failed to see anything special about that but refrained from commenting on that fact.

"If it were my family," she went on, "they would have a space for me on the other side of the church."

Dylan turned to look at her. She'd made the statement matter-of-factly, as if it were of no consequence. Yet he heard the underlying sound of hurt.

"What are you talking about?" he asked.

She leaned her head back and stared at the sky. "It was a long time ago, so I understand why you don't remember what it was like at my house, but ours was not a close family. Janet and I fought constantly, my mother seemed to find fault with everything I did and my father—" She sighed. "He was physically in the house, but emotionally he disappeared a long time ago."

"I remember you and Janet fighting," he said, recalling how Janet would go on about Molly and how annoying she was. "From what I've seen, all siblings fight." He didn't have any personal experience. His parents had only had one child. With all the drinking and violence in his household, he couldn't say he was sorry.

"It took me a long time to figure out what was wrong," Molly said. "I thought things would get better when Janet left for college, but they didn't. I still felt like an outsider.

One day, when Janet was home on one of her breaks, she asked me out to lunch. She told me she'd finally realized that our mother was encouraging us to argue with each other. As if she didn't want us to get along. I hadn't thought of it myself, but I knew as soon as she said it that she was right. The problem was to figure out why.''

Dylan stretched his arm across the back of the stone bench. He let his hand rest against the back of Molly's neck. Her skin was warm and soft. He rubbed the tension from her muscles.

"What did you do?" he asked.

"I tried raiding the attic, looking for old papers. The problem was, we really didn't have an attic and I couldn't find anything interesting in the garage. One day, when my mother was going at me for not hemming a dress correctly, I lost it. I started screaming at her to tell me why she hated me so much. I think I really wanted her to tell me she loved me.''

Dylan didn't have to ask to know the news had been bad. "I'm sorry, Molly.''

"Don't be. In a way it was nice to have the information out in the open. It seems that after Janet was born, my father got very involved with his career. He was hardly ever home. My mother was lonely and unhappy. She had an affair. It was over quickly, but I'm the living, breathing reminder that it happened. She wouldn't tell me anything about my biological father, and I don't really care about him anymore. The man who raised me as his never took any interest in Janet, either, so I don't blame him for ignoring me. My mother is another matter.''

Dylan had trouble absorbing what she was saying. "Janet's only your half sister?"

"That's it. I told Janet when I found out the truth and she said she'd thought it was something like that. It doesn't matter to us. Since I went off to college, I haven't had much contact with my mother. I tried to make peace with her a couple of times, but she isn't interested. She told me she was glad I was out of her life. Finally."

Dylan thought about all he'd endured while he was growing up. Coming home to find both his parents drunk, the pain of the frequent beatings when they were sober. But always, he'd been able to blame the alcohol. He'd carried around the fantasy that if they stopped drinking, everything would be all right. Molly didn't even have that. All she had was the stark reality that her own mother resented that she'd ever been born.

He leaned toward her, but she raised her hands to ward him off. "Don't worry, I'm fine."

He raised his eyebrows. "Why don't I believe that?"

"I'm not sure. But it's true." Her hazel brown eyes clouded a little. "Okay, I'll admit that I would rather have a loving and close relationship with my mother, but at least I know why things happened the way they did. You'd be amazed how much that helps. Now my past makes sense to me. Janet and I have become very close and that means a lot to me."

It was something, he supposed, but he wanted her to have more. He wanted there to be lots of people who cared about her. Funny how so much more about Molly now made sense. Her independence, her statement that she wasn't sure she believed in love. They had that in common.

"If you're sitting there feeling sorry for me, I'm going to have to punch you in the stomach," she said, her expression fierce.

He grinned. "Don't start something you can't finish. If we have a contest of physical strength, I'm going to win."

She smiled back at him. "You couldn't be more wrong."

"How do you figure? I'm a lot stronger than you'll ever be. Just by virtue of being a guy."

"My point exactly. You're a guy. You can't hit back."

He opened his mouth, then closed it.

She batted her eyelashes at him. "I do so love it when I win."

"It was nothing but a cheap trick. I'd find a way to win."

She leaned toward him and wrapped her arms around him. He hugged her back. She felt good to hold. The wanting, never far under the surface, sprang to life. Fortunately, Molly didn't seem to notice.

"Thank you," she said. "For all of this. For coming away with me, for being a good friend, for showing me a good time and for caring."

He stared at her. They were close enough that he could kiss her. Only he didn't, because...hell, he wasn't sure why he didn't. Maybe because he knew she wouldn't just accept it. She would want explanations and assurance it wasn't about pity or anything else. Couldn't a man just want a woman because he wanted her?

"I do care about you," he said.

"I would have sold my soul to hear those words ten years ago." She rested her forehead against his chest. "I was so gone on you. It's kind of funny to look back now, but at the time, I was convinced I would never want another man."

"Of course you wouldn't."

"What?" She looked at him.

"Hey," he teased. "This is me. What else would I be if not the man of your dreams?"

She shoved him away and sat up straight. "Talk about an ego."

"I'm just being honest."

She angled away from him, crossing her legs and folding her arms over her chest. She was adorable.

"If I'd known what you were really like, I wouldn't have wasted my time mooning over you," she grumbled.

"Sure you would have."

"Do you have to have the last word no matter what?"

"Uh-huh."

She was laughing now. He'd always liked the sound, but it was more important to him since he'd learned what was on her mind when she was quiet.

She shifted until she was facing him again. "You are good for me. Actually, you've always been good for me. I appreciate how kind you were—back when I was still in high school."

"I'm willing to take credit for a lot of things, but I was never 'kind.' I liked you, Molly."

"As I said, you were kind. I was not a pretty young woman."

"What does that have to do with anything? Do you think I'm that shallow? Besides, you make it sound like you were a mutant. You were a little awkward, that's all."

"Awkward? It was more than that. I remember how much I hated Janet for being so incredibly beautiful. If she'd just been pretty, it would have been a whole lot easier to deal with." Molly sighed, remembering. "She was so tall, with those long legs and that face. All her friends were stunning, too. I remember walking into the living room once. She was there with five or six other girls. Our mother had also joined them. When I showed up, they just stopped talking and stared at me. At that exact moment, I realized I would never be like Janet or my mother. I felt as if I'd been dropped off from another planet—an ugly one. I was about thirteen at the time. I went into my room and stayed there for three days. Then I got bored and decided to just ignore them and make my own life.''

Dylan wasn't comfortable hearing the story. He was torn, knowing that Molly hadn't been pretty as a child, yet wanting to tell her she had been. He always remembered her as someone he liked, and her appearance had little to do with that. But for her, appearance was important. He shifted the conversation in a different direction.

''I'm glad you and Janet finally became friends,'' he said.

''Me, too. She's been so wonderful through all of this. I couldn't have made it without her.'' She laced her fingers together and frowned. ''You've done so much, Dylan. You came from a troubled childhood and you've made something of your life. It's very impressive.''

''Thanks. Some of it was hard work, but some of it was just being in the right place at the right time. I can't take credit for dumb luck.''

''It's more than that. You haven't been afraid.''

He sensed they were on shaky ground, but he couldn't figure out why. ''Everyone is afraid sometimes.''

''I know, but I've lived my life in fear. I see that now. I've had a lot of time to think and one of the things I've learned is that clichés are clichés for a reason—they tell the truth. If something happens to me, something bad, what I'll most regret is what I didn't do. I've lived such a small life. It's as if I made a deal with God and promised not to expect too much. In return, nothing bad would happen to me. There would be no great joy, but no great sorrow, either.''

That he could understand. ''Now you're thinking you didn't really make a deal.''

''Exactly. I'm facing potential sorrow and I haven't done anything with myself. There has been no joy. There were so many things I wanted to do or thought about doing, and I did none of them. Now I look at where I am and it's incredibly tragic. It's one thing to regret not living longer and having more time. It's another to regret having wasted the time I was given."

Her eyes filled with tears, but she blinked them back. Frustration filled him. Here was one more situation he couldn't fix. He could only stand helplessly by while Molly wrestled with her pain.

She leaned against the back of the stone bench. Sunlight filtered through the trees and illuminated her face. For a moment he thought he was staring at an angel.

"Maybe this is my lesson," she said. "Maybe this is what I'm supposed to learn from this experience. That I have to take all the time I'm given and use up each hour as best I can, because time is precious."

He couldn't help himself. He slid toward her and hugged her close. She came willingly into his arms. After clasping one hand behind her head, he began to rock, comforting them both with the action.

"I'm sorry," she whispered. "I didn't mean to upset you."

"You didn't. I'll admit the conversation is a little unusual. I don't usually discuss the meaning of life."

She was silent for a while, then she asked, "Do you believe in God?"

"Yes," he answered without hesitation. "I suspect we are physiologically unable to grasp Him as He is and that our view of Him is simplified, but I believe a great power exists."

"Me, too. I've been thinking about that a lot. For obvious reasons. There's nothing like the reality of facing death to make one think about God and heaven, and what happens after we die."

He did *not* want to be having this conversation with her, but he knew that she needed to talk about it. If not to him, then to whom? Right now he was her whole world. At one time that thought would have scared him into running as far and as fast as he could. But now—now he wanted to stay here, holding her, helping in any way he could.

"You are very brave," he murmured against her hair.

"Stop saying that. I'm just trying to make peace with circumstances that I can't control. There's a difference."

"No, Molly. You're amazing. Just quit disagreeing with me and accept the compliment graciously. All right?"

She looked up at him and smiled. "I love it when you talk tough. I'm hungry. Let's be wild today and have ice cream for lunch."

"You're on."

Dylan was as restless as a mountain lion in a cage. He paced their small house from end to end, pausing only to stare out into the darkness before resuming his route. Molly curled up in a corner of the sofa and watched him. Despite the pep talk she'd been giving herself for the past hour, she couldn't seem to shake off the feeling of sadness overwhelming her. Maybe because there was no way to avoid the truth.

Dylan wanted out.

Last night he'd taken the news very well. This morning he'd seemed fine, both at breakfast and when they'd visited the mission. After a decadent lunch of ice cream, they'd gone to the movies and then shopping. He'd been friendly, supportive and solicitous, holding her hand during the film, inquiring about her comfort when they'd been at the restaurant. She'd basked in the glow of his attention, but now she wondered if it had all been a cover.

She shouldn't be surprised. It had been over two weeks,

and she still hadn't adjusted to the reality of having found a lump. It was impossible for him to accept it in twenty-four hours. Despite the past ten days, they were relative strangers. He didn't owe her anything. She was wrong to expect him to stay. The true act of kindness would be to release him.

She watched him as he paced by her. He didn't look at her; in fact, he barely seemed to notice she was in the room. She'd hoped... Molly shook her head. She'd had a lot of hopes, but none of them had been realistic. She was a grown-up. She'd been alone before and she would be alone again. She was tough. He'd given her ten wonderful days and that was more than she'd expected.

"I understand what's wrong," she said.

Dylan stood by the window, his back to her. "I doubt that."

At least he hadn't tried to deny there was a problem. "You're frustrated by the situation. You want to leave but feel you have a responsibility to me. Don't worry about that. I'll be fine."

He turned to stare at her. Tension tightened the lines of his face, drawing his cheekbones into stark relief. His mouth was straight, his eyes unreadable. "What the hell are you talking about?"

She didn't flinch at his harsh tone. She knew he was more angry with himself than with her. "You've already given me so much more than I'd imagined was possible. These days have been a terrific adventure. I'll remember them always. Not just because you helped me through a difficult time, but because I've enjoyed getting to know you again."

Dylan shoved his hands into his jeans pockets. "You're missing the entire point."

"No, I'm not. You're a good man. You want to fix me,

and you can't. It's out of your hands. So let it go. Let *me* go. I'll head on up to see Janet, so you don't have to worry about me being alone.'' She drew in a deep breath. "I don't regret a minute of the time we've spent together. I don't want you to regret it, either. Say goodbye, Dylan. Go while it's still good between us.''

He crossed to her in three long strides, then sat on the sofa next to her. After taking both her hands in his, he gazed at her face. "You think you're really bright, and you are about some things, but, Molly, you couldn't be further off base with this one."

He looked incredibly sincere. "If it's not that, then what? What's wrong?"

He touched a finger to her cheek. "I don't want to leave. I want to stay.''

He was not making sense. "Then stay. What's the problem?"

"I want to be with you and it's making me crazy."

His words came out in a rush. Molly heard them. They turned over in her brain. He wanted to be with her. Okay. He was with her. They were with each other. They'd spent the past ten days together.

"You *are* with me.''

"I want to make love with you.''

Her mouth dropped open. She felt it. She also felt all the air leaving her lungs. In a couple of seconds she was going to start gasping, but for now, she would only stare at him in disbelief.

He *wanted* her? *He* wanted *her*?

She managed to draw in a breath and close her mouth, but that was it in the bodily function department. Nothing else was working.

She wanted to believe him. Desperately. She'd thought about them being together—it was one of her favorite fantasies. But the reality was very different. He was Dylan Black, an amazing man who was incredibly good-looking and successful and whatever would he want with a woman like her? She was short and pale. There was the issue of those extra twenty pounds. She'd found she could not enjoy the sexual act and try to hold in her stomach at the same time. And what about her breast? She had an incision with stitches. The shape was weird on that one side and the bruise was gross.

He couldn't really want her. This was about feeling sorry for her or—

"Dammit, no!" he growled, and grabbed her shoulders. "Confusion is acceptable. You can blink at me and tell me it's too sudden. You can even slap me across the face and remind me I'm breaking the rules, that you aren't interested in a guy like me. Any of that. But I won't let you doubt yourself or the fact that I want you."

Dear Lord, he could read her mind.

"How'd you know what I was thinking?"

"I know you, Molly. Better than you think."

She was too confused to be able to say anything. "I don't understand. I'm so not your type."

"Why is it so hard to believe I want you?" He scowled. "Just for the record, I want to make love with you. I don't want to 'get off.' Don't be confused about that. If you're not interested, say so and I'll leave you alone. We'll pretend this conversation never occurred."

He was kidding, right? He had to be. But she saw the uncertainty in his eyes. The fear that she would reject him. Beneath that, she saw desire. The flickering flames of wanting and needing.

She believed him. Maybe because she wanted to, but that was all right. She'd promised herself no regrets. Dylan said he wanted to make love with her. She'd wanted to be with him since she'd first seen him. Both ten years ago and recently. That hadn't changed. It didn't matter that it was only temporary. For reasons she would never understand, Dylan had engaged her heart in more ways than any other man, even Grant. She could deny him nothing. More important, she would not deny herself this chance...this miracle.

She touched a finger to his lower lip. "I want you, too," she whispered.

Chapter Eleven

She had to clench her teeth to keep from screaming. Had she really said that? Admitted that she wanted him? What if he'd been kidding? What if it had all been a joke and she'd taken him seriously and—

He stood up and pulled her to her feet. "You make me crazy," he said.

"What? How? What did I say?" She went with him, only because he was tugging her along. She tried not to notice that they were heading for her bedroom, for the very large bed she'd been sleeping in, until last night, alone. Maybe if she concentrated on his words she wouldn't have the chance to think about other stuff, such as maybe they *were* going to do it and then she would have to think about being naked in front of him and oh, Lord, this really, really wasn't happening.

"Stop doubting yourself," he said when they reached the side of the bed. "I can practically hear what you're saying. Why can't you get it through your head that I'm serious about this?''

"Because you're telling me something wonderful and the bad stuff always makes more sense than the good stuff." She raised a hand to ward off his comments. "I know, I know. I should get over it. It's not that I haven't done this before. I mean, I'm even on the pill. But I'm not hugely experienced." She and Grant had been intimate a few times, but it wasn't a real regular occurrence. Maybe that's what had gone wrong between them. She pushed the thought aside. "The bottom line is, if I started therapy right this minute, it would still take a couple hundred years for me to believe the good stuff first. Trust me, Dylan. I'm not alone in this failing. A lot of women are blessed with confidence about their looks, but many of us are filled with insecurities.''

"That's just plain silly.''

They were in the dark. She told herself to go ahead and relax. In the dark he would only be able to feel, not look. If she kept his hands away from certain parts, then it would be—

The light on the nightstand sprang into life. She blinked in the sudden glare.

"You turned the light on," she said.

"Yes. I want to see you. Is that a problem?''

Define problem, she thought grimly. "No, of course not," she lied cheerfully. "I like it with the lights on.''

"Like I believe that," he said. "But thanks for pretending. Come here.''

He sat on the edge of the bed and pulled her down next to him. He shifted them until they were stretched out on the mattress, facing each other. They were just a few inches apart. Molly could feel herself shaking, and it wasn't from anticipation. If only they didn't have to be naked to have sex, she would be a lot more comfortable with the whole procedure.

"You are lovely," Dylan said, and touched his finger to her forehead. He traced both her eyebrows, then moved down to stroke her cheek. The contact was light and teasing. When he brushed back and forth against her lower lip, she opened her mouth and nipped him.

He chuckled. "So you want to play, do you?"

She thought about that for a second. "Actually, I don't. At some point I would like to laugh and tickle and tease in bed, but not tonight. I'm scared. I want to do this. I want you, but I'm trembling with fear. It would be too easy for me to think that laughing with me was laughing *at* me."

"I would never do that. I would never hurt you."

If only she could believe him. "You wouldn't hurt me on purpose," she agreed. "But things happen." The problem was, he didn't understand how much power he had over her. Better for both of them to keep it that way.

He slipped his hand behind her so he could cup her head. "The world hasn't always been kind to you, has it? No," he added before she could speak. "I'm not feeling sorry for you. If anything, I admire your strength and character. And you're not allowed to do anything but politely accept the compliment."

"All these rules," she said. "I thought it would be simpler than this."

"Making love is wonderful," he said, "but it's almost never simple."

Before she could ask what he meant, he leaned forward and kissed her. They'd done this part before...the kissing...and she'd liked it very much. His mouth worked the same magic she remembered, his lips moving against hers, his tongue sweeping inside. She liked how he tasted, the texture and scent of him. He made her feel safe and alive.

He also turned her on in a big way. Despite the fear and the shaking, she felt the first stirrings deep inside her. The initial hints of arousal began as a faint pressure low in her belly. She found herself wanting to get closer to him so they could kiss more deeply. She slipped one of her legs forward and he squeezed it between his.

The hand in her hair began to move. He tugged at the rubber band at the bottom of her braid and pulled it free, then he began to finger-comb her thick curls.

She let the needing overtake her. Passion gave her courage. She touched his face. Smooth skin gave way to stubble. She liked the contrast and the soft scraping sound her fingers made as she ran them down to his chin. He must have liked it, too, because as she learned the intimate details of his features, he moaned and surged toward her.

She let her hand fall to his shoulder. He was strong and broad. She could feel the heat of him, even through his T-shirt. Without thinking, she drew her fingers down his chest and explored the muscles there. Her thumb grazed his nipple. She felt the tight peak and the way he jumped. Instantly she pulled back, both from touching him and from the kiss.

He grabbed her hand and placed it against his chest. "Don't stop," he said, his voice low and husky. "I like it."

"Are you sure?"

"Of course. That just took me by surprise. In fact—" He rolled away from her, tugged his shirt out of his jeans, then pulled it up and over his head. Then he stretched out next to her again. Topless.

Molly stared at him, at the breadth of him, at the faintly tanned skin, the tempting pattern of hair that swirled across his chest, then narrowed as it moved down toward his waist. Her mouth went dry and she was suddenly thrilled they'd decided to leave the light on. Looking at his chest was more than worth the price of admission.

"Touch me," he said.

When she hesitated, he took her hand and once again pressed her palm against him. This time, instead of the soft cotton of his T-shirt, she felt crinkly hair and smooth skin.

Involuntarily, her fingers curled against him. She moved in a circle, exploring him, reveling in the tension that filled his muscles as she slipped over different parts of his chest, enjoying the way his breath caught and the passion brightening his dark eyes.

"You have no idea what you're doing to me," he murmured, then bent his head to kiss her.

There were no preliminaries this time, no pausing for permission. Instead, he kissed her openmouthed, seeking as soon as they touched, going deep inside. His tongue circled hers, then moved back and forth. They began the sensual dance that re-created what their bodies would do later—when they were both undressed and she was beneath him.

She moved her hand to his back, both touching him and drawing him closer. She moved up and down, tracing a line from his shoulders to the waistband of his jeans. The tight curve of his rear tempted her, but she wasn't that brave. A part of her was still stunned that this was actually happening. She knew it had to be real. While she had often fantasized about making love with him, all her imaginings combined didn't come close to the wonder that was reality.

His hands were warm and sure as they rolled her onto her back. She went willingly, angling her head so they could keep kissing. She liked the way he rubbed his open palms up and down her arms. Then he stroked her neck. That one hand slipped lower, toward her breasts. She froze.

Dylan didn't appear to notice. Nothing about his kiss changed, even though she'd stopped participating. Her hands fell to her sides, where she curled her fingers into fists. Fear, embarrassment, confusion all blended. She couldn't do this. Not with him. Not ever.

She would have told him, too, if he had stopped kissing her long enough. But he didn't. His mouth continued to move against hers; his tongue continued to stroke her own. She wasn't held in place—she could have easily pulled away or pushed him off. She almost did, too. Except—

She wanted him. That hadn't changed. If only she didn't have to be afraid.

Want and fear continued to battle it out. She tried to focus on what he was doing, on the heat and dampness growing between her thighs. She told herself she would have to get over this sometime and wouldn't it be easier with Dylan?

The questions and concerns continued to circle in her mind. As there were no answers, she decided it wouldn't hurt to kiss him back. After a while she noticed that his hand was still sliding up and down between her breasts, getting close but not actually touching either one. The outside of her left breast was still a little tender from the surgery, but nothing was wrong with the nipple. Like the right one, it was tight, almost uncomfortably so. The soft cotton of her sports bra irritated her skin. She shifted to try to make it better, but that didn't help at all.

She wanted... She wanted him to touch her there.

Her breath caught in her throat as she realized her breasts were both swollen and aching with desire. Instead of just being clenched, her hands were opening and closing against the bedspread. Her legs had parted a little and the heat between them had returned.

She wrapped one arm around his shoulders and stroked his hair. When he withdrew from her mouth, she whimpered in protest and followed him. Once inside, she teased and explored, savoring the taste of him. Excitement rose between them. This is what she wanted—Dylan, always Dylan.

His hand continued to stroke up and down on her chest, moving from her belly to her throat. On one of the return trips, he moved his fingers a little to one side. His warm palm cupped her right breast. Slowly—gently—perfectly. She dug her fingers into his scalp.

"Yes," she whispered against his mouth, giving them both permission to enjoy that part of her body.

He stroked every part of her curves, discovering the possibilities, teaching them both what made her squirm, what made her sigh and, when he finally teased the tight nipple, what made her clutch him close and moan his name.

Without warning, he broke away. Before she could ask what was wrong, he tugged on her T-shirt and pulled it out of her jeans. In a matter of seconds, he had it over her head and sailing toward the floor. Her seeing him topless was one thing, but him seeing her was quite another.

"This isn't a good idea," she said, folding her arms protectively over the sports bra that kept her breasts from moving around too much. What a time not to be in satin and lace.

He looked into her eyes. "Why?"

She could feel heat on her cheeks, and it wasn't from passion. "I don't want you to take off my bra. The incision is still red and bruised, and I just don't want you looking at it."

"Because I'll think it's ugly."

He wasn't asking a question, but she nodded anyway. Not that it mattered. The mood had been broken. "This wasn't a good idea," she muttered. "Just forget it." She started to get out of bed.

"Don't," he said, taking hold of her arm. "Don't leave

me like this. Do you really think it matters that you've got a cut and a few stitches? I don't want to look because I have this morbid fascination with your surgery. I want to see you naked because the thought of it turns me on. I've been imagining us doing this for a long time. I want to touch and taste every part of you."

He certainly had a way with words, she thought, and realized the mood might not be as broken as she'd first believed. "Can't we still do this if I leave my bra on?"

"Yes. Of course. But I'd rather you took it off."

"Why is that so important to you?"

"It's not. It's important to you."

She pressed her lips tightly together. All right, so she didn't need a degree in psychology to figure out what he was trying to say. If she could allow him to see her naked, scar and all, she would feel less self-conscious about her breast. "You don't know what you're asking."

"I do know. You'll never believe that I'm not going to reject you because of how you look until you put me to the test. If I have to, I'll play it your way, but I'd rather you trusted me. I won't let you down, Molly. You matter too much to me for me to want to hurt you."

How was she supposed to resist that? she thought unhappily. Why couldn't the man be an insensitive jerk and just do it without worrying about her psyche or her breasts? But no, he had to go and be all warm and caring. She hated that.

The absurdity of her complaints made her laugh. "Dylan, there is absolutely no hope for me."

Before she could change her mind, she reached behind her and unfastened her bra. Holding it in place, she pulled her arms free of the straps, then she flopped down her back, leaving the garment loose but in place. She could make it easy for him, but she couldn't actually take it off. He would have to do that himself.

She closed her eyes for good measure. She didn't want to see the disgust on his face.

She braced herself for the inevitable. Nothing happened. Then she felt warm breath on her stomach. Something tugged and unzipped. She realized he was undoing her jeans. Great. Now she had to worry about sucking in her stomach. Talk about romantic.

Warm, moist heat settled just above her belly button. Her eyes sprang open and she looked down to see what he was doing. Her throat closed as the visual image combined with the sensual pleasure to make her nearly faint. Using his tongue, he circled around her navel, then dipped inside. Her muscles jumped and she gave a strangled laugh.

"That tickles."

He smiled against her belly but didn't stop. Instead he moved slowly up, leaving behind a wet trail. His breath puffed against her sensitized skin. She shivered in pleasure and anticipation. Talk about attention to detail—she liked this quality in a man.

Farther and farther up toward her chest, toward her breast. She felt herself tensing and tried to relax. But she couldn't. What was he going to say? Would he try to fake interest? There were some things a man couldn't fake and she didn't want to touch him *there* only to find out he wasn't aroused.

Dylan changed course. He moved a little toward her right breast and her breathing relaxed. She didn't mind him touching her there, although her bra was in the way. Still, he could go underneath it or around it or—

He licked the underside of her breast. Somehow he nudged the fabric out of the way just enough to gain access to the sensitive skin. She actually called out something, although she wasn't sure what. His warm, wet tongue moved back and forth, caressing her, shifting ever so slightly toward her nipple.

She was practically whimpering with pleasure. Her hips rose slightly, as if that action would encourage him to continue. She wanted him to move higher, to take the tight peak in his mouth and suck it. She wanted—

He read her mind. It was another excellent quality in a man, she thought in the split second before the wonder of it all washed every other thought out of her brain. She reveled in the way he circled the tiny bud, then drew it deeply into his mouth. She raised her arms so she could run her fingers through his hair, both caressing him in return and holding him in place.

Dampness flooded her panties. She wanted him to touch her there, too. She wanted him inside her, filling her, making her feel whole and special.

He kissed the valley between her breasts. As he moved up her left breast, his fingers continued the ministrations his tongue had begun, teasing her tautness, rolling it between thumb and forefinger, making her whimper and beg that he never stop.

He kissed around the bottom curve of her left breast, then up to the nipple. Again he took the ready nipple in his mouth and licked it. Pleasure doubled as tongue and fingers worked in cadence. Unable to bear it, she let her arms fall to her side. Her fingers got tangled in her bra. The bra that was now resting on the bed and not on her.

She grabbed his shoulders. "Dylan?"

He raised his head and looked at her face. Not by a flicker of a lash did he lower his gaze to her left breast or the ugliness there.

"Don't try telling me you don't like it, kid. Your body gives you away."

Amazingly enough, he could still make her smile. "I wasn't going to try to tell you that. It's just—"

"What?"

"Look," she whispered. "Go ahead and look. But it's awful."

"I did and it's not."

She stared at him. "You already looked?"

"Uh-huh." He shrugged and straightened so that he was kneeling at her side. "When you laid back down on the bed, your bra kind of hitched up on that one side. I could see the incision then."

She didn't know what to say. "You saw it and you still wanted to touch me?"

He shook his head. "And here I thought you were so damn smart. Goes to show what I know." With that, he unzipped his jeans, pushed them open and reached in to draw out his arousal. "I want to do more than touch you, Molly. I want to make love with you." His expression got fierce. "Don't for a minute think it's going to be anything else, either. You and I are making love."

He was beautiful. She touched him, stroking the head, then the length of him. He flexed in her hand. He was turned on. Really turned on. She had proof.

"Enough," he said, pulling back. "You'll start something that I don't want to finish just yet."

He swung around and sat on the edge of the bed, pulled off his boots and socks, then pushed down his jeans and briefs. When he was completely naked, he pulled off the rest of her clothes and settled next to her.

"Where were we?" he asked.

Molly threw her arms around him and held him tight. "How did you do that?" she asked. "You made me feel so incredibly wonderful. Not just in how you touched me, but in how I feel about myself."

He tucked her hair behind her ears and gazed at her. "I want you, Molly. I'm not doing anything special."

If only he knew the truth. Wanting her was the most precious gift he could have given her. No matter what, she would be able to remember this for the rest of her life.

He kissed her. She met him more than halfway, her mouth open, her body ready for him. When his hand came down toward her breasts, she turned toward him, giving him room, wanting him to touch her there. She knew that he would be careful on the side where she was tender. He'd seen the stitches and the reddish purple bruising. He was a warm and sensitive man—she didn't know what she'd done to deserve him.

Dylan held Molly protectively. While he was glad he'd finally convinced her that he really wanted her, taking off his clothes had been a pretty stupid idea. He was ready to take her. It was all he could do not to kneel between her thighs and drive home to paradise. He did still plan to do that, but not for a while. Not until he was sure she'd already had her pleasure and that she was completely prepared for his entry. He didn't want any part of their lovemaking to be less than perfect for her.

He eased her onto her back and started trailing kisses down her neck and chest. He only touched the inside of her left breast, being careful not to jostle it or bump the incision. He hadn't been sure what to expect, but it wasn't ugly at all. There was a small red line where they'd cut her, and a bruise surrounding the area. The breast was obviously tender and swollen. The shape might have changed slightly, but he hadn't seen her before the surgery, so he couldn't be sure. He didn't really care. As far as he was concerned, she was lovely.

He moved until he was kneeling between her legs, then he continued to kiss his way down her body. She was soft and sweet. Both her taste and scent appealed to him. He cupped her hips, liking the swell of flesh that filled his hands. Molly was all womanly curves, welcoming and yielding. She had no sharp angles like all his previous lovers, and he found himself enjoying the differences. He knew she was a little self-conscious about her body and the extra few pounds she frequently complained about. He wished there were a way to convince her none of that mattered to him. However, he figured that if he brought it up, she would start thinking about it and that would make them both crazy.

He reached her belly button. He'd already tasted her sweetness there and he'd liked it, so he dipped inside. Molly writhed and giggled beneath him.

His response was to grin and do it again. As she twisted, her breasts moved. She cupped the left one to hold it still, probably because it was still tender. The right breast bounced and swayed. He loved watching it and decided that when she was healed he was going to insist on a wrestling match—but they both had to be naked.

He slipped lower, licking the soft skin right above the protective vee of hair that concealed her feminine secrets. He could feel the heat of her there. He wanted to hurry, to touch her and discover her taste, to feel how ready she was for him, how wet he'd made her. Just the thought of it aroused him even more. His body pulsed with wanting her.

"Dylan." She breathed his name.

He urged her thighs apart, then bent down and licked her most secret place.

Her legs tensed and her hips came up off the bed. She moaned, her head moving from side to side. She tasted as sweet as he'd thought she would. She was hot and slick.

He explored her and quickly found the spots that made her beg for more. He teased at the tiny button nearly buried

inside her. He moved over it and around it, making all of
her swell more, bringing the small place to the surface. He
listened to her breathing, felt her tension and continued
accordingly. He wanted this to be incredibly special for her.
Not just the release, but all of it. When she thought of him,
he wanted this night hardwired into her brain.

He moved faster. She flexed her hips slightly, telling him
that she was getting closer. Slowly he slipped one finger
inside her.

Instantly her muscles clamped around him. He began
moving the finger in and out, preparing her for what they
would soon be doing. He tried not to think about thrusting
himself there, afraid that if he thought about it too much,
he would completely lose control.

As her breathing quickened, he felt her collecting herself.
He licked lighter and faster still, urging her on, silently
demanding that she give him everything.

"Oh, Dylan," she moaned. "I can't believe what you're
doing to me."

He was torn, wanting to love her like this forever, yet
desperately wanting her to find her release. He closed his
lips over the tiny knot and sucked gently. She froze, gasped
once, then seemed to explode.

She called out his name even as her body convulsed
around him. The muscles deep inside her rippled as contraction after contraction pulsed through her. Her legs fell
open, her hips thrust him. He continued lighter and lighter
until he was barely touching her, until the last of the shud-
dering ceased. Then he stretched out beside her and held
her close.

The tears began slowly. Then they flowed faster and she
started to sob. He wasn't surprised. After all that she'd been
through, she needed an emotional release as much as a
physical one.

"I'm sorry," she managed, her voice choked. "I don't know what's wrong with me."

"It's okay. I know. You're just reacting. I'm not offended, so go ahead and get it out of your system."

"I just—"

Another sob tore at her. She clutched his arms and buried her head against his chest. Her tears were hot and wet on his bare skin. He could smell the scent of their bodies and the lovemaking.

As she clung to him, he felt a tightness in his chest. A need to be close to her for a long time. He supposed the situation should have terrified him, but he didn't want to pull back. He liked having her depend on him.

Molly sniffed. She was pretty sure the crying jag was over, but how on earth was she supposed to face Dylan? He'd just treated her to the most amazing experience of her life and she'd rewarded him by bursting into tears.

"You probably think I'm crazy," she mumbled against his chest.

"Nope. I think you're great."

She didn't want to look at him for two reasons. First, she wasn't sure what she was going to see in his eyes. There was that whole pity-fear, plus they'd just been so intimate. Second, she wasn't one of those "pretty" criers. When she gave in, her eyes got all red, her mouth puffy, her skin flushed and blotchy at the same time. It was not an attractive visual.

But she couldn't lie here with her nose pressed against him forever. Slowly she raised her head and looked up. Dylan smiled at her.

"Hey," he said. "You all right?"

He wasn't mad. She could tell. And if the large, hard object poking into her stomach was anything to go by, he still wanted her.

"I'm fine. How about you?"

His smile turned into a grin. "I've been thinking that I'm pretty hot stuff in bed."

She laughed. "You'd be right on that account. I'll be happy to give you a written testimonial."

"Gee, thanks."

Her smile faded. "Thank *you*," she said. "For everything. For what you did, for understanding when I lost it. Actually, I do feel better."

"I'm glad."

She continued to look at him. Making love, he'd said, and he'd been right. This had been about more than just sex, and that made her feel very special. Now she wanted to do the same for him.

She rolled onto her back and urged him to follow. "Be with me," she whispered. "Be in me."

Again he knelt between her legs. She was more than ready for him—she *needed* him inside her. While her body was still tingling with the pleasure of her release, she wanted the same for him. If she was willing to admit even a tiny bit more, she also wanted them to bond in that age-old way.

He entered her slowly, stretching her, filling her until the pressure began to build and she knew it was just a matter of time until she climaxed again. His face tightened as he groaned. They were, she realized, a perfect fit.

"I don't think I can hold back very long," he managed between gritted teeth.

He withdrew, then entered again. The pressure built even more. She gave herself over to it. "I don't need very long."

She tried to wrap her arms around him. He shook his head. "Don't," he told her. "Don't pull me down on you. It will hurt."

If she hadn't been all cried out, she would have started

sobbing again. The man was deep inside her, close to finding his release, yet he was still concerned about her physical well-being.

They moved together. She felt the tension in his body as he got closer and closer. She went with him, pulled along by the miracle that was their joining. At the last possible second, when her body collected itself to once again take her to paradise, she opened her eyes and found him looking at her.

"Now," he breathed.

She let herself go, feeling him do the same, and for the first time in her life, she understood the concept of two people becoming one.

Chapter Twelve

For the second time in as many days, Molly woke up with the realization that she'd spent the night in Dylan's arms. It was, she thought sleepily, a great way to start the morning.

This time he was still with her, still asleep, stretched out on his back, his head on the pillow close to hers. He was warm, generating enough heat that were this winter, she definitely wouldn't need an electric blanket. What a lovely thought, she told herself, and wondered if she dared fantasize about what it would be like to wake up next to Dylan every morning.

She rolled onto her side and looked at him, at the strong profile, the straight nose and firm mouth, at the stubble covering his cheeks and jaw. She knew he wasn't for her; he never had been. Through a series of circumstances she could neither explain nor hope to duplicate, they'd ended up here—together. It was only for a short period, but that was all right with her. He'd been so kind about everything. Even before he'd known her secrets, he'd been a good friend. She couldn't ask for better.

So this was going to be enough. It might take her a while to believe it. After all, she was a normal woman who would hate to give up the best man she'd ever known. But in time she would be able to put all this in perspective and just remember how wonderful everything had been.

Molly stretched. Several muscles ached pleasantly. She smiled. Must have been all that unfamiliar activity, with her body tensing, then relaxing. Last night had been... indescribable. Maybe there were words, but she couldn't think of them. It was as if they'd discovered a different kind of lovemaking. She'd been with men before. Okay, just two, but she wasn't a virgin. She not only understood the mechanics of what went on between men and women, she'd participated in the event herself. Yet except for the most basic of descriptions, what she and Dylan had done together bore little or no resemblance to the other experiences in her life.

He'd been so incredibly tender. And not just about her breast. He'd treated her as if she were someone special, as if her body were precious, almost sacred, and deserved to be worshipped. She still couldn't believe that he'd, well, *kissed* her down there! No one had done that before. She'd read about it and had thought it was kind of weird. Now, after having experienced it for herself, she could understand the appeal.

They'd made love again in the night. After dozing for a while, she'd awakened to find him stroking her. This time it had been dark and they'd been forced to find their way by touch alone. She'd enjoyed the mystery and the discoveries. If his groans of pleasure, his rapid breathing and the way he'd called out her name over and over were anything to go by, he'd had a good time, as well. She smiled at the memory.

"You're obviously happy about something," he said.

She looked at him and saw that he was awake. "Good morning. How'd you sleep?"

"Great."

He shifted so he could put his arm around her and pull her close. She went willingly into his embrace. She supposed that she should be embarrassed about everything, but she couldn't summon the strength. Dylan had, through his actions, restored her to herself. She would always be able to carry that with her. With him, she'd learned that her body was still lovely and that all the important parts worked.

"Me, too." He glanced at the clock on her nightstand. "Looks like we slept in."

"Are you surprised?"

"No." He kissed her forehead. "After all, you kept me up half the night."

"Me? What are you talking about?"

"Don't pretend innocence," he teased. "You were hanging on to me, touching me, waking me from a sound sleep with your insatiable appetites."

She heard the laughter in his voice, read his pleasure in his expression. "That was you. You have things mixed-up."

"No way. You were grabbing me in the night."

She pulled back far enough to start tickling him. He grabbed her hands to stop her. She wriggled free and continued her attack.

"I don't want to hurt you," he warned.

"Oh, yeah, like I'm scared." She attacked him again, this time going for his feet.

He yelped and jumped out of bed. "That is unnecessary," he said, his voice stern.

She laughed. "Since when do you get to set the rules?"

"I've always set the rules. I'm completely in charge of this situation."

Soft morning light filtered through the blinds. He looked so beautiful standing there, his lean body exposed to her gaze. Even as she watched, he started to get aroused.

"Yup, you're in charge," she said. "Nothing happens without your express permission. That's good to know."

He glanced down. "Damn. Betrayed by my own body." Then he lunged at her.

She didn't have enough warning. She tried to scramble off the other side of the bed, but it was too late. He got hold of one of her ankles and pulled her back toward him.

When he'd wrestled her into submission on the bed, he smoothed her hair off her face and smiled at her. "I'm glad you're like this," he said.

"What are you talking about?"

"I was afraid you'd have second thoughts about last night. About us being lovers."

The word made her shiver. Lovers. That was nice. It implied that they would be doing it again, that last night hadn't been a one—make that a two—time thing.

"I don't regret anything," she said. "I'm not even going to grill you on why you did it."

"I made love with you because I wanted you. No other reason."

"Oh, sure, go ahead and be logical." She softened the words with a smile. "My natural inclination is to doubt myself, but in this circumstance, I'm going to let it go and just believe you."

"You make it sound like that's difficult to do."

"You'd be amazed at how hard it is."

"I knew I'd impressed you."

It took a second for her to register the teasing glint in

his eyes, not to mention the other meaning of his words. She slipped a hand between them. Instantly her own body came to life.

"No!" he said quickly and stood up. He took her hand and tugged her until she was sitting on the edge of the bed. "I plan to make love with you over and over, but I insist we at least pretend that we're going to get up and start our day."

As always, he made her laugh. "If you say so." She gave him one last stroke, making it slow and sensual, forcing him to catch his breath. "We could start with a shower."

She felt bold issuing that kind of invitation. But while she was a little scared, she was comforted by the fact that this was Dylan and she believed him when he said he wouldn't hurt her.

"I'd like that," he said as he took her hand and led her into the small bathroom.

Five minutes later they were under the spray, washing each other. As she rubbed his chest, he rubbed hers. He was careful not to bump her near her incision. Even so, they kept getting in each other's way.

"We can't do this," she said, and laughed. "You go first. Wash me, then I'll wash you."

"Fine by me."

She stood quietly while he soaped her body. Even as she told herself this was just a way of getting clean, she found herself leaning into his touch. She liked the feel of his slick hands all over her body. He seemed more interested in cleaning some spots than others. Her breasts received an extra dose of sudsy attention, as did her fanny and her legs. He was gentle between her thighs, careful not to make her sore.

When it was her turn, she worked as slowly, building up

a rich lather before smoothing the soap all over his body. The warm water sluiced down her back as she knelt in the tub to wash his legs. The proof of his desire jutted out at eye level and she wondered what it would be like to take him in her mouth.

Without pausing to consider the question, she licked the tip of him, then drew him inside.

Dylan swore softly, then tensed. "Molly, you're killing me."

She had to release him to talk. "I assume in a good way."

"In a very good way."

"Hmm." She returned to what she was doing. He tasted clean and wet. He was so aroused, she could feel the ridge of veins pressing against his skin. As she moved back and forth, she brought up her hands and gently touched the sac hanging between his legs. He shuddered.

"You're going to make me explode," he said.

"That was sort of the idea," she told him.

"Not like that. Not yet."

He drew her to her feet. A warmth spread through her belly. Not yet. That's what he'd said, implying that they would have other times to be together. Other times when they would do new things and enjoy taking each other to the edge.

He pulled her close and kissed her. She went willingly into his embrace. As the water poured over them, he ran his hands up and down her back. His arousal jutted against her belly.

There had been a time in the night when she'd awakened to wonder if it was all just a dream. In the darkness, she'd worried that he had made love with her because he felt sorry for her. That it was an act of mercy, not desire. As she'd thought it through, she'd realized that Dylan wasn't that kind of man.

He turned off the shower and reached for the large towels hanging on the rack. After he wrapped her in one, he quickly dried off himself, then led her to the counter.

"What are you doing?" she asked as he urged her up on the counter next to the sink.

"Nothing," he said, stepping between her legs.

He cupped her face and started to kiss her again. They were both naked, both still damp from the shower. Her secret woman's place was also damp, but from other things. She couldn't believe how much she wanted him again.

"Is this going to make you sore?" he asked, his voice hoarse with need.

"No." She shifted closer to the edge of the counter and opened more fully.

He deepened the kiss. His hands moved up and down her back. She felt the maleness of him probing, so she reached down to guide him inside. The kiss intensified as their bodies moved together. Molly felt herself quickly reaching for release.

As she neared the peak, she realized Dylan was carefully holding his torso slightly away from hers. In this most physical moment, he was hyperaware of her left breast and that it was tender. She wanted to weep from the wonder of it. From how special he was and how he made her feel.

He continued to thrust in and out, drawing both of them up toward the pinnacle of pleasure. Thoughts blurred in her mind. Later she would tell him how much she appreciated his concern. Later she would explain that he was an amazing man.

Her muscles tensed in readiness. Dylan grabbed her hips and pulled her nearer as he, too, soared to completion. And then she knew. At the exact moment they gazed into each other's eyes and watched the explosion, she understood that what she'd thought was merely the continuation of her crush was so much more. Perhaps it had started that way, but something had fundamentally changed between them. At least for her. She wasn't with Dylan because he was good to her, or handsome or funny or bright. She was with him because she loved him. Perhaps she'd always loved him.

It wasn't part of the rules, it wasn't supposed to be allowed; but there it was.

And then all she could do was feel as her body lost itself in the inevitable. She caught him round the waist and held him to her, feeling the tension slowly fade from him.

When they'd both caught their breath, she leaned her head against his chest and listened to the rapid beat of his heart. She'd broken the rules. This was supposed to be for fun, an escape. She wasn't supposed to fall in love with him.

But there was no going back. Molly figured that if she had to get stuck on someone who couldn't possibly love her back, she would prefer it be Dylan. He would never be cruel. If he found out the truth, he would never use it against her. Of course, if she had her way, he would return to his life ignorant of her feelings. Better for both of them, she thought, to part as friends. As for her, she'd promised herself no regrets and she was going to keep that promise. No matter what, she wouldn't be sorry about loving him. Not ever.

"How many permanent pounds does the average woman gain with each pregnancy?" Molly asked, reading from the card. She scanned the answers, then read the four possibilities aloud. "Huh. I would have thought it was a different amount."

Dylan stared at her. "You have to be kidding. They expect me to know this?"

"I believe this game was your idea. Are you saying that I know more about men than you know about women?"

Her self-satisfied smile made him want to grin in return. They were sprawled out on the living-room floor playing a board game they'd purchased that morning. The object was to pit the sexes against each other, with men answering questions about women and vice versa. After failing at a question about tightening lug nuts on a car, Molly was holding her own. Dylan was beginning to think he'd made a mistake in picking this game. Every other question he got seemed to be about weight gain, cosmetics or decorating tips.

"Read me the answers again," he said.

Molly rolled onto her back and did so.

He'd never had much contact with pregnant women and didn't know how much weight they gained altogether. "Three pounds," he guessed.

Molly waved the card at him. "Five. That's good to know."

If. She didn't say the word, but he heard it anyway. If she got through this thing with her breast. If she found out the news was good and she was going to make it.

He watched her as she tossed the single die that would tell her which category her next question would come from. She wore her hair loose. The afternoon was warm and they were both in jeans and T-shirts. He liked looking at her, at her pretty face, at her body. He liked watching her move. Sometimes he would come up behind her and just hold her, wanting to feel her close to him.

It wasn't just about sex, although there was plenty of that between them. It was about a kind of skin hunger. As if he couldn't get enough of touching her and being next to her. It had only been a couple of days since they'd become lovers. Sometimes he felt as if he'd been with her for a lifetime. She was all he could think about, all he wanted. When the outside world intruded, he resented that.

But intrude it did. Now that he knew the truth about why she'd come away, she no longer went in the other room to make her nightly phone call. She sat next to him and dialed her home number to listen to the answering machine. She was quiet for a minute, then she would slowly shake her head as she pushed the off button.

Nothing. Not a single word from the doctor. How long did these things take? Didn't they realize how hard it was for Molly to wait to hear the news? He ached for her and could do nothing about it.

Even so, even though they both just waited, this was still a special time. He really enjoyed being with her, perhaps more than he'd ever enjoyed being with anyone. She was fun to be around. She was too intelligent to be easy, but he didn't mind that. He was glad that she'd come to him when she'd wanted to run away and he'd been smart enough to go with her.

He'd never felt this way about anyone, he realized. That should have terrified him, but he was getting used to feeling strange when he was around her. He tried hard not to think about what would happen if she was taken from him. He couldn't bear the thought.

"Don't, Dylan," she said, rolling over and staring at him.

"What am I doing?" he asked.

She reached out and touched the back of his hand. "You're looking sad. Your eyes get this faraway gaze and I know you're worrying about me."

He thought about lying, but what was the point? "I do think about the possibilities," he told her. "Not just about what the doctor might tell you, but also the future. Our time together is almost up."

"I know. I'll miss you."

Which meant she had no expectation of ever seeing him again. He supposed he shouldn't be surprised. He was only ever going to be a temporary part of her life. Yet sometime in the past few days—even before she'd told him about the lump—he'd toyed with the idea of making it more.

The thought should have sent him running for the hills. He knew better than to get involved. And yet... There was something about being with Molly that felt so damn right.

"I'll miss you, too," he told her. It was an understatement. He couldn't remember what his world had been like without her and he didn't want to find out now. Only he didn't have anything to give her. Oh, he had money and could offer to share his big house, but that wouldn't matter to her. He couldn't promise to love her. What was love? He'd never figured that out. Besides, she deserved someone as wonderful as she was. He was just some motorcycle loser from the wrong side of town. He'd grown up with alcoholic parents who hadn't given a damn about him. If they hadn't cared, why should anyone else?

She braced her head on her hand and stared at him. "You've changed me," she said.

"What do you mean?"

"I'm less afraid. I feel stronger."

That had nothing to do with him. "You did that all on your own. I was just along for the ride."

She shook her head. "You're so wrong, Dylan. I wouldn't have made it without you. You got me to believe in myself and I don't think I ever have before. You helped me see the possibilities. I know I can get through whatever I have to deal with." Her smile turned shy. "You've made me feel pretty and I would have assumed that was impossible.''

He leaned down and kissed her. "You *are* pretty. If you can't see that, go have your eyes checked. You obviously need glasses.''

She chuckled. "You make me laugh and sometimes that's been the best gift of all.'' Her humor faded. "You've given me the courage to do what I have to so I won't have regrets. I'm going on with my life. I can do that, all because of you.''

He touched her cheek. "You don't know how much I want to claim credit, but I can't. You did that on your own, Molly. Believe in yourself. I believe in you.''

"That's a hard one. Tell you what. I promise to continue to make the right choices so that I don't ever have regrets. And I promise, when I get scared or start doubting myself, that I'll ask what you would tell me to do. Then I'll do it.''

She was so earnest, and so honest, cutting right to the heart of the matter. He didn't know when he'd ever respected anyone as much.

"Okay. I promise to take more adventures," he said. "I'll ride my bike every week. I'll take time for what's important.'' He pulled her hard against him. "I don't want to lose touch.''

She hugged him. "Me, either. Promise me that won't happen.''

"I promise.''

Emotions flooded him. He didn't dare identify them because he couldn't do anything once he knew what they were called. So what if his feelings had changed and grown? Molly had to make her own way, without him. He would only hold her back.

He felt the familiar wanting fill him, but he resisted the urge to make love. They had already been intimate once that day and he didn't want her to get sore. Instead he smoothed her hair out of her face.

"You haven't called home to check your machine," he said.

"I know, but it's Saturday. There isn't going to be anything from the doctor."

"You never know. Go on. Check. Then we'll finish the game." He glanced down at his marker, several spots behind hers. "You know, I'm *letting* you win."

She pushed on his shoulder. "Oh, please. Like I believe that." She stood up and crossed to the kitchen counter where they kept the cellular phone. "Actually, Dylan, I'm not the only one who should make a call. Two days ago you said you needed to check in with your office and you haven't. Don't you wonder what's going on?"

Not anymore, he thought. The company and the buyout offer weren't real to him. Not since Molly. But he supposed he should phone and make sure there hadn't been a major crisis. "All right. You want to go first?"

She shook her head. "You call. I'll wait."

As he took the phone, he wondered if she was putting off the inevitable, just in case it was bad news. For the hundredth time, he wished there were a way to make it easier for her. If he could take her fear and even her illness on himself, he would.

He punched in the familiar number for his voice mail. The computer said he had several messages waiting.

"How many?" Molly asked as he entered his private code.

"Eight."

"Oh, all the ladies are missing you."

"To quote you, 'Yeah, right.' There aren't any ladies, unless you want to count yourself."

She sat next to him and leaned her back against the sofa. "A fan club of one."

"Are you my fan?"

She rested her head against his shoulder. "Always, Dylan."

Her words produced a warm glow inside him. Maybe they could make love slowly so he wouldn't have to worry about her becoming sore. Later, he promised himself as the first message began.

He recognized Evie's voice. "My secretary," he said as he listened. She yelled at him for not calling. For all she knew, he was lying dead in a ditch somewhere, and if so, she hoped it had been a slow, painful death. Then she mentioned a couple of nonpressing issues and said that his attorney had been calling to talk about the buyout offer. The remaining messages were more of the same, including one from his attorney begging him to at least take a look at the offer. Apparently the large motorcycle company had delivered it sometime last week.

He left Evie a quick voice mail telling her that he was fine and would be in touch soon, then he hung up.

"News?" Molly asked.

"Nothing important. The other company is really pushing for the merger. They've sent an initial offer to my lawyer and he wants me to take a look at it."

"Are you going to?"

He shrugged. "I don't know. I still can't decide if I'm going to sell out or not." He glanced at her. "What do you think?"

She tilted her head. "It doesn't cost anything to look. If you don't like what they have to say or decide you want to keep sole control of Black Lightning, you can always tell them thanks but no, thanks."

"Good point." He thought about the logistics. "Would you mind if I had him send me the package here?"

"Of course not."

"Would you look at it with me?"

She blushed. "If you want me to. I don't know that I can be any help."

"Of course you would. You have a degree in business. Besides, I'd like your opinion of the offer."

"Sure."

He called his attorney's home and left a message there, telling the man to send the offer to him. Then he handed the phone to Molly. "Your turn."

"This is a complete waste of time. The doctor isn't going to call on the weekend." She held out a hand before he could say anything. "I know, I know. If it makes you happy, I'm glad to do it." She pushed the button to activate the phone, then punched in a number. After a couple of seconds, she frowned. "There's a message."

As she entered more numbers to access her machine, he sat up. Fear knotted his gut. Dear God, please don't let it be bad.

Molly listened intently. He couldn't read much from her face. There was no elation, but there also wasn't any panic or even resignation. Finally she pushed a button to end the call and stared at him.

"You're never going to believe it," she said. "That was my boss, Harry. Actually, he would be my ex-boss. He said that the company has reevaluated the situation and they want me to come back to work for the firm. Not only that, they're offering me a promotion and a raise."

Relief filled him. She was all right—at least for now. "You sound more confused than happy."

"I guess I am. I never thought about going back there.

I didn't hate my job, but it wasn't wonderful. I'm still kind of annoyed at how they handled the situation."

"You've got some money. You don't have to make a decision tonight."

"You're right. I couldn't anyway. I can't do anything until I hear from the doctor. I mean, if the news is bad—"

"I know."

She leaned against him and sighed. "I never thought I'd hear from them. Life certainly takes unexpected turns."

"I agree."

Three weeks ago, he would have had a hard time remembering who Molly Anderson was. Now he couldn't picture his world without her.

"Everything is on hold until I get the results of one slide. Isn't that incredibly strange?"

He tucked her head into the crook of his neck. "I'm sorry you have to go through this."

"Me, too, but I'm glad we're together. There isn't anyone else I would rather do this with than you. You've made the waiting a lot easier."

"That's because I care."

She hugged him close. "Thank you for that. Not many men would be willing to go through this."

"You're wrong. They'd go through a lot more if you were the prize."

He would go to hell and back if it would help her. Instead, all he could do was hold her and wait.

Chapter Thirteen

Late Monday afternoon Molly set the cellular phone down on the counter. As she'd learned over the past few years, life was nothing if not a constant surprise. She just wasn't sure what to make of this latest one.

"From the look on your face, you haven't heard from the doctor," Dylan said.

She shook her head. "No, but there was another message from my boss, Harry."

"He still wants you back?"

"Yes." She frowned. "I don't understand. Apparently it's very important to them. He's offering me a larger starting salary and a bigger office."

Dylan stretched in his chair and grinned at her. "Great. If you hold out for a little longer, you can squeeze some stock options out of them."

She crossed the worn linoleum floor and took her seat. They were at the small table in the corner of the kitchen.

She rested her chin on her hands and looked at him. "That's what's so weird. I'm not saying that I didn't do a good job—I did. I ran a strong department. Everything was always organized. I worked with purchasing to get the best deals, the most beneficial payment plans. I was a good employee. But I wasn't extraordinary. It's not as if I was the sales manager and with me gone they're losing their biggest clients. This is strictly internal."

"Why are you complaining?"

"I'm not. I'm just confused."

"Businesses often get overly zealous when they purchase and downsize. I would guess that old Harry let too many people go. Now he's scrambling to get a few of them back. Obviously he considers you worth quite a bit to the company."

Dylan's points made sense. Harry had been on a pretty vigorous slash-and-burn when the merger went through. She'd been the one to prepare a memo on the virtues of waiting to see how the business would be affected by the change in ownership, before they started to eliminate personnel. Harry had thanked her for her opinion, then proceeded to toss the document in the trash. Looks like he'd had to read it after all.

She smiled. "It's very nice to suddenly be popular."

"I'll bet. What are you going to do?"

"I don't know. For now—nothing. It's not even about my job. That was fine. Not the greatest in the world, but not hideous, either. I might think about going back, but I'm not making any decisions until I hear from the doctor."

He stroked a finger up and down her forearm. "That's wise."

She liked that he didn't try to pretend everything would be fine. With Dylan she felt safe discussing her fears, even showing that she was afraid. Sometimes he told her that he was scared, too; sometimes he just held her. Either way, she felt that he was someone she could depend on. It was a pleasant and unfamiliar feeling. Being with Dylan made her realize that she'd never really trusted Grant. Until he'd broken off their relationship, she hadn't seen that she'd been living in anticipation of the other shoe dropping. She'd been furious and hurt by his reckless behavior, but she couldn't truthfully say she'd been complete shocked. On the surface he had it all, but underneath the slick exterior, he was self-centered and shallow.

Her only regret was that it had taken his leaving for her to see the truth. What if she'd hadn't seen it and they'd gotten married? She shuddered at the thought. She would never have wanted to have children with that man. He would be a horrible father. It was, she acknowledged, better for everyone that he was out of her life.

So out of her three crises, she was down to two—the lump and her job. "I promised myself not to have regrets," she said. "I don't want to forget that lesson. Even if the news from the doctor is good, I don't want to go back to my old way of doing things. I played it safe all the time and lived only half a life. I deserve more than that."

"There's not a doubt in my mind that you're going to start kicking butt," he said.

His expression matched his words. He believed in her and her ability to change. That was only one of a hundred reasons why she loved him. And love him she did. Even though they only had a short time left together, even though he would return to his world and probably not give her much thought, she was still glad to know the truth. Loving him was the best part of her. Loving him made her willing to take chances, to really live. If the lesson of all that had happened in her life was to bring her to this moment, to loving him, then it was worth it.

She straightened and slapped her hands on the table. "Enough about me," she said. "What about this offer of yours? I still can't believe someone from your office drove it up this morning."

He shuffled through the thick sheaf of papers that had arrived while they were at lunch. "I don't know. It looks good. My attorney thinks I would be crazy not to agree. There are several reasons to accept their offer and very few reasons not to."

"But?" she prompted.

He shrugged. "You tell me. The numbers are in place. My employees' jobs are protected for five years. There's no reason to turn down this offer."

"Of course there is. There must be several—otherwise you wouldn't be sweating it. How much control will you maintain?"

"I'll run a division that will be strictly custom design. Any innovations belong to them and can be applied to their stock bikes."

"You'd lose out on any patents, right?"

"Sure," he said. "But that's standard in industry. If you invent something while in the employ of a company, the invention belongs to them. After all, you're using their resources, their facilities, and they're paying you for your time."

"Would that bother you?"

He reflected for a couple of minutes. "I don't think so. I've had to put a lot of ideas on the back burner. Some of the problem is time. I'm taking care of a lot of day-to-day issues that suck up the hours. I don't have as much capital as I would need, or if I have it, I think it would be better spent somewhere else. If I sold to them, I would have a generous design budget and not have to worry so much about making the payroll."

"You'd also be financially secure for the rest of your life."

"There is that," he said, and leaned back in the chair. He swore softly. "Sometimes I feel like just flipping a coin."

Molly looked at him. His dark hair gleamed in the overhead light. He was the most handsome man she'd ever met. She knew in her head that she was really sitting in this kitchen with him, that they were talking about something important and that he valued her opinion. She also knew that later that night they would go into the bedroom and make love. He would kiss her and hold her and touch her in ways she'd never even imagined. She knew that they would talk and laugh. She had physical proof that all this was happening.

But in her heart it was a very different matter. She wanted to laugh and run around the room shouting from the happiness of it all. If this was a dream, then she was determined to savor every second of it. If this was denial or a mental breakdown, then she would cling to it for as long as possible. It was so incredible that this was happening to her, and Dylan Black was the man making it happen. Dylan! After all this time!

"Tell me what you think," he said. "What should I do?"

"I can't make up your mind for you."

"I know. Let me rephrase the question. Tell me what you would do if you were me. I really want to know. Not only because you've got a great head for business, but because I know you're genuinely concerned about me."

Both his compliments filled her with a warm glow. She rested her elbows on the table and leaned toward him. "It comes down to choosing between financial security and professional freedom. Which is more important to you?"

"They both look good."

"You've always been a free spirit," she reminded him. "Are you ready to start taking orders from someone else?"

"Excellent question."

"Do you have an equally excellent answer?" she asked.

"Not yet."

"There are reasons to do it either way. I know it would be a whole lot easier if all the positives came down on one side, but life doesn't work that way."

"Tell me about it." He reached across the small table and took her hand in his. "Thanks for listening," he said. "You're a good friend."

There was something in his eyes. Something that, if she'd been a risk taker, she might have dared to call affection. Romantic affection. But she wasn't sure and she didn't dare ask. She also didn't dare tell him about the love filling her. Love for him.

She was torn between her promise to herself not to have any regrets and her not wanting to put Dylan in an uncomfortable position. He'd been very good to her. He'd made her feel special and wonderful. She didn't want to repay that by trying to force something that wasn't meant to be. Dylan was a kind and gentle man. She didn't doubt that he cared about her, but caring wasn't love. Despite his claims to the contrary, she knew she wasn't his type. All the time in the world wouldn't change that.

So she held in the feelings and the words. Maybe there would come a day when she would have the courage to be honest. But not now.

Dylan turned slowly in the shower, then rinsed the shampoo from his hair. It was the first shower he'd taken alone in several days and he missed Molly's presence. However, he'd been the only one chopping firewood after dinner, so he'd been the only one to get sweaty. She'd offered to join him and wash his back, but he'd declined. They were going to sit by the fire and watch a movie they'd rented. He was determined to go at least a couple of hours without taking her to bed. He didn't want her to think that was all he cared about.

His thoughts turned to their earlier discussion about his business. The buyout offer was generous. When he lined up the pros and cons, it made sense to sell. But something inside him kept resisting. He remembered what Molly had said about his not working well for someone else. That was a serious consideration. If he didn't have autonomy, then he might find himself hating his job. He didn't want to live like that.

Molly knew him pretty well. He smiled as he remembered her earnest expression when they'd talked about his options. She really cared about him and he appreciated that. In a short time, she'd come to mean the world to him. In fact—

The bathroom door swung open. "Dylan!" Molly screamed, then she pulled back the plastic curtain and jumped in with him. "Dylan, I called! I called!"

She was laughing and crying and holding on so tightly he couldn't catch his breath. Her clothes were completely soaked. She kissed him on the mouth and then he knew.

Elation filled him. It was as if the band that had tightened around his chest when he'd first heard about her lump suddenly loosened and dropped away. He squeezed her hard, swinging her around in the tiny space.

"You heard from the doctor," he said.

She looked at him and nodded. Her wet hair hung down her back; her T-shirt clung to her. Her grin was a mile wide.

"I don't even know why I called. I just checked a couple hours ago, remember? It was like someone whispered in my ear and I had to call. She'd left the message all of ten minutes before. I'm fine. The lump was completely benign. No cancer, nothing. I just have lumpy breasts. Isn't that great?''

It was a gift from God. "It's so terrific," he said, and kissed her.

The water pounded over them both. He parted his lips and she did the same, then he slipped inside. She tasted as sweet as she always did. Warm and welcoming.

She was okay. The message sank into his brain and freed him from the fear. He wasn't going to lose her. She wasn't going to die any time soon. His throat tightened and his eyes burned. He didn't know if the water on his cheeks was from the shower or from tears of joy and he didn't much care. Molly was going to be all right.

The water started to get cool. Dylan broke the kiss, then turned off the taps. "You'd better get out of those wet things," he said.

She laughed. "Sorry. I didn't mean to interrupt your shower."

"Yes, you did, and I'm glad." He touched her cheek. "About all of it."

"Me, too. Oh, Dylan, do you know what this means? I get a second chance. I swear I'm not going back to that pitiful excuse for a life. I swear it's going to be different."

Her gaze was intense, her face set. "I believe you," he told her.

She pulled off her wet clothes, then wrapped a towel around herself. "Do you mind if I make a quick call to Janet? She's been worried, too."

"Go ahead."

She scampered out of the room. In a couple of seconds, he heard her excited voice, followed by laughter. He was so happy for her. This was what she deserved. She had her job back, if she wanted it, and a second chance to make things right. Very few people had that opportunity. The best part was, not only did Molly deserve it, but he knew she would make the best of it.

He dried off. His clean clothes were in the bedroom, so he secured the towel around his waist, then walked to the kitchen. In the bottom shelf of the refrigerator, tucked behind a plastic bag filled with broccoli, he'd stored a bottle of champagne. He'd bought it one afternoon when she'd wanted to take a nap and he'd gone for groceries. He didn't think she'd seen it.

If the news had been bad, he would have kept the bottle hidden, then left it behind when they went back to L.A. But he'd hoped they would have a chance to use it. Now, while she talked to her sister, he got out two glasses, then the bottle, and opened it.

When she saw what he was doing, her eyes widened. She quickly told Janet she had to go and promised to call the next day.

"What's that?" she asked.

"What does it look like?"

"Champagne. Are we celebrating?"

He handed her a glass and grinned. "You have to ask?"

"I guess not." Her happy expression turned serious. "Thanks, Dylan. For everything. For being so supportive, for helping me get through this, for just being around. Oh, and for the champagne. I'm impressed that you managed to sneak it in the house without me knowing."

"I'm a very clever guy." He touched his glass to hers. "Here's to many years of continued good health. To your future."

She laughed. "Thanks."

They sipped. He watched her, noting how the overhead light from the kitchen illuminated her features. She was so pretty, and so happy she glowed. How could he ever have thought of her as less than beautiful? he wondered. She was an amazing woman and he was fortunate to have this brief time with her. He only wished there could be more.

But it was enough that she was going to be okay.

"I'm relieved and happy, but you must be thrilled," he said.

She leaned against the table and nodded. "I'm shaking inside. I can't believe I finally have my answer and it's such good news." She pressed a hand to her chest. "My lumpy breasts and I are thrilled."

"Me, too."

She giggled. As she turned to pull out a chair, her towel got caught against the table. The corner tucked by her arm loosened and the covering threatened to fall away. When Molly reached for the end, Dylan grabbed her hand to stop her.

"Let it go," he said.

Her breath caught. She swallowed and stared at him, while the towel slowly slipped to the ground.

There was a time when she would have covered herself, when she would have been shy about standing naked in front of him. One night, in the dark, she'd talked about her body, how she hated the way her breasts weren't perky, and thought her stomach stuck out too much and her legs were chunky.

He didn't see any of that. He saw the perfect curves, the pale, soft skin, the sweet place between her thighs where he found respite. He saw Molly and he wanted her.

Her gaze moved lazily over him, then she reached out and tugged on the towel wrapped around him. "You seem a little overdressed," she said, her voice low and husky. He was ready before the cloth hit the floor.

"Nice," she said, and stroked his length. "Very nice."

She took a mouthful of champagne, then set the glass on the table. After sinking to her knees, she moved close to him and took him in her mouth.

He thought he was going to die. Or at the very least, his legs would give out and he would find himself sprawled on the floor. The contrasts were more than he could absorb—the heat of her mouth, the coolness of the champagne, the softness of her lips and tongue, the sharp fizzing of the liquid.

She circled him, then drew him in deeply. He had to stop her. For one thing, it felt too good and he was about to lose control. For another, he wanted this to be about her, or at least about them both.

So he placed his hands on her shoulders and gently pulled back. She swallowed and grinned. "I felt you pulsing. Gee, Dylan, you were about to—"

He bent over and silenced her with a kiss. Several minutes later she broke away and sighed. "Okay, you win. I'm putty in your hands. But don't think for a minute that hot kiss made me forget you were about to lose it like a teenager."

"You love that you can do that to me," he told her as he knelt in front of her.

She cupped his face and stared deeply into his eyes. "Absolutely. It makes me wet just thinking about it."

He touched her and found out she was telling the truth. She was wet and ready. He wanted to hold back. They were only a few feet from the bedroom and it made sense to be comfortable. But he couldn't wait anymore.

"I need you," he growled, and pulled her close.

She clung to him as if she were just as frantic. "Yes, Dylan. Take me. Make love to me. Help me celebrate the beginning of my new life."

Even as he moved between her legs, she stretched out

on the rug and welcomed him. He entered her in one, long thrust, making them both gasp. He braced his weight on his haunches so he could cup her breasts. Her nipples were already hard and he teased them with his thumb and forefinger.

She gasped, then placed her hands on top of his. "Don't stop," she gasped. "Don't stop because I—"

The first release made her convulse against him. He felt the contractions deep inside her. He kept moving in and out, taking them both higher.

He stared deep into her eyes, bonding with her. She cried out two more times, then he felt himself reaching the pinnacle. He dropped his hands to her hips and held her still so he could go in all the way. She half rose into a sitting position and called out his name.

He felt himself explode. Even as he plunged inside, her body contracted around him as she lost herself in yet another moment of release. He couldn't imagine being with anyone else, ever. She was the very best part of him. Together they created pure joy.

Later, when they'd recovered their breath, they made it to the bedroom. Molly snuggled against him and sighed. "I don't want to get up, but we forgot the champagne and I have to call my answering machine again. The doctor wants me to phone tomorrow and I didn't write down the number."

"I'll get it," he said, and rolled off the bed. After collecting the glasses and the bottle, he set them on Molly's nightstand. The phone was where she'd left it on the counter and there was a pen and pad of paper in the living room. He brought them into the bedroom. She was busy pouring the bubbly liquid into their glasses.

"Want me to call for you?" he asked.

"Thanks."

She gave him her home number, then the access code. He listened to the message and wrote down the doctor's phone number. He was about to hang up, when he realized there was a second message.

"Someone else called," he said.

"Probably Janet." She waved at him, indicating that he should go ahead and listen while she took a sip of champagne.

But the voice didn't belong to a woman.

"Hey, Molly, it's me. Grant."

There was a pause. He knew he should hand the phone to Molly. Whatever her ex-fiancé had to tell her wasn't his business. But he couldn't move. He realized he couldn't breathe, either.

"I've wanted to call for a couple of days now, but I didn't know what to say," the voice continued. "I've been such an incredible jerk. I can't believe how stupid I was. I guess I got kind of crazy, what with us getting engaged and all. It was that guy thing, about losing freedom or whatever. I'm not sure." Grant cleared his throat. "The point is, I'm back. I'm not with my secretary. I never really cared about her. It was just a fling. I want to see you. Molly, I miss you and I still love you. Please, can't we talk? We had something really special together and I'd like another chance. I know I have a lot to make up for and I—"

"Dylan?" Molly was staring at him. "What's wrong."

He pushed the end button and handed her the phone. The message probably went on, but he couldn't listen to it.

"It wasn't Janet," he said, and was surprised that his voice sounded almost normal. There was no way Molly could guess that he was being ripped up inside. He felt as if someone had sliced him open from throat to groin and he was bleeding to death. The problem was, he had no injury. The pain was real enough, but he wouldn't die from it. He would only wish he could.

Chapter Fourteen

"What's wrong?" Molly asked, not liking the shock on Dylan's face. Her stomach knotted. "Did the doctor call back?"

"No." Dylan cupped her face. "No, it's nothing like that. You're fine. You can phone her in the morning and talk to her. Just check your machine and listen to the second message."

She did as he requested. She was shaking inside—she could feel it. But there was no way she could not know what had happened. She listened to the happy voice of her doctor, then sucked in a breath as the second message began.

"Hey, Molly, it's me, Grant."

His words rolled over her. She absorbed phrases about the mistakes he'd made, that he didn't love his secretary but loved her, instead, that he wanted another chance. She listened, but the sentences had no meaning. When the message was finished, she hung up.

"It was Grant," she said unnecessarily, knowing Dylan had already heard the message. "He wants a second chance."

"There it is, then," Dylan said. "Everything is back in place."

She felt as if she were in a thick fog. She could make out shapes, but everything was a little blurry and she wasn't sure where she was going. She stared at Dylan, knowing that if she could make him come into focus, everything else would, too.

"What do you mean?" she asked.

"One by one the pieces of your life have been restored. You have your job back if you want it—actually, it's a better job, with a raise. You've found out you're healthy. Now Grant is begging forgiveness. It's as though none of this ever happened."

He was right. It was almost as if she'd gone back in time, before the nightmare began. Only she hadn't. She'd had to live through it and come out the other side. Her life was restored, but it was so different. The pieces didn't fit anymore.

"It's not that simple," she said slowly.

"You'll figure it out."

He sounded so normal, she thought as she watched him. Dylan sat up and casually pulled on his briefs. Same graceful actions, same handsome face. He'd distanced himself from the situation. She wanted to scream in protest. This was supposed to matter—*she* was supposed to matter. But she didn't.

Oh, he cared about her as a friend. He'd been wonderful to her. She knew that and was grateful. But he hadn't grown to love her. If he had, he would have been furious about Grant or at least threatened.

Until that moment, until she'd hard evidence that Dylan didn't think of her as more than Janet's little sister, she hadn't realized how much she'd hoped. In the back of her mind had been the foolish dream that they could be more. That their time together had worked a miracle. One where he finally realized that she was exactly right for him, just as he was right for her. That they belonged together.

Something inside gave a sharp jolt and she wondered if hearts could actually break. He didn't love her. He would never love her.

Her happiness at the news from her doctor, the confusion generated by Grant's call and the death of the dream combined to make her feel sick to her stomach. She sank onto the pillows and pulled her knees to her chest. It was only then that she remembered she was naked. Just a short time ago, they'd been making love.

"What are you going to do?" Dylan asked.

She searched his face, hoping for some hint that this was hard for him. He'd been stunned when he'd handed her the phone, but it hadn't been anything but surprise. If only... Yeah, right. She was a grown-up and she knew better than to count on wishes to make things right.

"About Grant," she said, but it wasn't a question. She knew what he was talking about. "I don't know. I don't know how I feel. As far as I'm concerned, he's a lying, cheating piece of trash and I'll never trust him again."

"That sounds definitive, yet I sense a 'but' in that statement."

She shrugged. It was odd to be having this conversation with Dylan. "But I don't know what to think. Is he telling the truth? Should I even care?"

"You have a history with the guy. At one time you were going to marry him."

Molly thought about that. Dylan was right. She had been engaged to Grant. So they'd been planning a future together. It felt like another lifetime ago. She couldn't imagine being with anyone but Dylan. But he didn't want her, except as a friend. Was she going to spend the rest of her life waiting for him to come around? What about living with no regrets? Was she going to give up her dreams of a husband and children because she'd fallen in love with someone who couldn't love her back? Talk about a recipe for regret.

"I don't know what to think," she said at last.

"You don't have to decide tonight," he told her, then tugged on the covers and pulled them up so they were covering her. He turned out the light and slid into the bed.

He was warm and familiar. In the dark she couldn't see much more than the shape of him, but she recognized his heat and his scent. She would always be able to find Dylan just by her sense of smell alone. He pulled her close.

"Don't tell him no out of hand," Dylan said.

"I can't believe you're saying that. You're the one who told me he should be shot."

"I still believe that, but maybe he's learned his lesson. You've put a lot into the relationship. If he's really changed, do you want to take a chance on losing it?"

Yes, she thought grimly but didn't say it. "I don't know."

"You have time," Dylan said as he stroked her hair. She put her head on his shoulder and snuggled closer. "These couple of weeks did what they were supposed to do. We both had the chance to escape our worlds and figure out what we wanted."

Molly closed her eyes. Maybe Dylan had decided, but

she was as confused as ever. As he'd said, one by one the pieces of her life had been restored. She should be thrilled. While she was delighted to find out that her lump wasn't anything to worry about, the rest wasn't so easily resolved.

"Thank you for getting me through this," she said, and to her dismay began to cry.

Dylan reacted by holding her tighter. "It's all right," he murmured. "You're going to be just fine."

She was, of course. She would survive. But she wanted it to be with him. She wanted the magic to continue. Still, she had no right to hold him against his will. He had been so incredibly generous with her—she could do no less.

He brushed his lips against her forehead. He whispered, "It's time for us to go back."

The tears flowed faster. "I kn-know," she stammered. Time to go home and pick up the pieces. Time to make decisions. But not tonight. Tonight was for them.

"Hold me," she said. "Don't let me go. Not until the sun comes up."

"I promise."

She continued to cry, wondering how the moment could be so perfect and so incredibly sad at the same time. They had come so far together and they had gone nowhere.

"I don't want to lose touch," Dylan said. "I mean that, Molly. I want more than just a card at the holidays."

"Me, t-too." She drew in a breath and tried to slow the tears. "I want you to be very happy."

"I will be. You're going to have great kids. I want to meet all of them."

Kids. She wanted children, but only with Dylan. He would be, she realized, a fabulous father. "Yours, too," she said. "I mean I want to meet them."

"I'm not the marrying kind."

There wasn't any more hope, so his words barely hurt.

Of course. She'd known that from the beginning. But that hadn't stopped her from loving him.

No regrets, she reminded herself. Even knowing what she did at this minute, with her heart breaking and her soul battered, she wouldn't go back and change a thing. She wanted to ask him if they could try to make it work, if maybe there was a chance, but she already knew the answer. Oddly enough, despite the pain, she could live with that. It was okay that he didn't love her back. Loving *him* had been enough. She'd given with a full heart and she'd kept her promise to herself. She could never regret what they'd shared.

Dylan took the long way back, turning off the 101 freeway onto the 126, which would take them through several small towns and acres of orange groves. He knew he was delaying the inevitable, but even an extra half hour with Molly was something he would treasure.

Their trip home was different from their ride out to Carpenteria. Now he was used to the heat of her pressed against him. The shape of her, the soft pressure of her thighs around his rear, the weight of her hands on his waist. She still turned him on. But more important, she'd taught him to care.

He didn't just want her—he liked and respected her. He admired her courage and her honesty. He wanted to be with her. He knew he was going to miss her after she disappeared from his life. He wondered how long it would take to get over her.

Was that love? He didn't have the answer to the question. He'd never been one to believe in love. That was for other people, if it existed at all. No one had ever loved him. He'd never loved another person. It shouldn't be any different with Molly. Yet it was.

He could imagine wanting to be with her for the rest of their lives. The world was a brighter place because she was in it, and he wanted to share in the light and the colors. She made him feel things he'd never felt. She made him think about a real home that he shared with someone. She made him think about having kids.

He swallowed. That was a new one. Children. Was he really considering being a father? He didn't know how to be a parent. No one had ever parented him...well, a few people had tried, but they hadn't been successful. He didn't think he was up to the responsibility of raising a human being from birth. The thought terrified him. But with Molly around, it wouldn't be so bad. He knew she would keep him from doing something too horrible.

Was that love? Was wanting to have a child with her more than just affection? She was so special to him. He would have done anything for her. He still would.

As they drove down the road and through the valley, he thought about asking her to stay. Even if it was just for a while. The house was big enough. She could have her own room if she wasn't comfortable staying in his. Maybe she could find a job out by him, or even come to work at his company. Maybe—

He shook his head. He was dreaming. These fantasies had no place in reality. Molly had her own life. She had a career with a company that would do just about anything to get her back. Even if he dared to ask, she would be crazy to consider his offer. What did he have to give her that she couldn't get ten times better somewhere else? He was reading too much into the situation.

The past few weeks had been incredibly stressful. She was living on pure emotion, nothing else. He knew she cared, and that was enough. Love, well, he still wasn't sure what he felt about love.

Now Molly had all the pieces back in place. She needed to get on with her life. He wanted to stay friends, but he didn't want to get in the way.

They reached Interstate 5, then the 405. Far too soon, he was pulling off the freeway and into her neighborhood. From there it was just a matter of a few miles until he slowed in front of her complex.

He stopped the bike. Molly slid off the back. Dylan fought against the pain in his gut and the incredible need to tell her not to go. That he wanted her with him always. But that wasn't what he was going to say. He was determined to set her free with a full heart, because that was the right thing to do.

She stood awkwardly on the sidewalk while he got her duffel bag.

"Do you want to come inside?" she asked as he handed her the luggage and she handed him her helmet.

He glanced at the building. It would be easier to let her go if he couldn't picture her in her world. "No, thanks. You have a lot of calls to make, I'm sure, and I need to get home."

Her hair was pulled back in a braid, exposing her face. She wasn't smiling, but the haunted expression had finally left her eyes. He was glad about that.

She stared at him. "I don't know what to say. Thank you seems so inadequate. I couldn't have made it through without you."

"Sure you would have. You would have been just fine. I'm happy to have helped, even just a little."

She took a step toward him. The afternoon was warm. Her T-shirt exposed all her curves. Lord, how he wanted her. Not just in his bed, but in his life. Would it be so wrong just to ask? She could always tell him no. Or he could set up a date for a couple of weeks from now. That would give her a chance to settle in and get used to believing she was all right. Then, if she was still interested, it wouldn't be just about what they'd been through...or gratitude.

"You'll never know how much you've meant to me," she said. Her hazel brown eyes glowed with conviction. "You listened—you held me—you let me be weak and reminded me how to be strong. Ten years ago I had a crush on a man I didn't really know. I'm very happy to find out the reality is even better than I imagined. You are amazing, Dylan."

He stared at her, not sure what to say. Maybe there was a chance. Maybe it wouldn't be so wrong to tell her what he was feeling. "Molly..." He paused.

She laughed. "I know, it's a little uncomfortable to be back in our regular world. I'm going to need some time to adjust."

"Just take it a day at a time," he said.

"I know. That's best. I don't want to make any hasty decisions."

"That's smart," he said, and gathered his courage. He would tell her now. Say all that he was feeling in his heart, maybe even explain that he wasn't sure if he loved her, but she was as close as he'd ever come. He could say that he wasn't ready for things to be over.

"Molly?"

The strange male voice came from behind him. He turned slowly, already knowing what he was going to see.

A man stood on the sidewalk, less than ten feet from them. He was of average height, with sandy brown hair and brown eyes. He wore a dark suit and conservative tie. Everything about him screamed lawyer, and Dylan knew exactly who he was, even before Molly confirmed the fact.

"Grant?" She sounded dazed. "Grant, what are you doing here?"

"Waiting for you."

Grant held a box of long-stemmed roses in his arms. Dylan guessed that the flowers were probably red, just to round out the cliché. So much for timing, he thought grimly. Just as well. Molly wouldn't want to know how he felt and he didn't want to embarrass either of them. It was better this way, he told himself, despite the disappointment and the pain moving up from his gut to his chest.

The fact that he wanted to rip Grant apart, limb by limb, didn't help the situation. Nor did the impulse to grab Molly and take off. This was the man she'd wanted to marry. That he'd run out on her, that he didn't look like anything special, wasn't Dylan's business. He should be grateful for the interruption. If Grant hadn't shown up just then, he, Dylan, would have made a complete ass of himself.

Molly touched her throat, wondering if the tightening there was going to cut off her breathing.

"Grant?" she repeated, still stunned beyond words. Grant had shown up here? Now? If it wasn't all so horrible, she would have started laughing. She'd never before had two men in her life at the same time, yet she knew other women who juggled multiple relationships regularly. The difference was, they could do it for weeks, while she got caught instantly. Then she reminded herself that Grant didn't have any rights here. He'd canceled their engagement and run off with another woman. She should hate him.

Unfortunately, she was too shocked to feel anything. Even anger.

Grant took a step toward her. "I tried to explain everything in my phone message." He glanced at Dylan, then back at her. "Did you get it?"

"Yes."

"You didn't call."

She'd forgotten how he could sound petulant when he didn't get his way. "I've been out of town."

"With him?" The sharp glance was unmistakably challenging.

Dylan moved forward and held out his hand. "Hi, I'm Dylan Black, an old friend of the family. I used to date Molly's older sister. You must be Grant. Molly's told me a lot about you."

Everything he said was the truth. His tone of voice and manner were so friendly and open that Grant responded in kind. Molly knew what Dylan was doing—trying to make it easy for her. Setting it up so she could return to Grant if that was what she wanted.

She watched as the two men shook hands and exchanged pleasantries. She felt as if her entire world had just tipped off its axis. Nothing made sense. Dylan was helping her with Grant, when all she wished was to run away. All of her life had been restored to her. What more could she want?

The answer came quickly and easily. Dylan. She wanted Dylan. She wanted to love him and be with him. She wanted to share her life with him.

But he had his own life, and there was no reason to think he would want her to be a part of that. She'd shown up without warning and asked him to take her away. Amazingly enough, he'd agreed. They'd spent the most wonderful two weeks together, but now that time was over and she had to let him go.

"I should be heading out," Dylan said, and gave her a quick smile.

"I'll be right back," she told Grant, then followed Dylan the two steps to his bike. "Thank you," she said, jerking her head toward her ex-fiancé.

Dylan shrugged. "It was the least I could do. He'd obviously figured out that we'd been away together. You don't have to go back to him, but if you do, I wanted to make it as easy as possible. A word of advice, kid," he said, and touched the tip of her nose. "If you do take him back, don't tell him we were lovers. He'll never be able to get over it."

"But I'm supposed to get over what he did?" She held up a hand. "Never mind, don't answer that. I understand that life isn't fair."

She searched his face. The familiar shapes and lines and features. How was she supposed to let him drive away? "I can't think of how to thank you."

"I don't want thanks. I want you to stay in touch with me. Promise?"

She nodded. "I swear I'll let you know every single detail of my life. Including when I go to buy panty hose."

He grinned. "Deal. Although I can pass on the panty hose information, I do want to know what you decide about your work. And Grant."

She didn't dare turn to look at her ex-fiancé. She didn't want to know what he was thinking. There would be plenty of time for that when Dylan was gone.

"All right, Molly, let's get this over with. Give me a kiss, then go put Romeo there out of his misery."

She wasn't sure if Dylan was telling her to take Grant back or kick him out, and she didn't much care. She moved close and hugged him, then pressed her mouth to his cheek. "Thank you," she whispered.

"No problem."

He released her and pulled on his helmet. Molly took a step back. Emotions flooded her. She didn't have any way of figuring them out right now. All she could do was absorb the feelings and know that she would deal with them later.

They shifted and flowed until one rose to the surface—one she'd promised herself she would never feel again.

Regret.

He started his engine.

"Dylan!" she screamed over the sound of the motor-cycle.

He turned toward her. She dropped the duffel bag and returned to his side. "Wait," she said.

He pulled off the helmet so he could hear her. "What's wrong?"

She flung her arms around him and pulled him close. "I can't do this," she said, speaking into his ear so that Grant couldn't hear her. "I don't want to just say thank-you. I want to tell you that you have changed my life. I will never forget your acts of kindness and generosity to me. You are so incredible and I wish you great happiness no matter what."

He drew back enough so that he could see her face. Molly felt the tears on her cheeks, but she didn't brush them away. "I promised myself no regrets," she went on, then sucked in a breath. "This is harder than I thought. Okay, here goes." She pressed her fingers against his mouth. "I don't want you to say anything back, because that's not why I'm telling you this. I just want you to know that I love you. You've made me believe in myself again, and for the first time in my life, you've made me believe in love. No matter what happens or where you go, know that you carry a piece of my heart with you."

She took her fingers away and replaced them with her mouth. This wasn't a friendly kiss between old family friends, but she didn't care. Passion blended with sadness, creating the sweetest of perfumes. His mouth, his lips, his scent, his taste were all painfully familiar. She tried to remember what it was like so that she could relive these memories when the nights were long and lonely.

Finally, they both pulled away. She offered him a shaky smile. "I have two more things to say to you," she told him. "Then you'll be free to go."

Dylan glanced at Grant. Molly didn't bother turning around. Grant could wait or not. It was up to him.

"First," she said, "don't sell out. Black Lightning is your heart and soul and you'll never be happy working for someone else. Just my opinion, but I mean it."

"What's second?"

His voice was low and thick, as if he wrestled with strong emotion. She was glad he was as affected by the moment as she was.

"This." She dug into her jeans pocket and pulled out the gold wedding ring that had first brought her to him. "If you ever need an adventure, come find me. No matter what, I'll go with you." She pressed the ring into his palm and closed his fingers over the band.

"What if you're married to him?" he asked, jerking his head toward Grant.

She thought about saying that was incredibly unlikely but didn't. "It doesn't matter. No matter what, Dylan, I'll be there for you. Not because I owe you, but because I want to be."

She stepped back to the curb. Dylan was in awe of her courage. It would have been so easy to tell her that he loved her, too, but he couldn't say the words. Not now. Not when everything she'd ever wanted had been returned to her. Maybe he thought Grant was a complete jerk, but at one time Molly had wanted to marry him. He owed her the chance to find out if any of those emotions were still alive. If he confessed his own feelings, that would change everything.

Maybe, in time, he could check on her. If she'd dumped Grant and still seemed interested, they could pick up where they'd left off. Maybe he was kidding himself. Why would Molly want a guy like him?

He tucked the ring into his jeans pocket and put on his helmet. Molly and Grant were already heading into the complex.

She stopped at the entrance and looked back at him. Grant put his arm around her. They made a great couple. What was the term? DINKs—double income, no kids. Grant would rise in his law firm, probably make partner. They could join the country club, send their kids to private school. Dylan would only ever be the bad boy from the wrong side of town. His business was successful, but he wasn't a white-collar professional. Given the choice, he would wear black leather.

Molly had come to him because she needed him, but she didn't need him anymore.

He put the bike in gear and started down the street. The last image he had of her was Grant ushering her into the building.

Chapter Fifteen

Molly stood still until the last sound of the motorcycle had faded, then she shrugged off Grant's arm. She was so confused, and there was no way she wanted to have this conversation with Grant. Unfortunately, she couldn't think of a reason to send him away. Maybe it would be better this way. They could just get it over with.

"I came by last night, but you were gone," Grant said. His tone was light, but she heard the annoyance in his voice.

"I told you. I was out of town."

As they approached the front door of her condo, he handed her the box of roses and pulled out his key chain. "Allow me," he said, and smiled.

She grimaced. She'd forgotten that she'd given him a key to her place. Not that he'd used it very much. Grant rarely spent the night and his hours at the law firm meant that she was home long before he ever showed up. Maybe it had been one of those symbolic gestures, designed to make them feel connected. At the time it had probably worked, but right now she was tired and annoyed.

They walked into her condo. The living room was exactly as she'd left it just two weeks earlier. A neighbor had picked up her mail and put it on the kitchen table. She could see the pile from where she was standing.

Grant moved to face her, placed his hands on her shoulders and kissed her. He'd probably been going for her mouth, but she turned her head and his lips brushed against her cheek. She closed her eyes and tried to find something familiar and pleasurable about the contact, but all she could think about was how much it hurt to breathe. Dylan was really gone.

"So," Grant said, placing his keys on the counter dividing the eating area from the living room and taking the box of roses. "You were gone for a few days."

She watched him search for a vase. He found one on the top shelf of the pantry, then opened the box and began arranging the roses. They were beautiful. Dark red and fragrant.

"Yes. I needed some time to think. There's been a lot on my mind." She motioned to the flowers. "They're very beautiful. Thank you."

He continued to fuss with the roses. Her gaze drifted to his keys. Without thinking, she dropped the duffel, picked up the keys and began separating her house key from the rest. It only took a second to slide the metal off the ring and slip it into her pocket. He never even noticed.

When he was done, he brought the display into the living room and set it on the coffee table. Then he settled on the sofa and patted the cushion next to him.

Molly walked over and sat at the opposite end of the

couch. Grant didn't take the hint. He slid over and took both her hands in his.

His eyes were medium brown—nondescript. Neither attractive nor unattractive. She told herself it was wrong to keep comparing him with Dylan. Grant was a corporate lawyer, Dylan a maverick entrepreneur. They were nothing alike. Odd that they had both had impact on her life.

"I know what you're thinking," he said.

"I doubt that."

He peered at her with what she'd always called his "owl" look. As if he were trying too hard to appear wise.

"You're thinking that I'm going to be upset about your motorcycle-riding friend. I'll admit that it looked pretty bad, but I trust you, Molly. I've always trusted you. You are such a great woman and I can't believe how stupid I was."

She tried to pull back, but he only tightened his hold on her hands. "It's like this," he continued. "There was that big case I was working on. My job has a lot of pressure. I know you understand. Added to that, you and I had settled into a rut."

She opened her mouth to protest but didn't know what to say. She couldn't be right. He couldn't possibly be trying to blame his actions on *her*, could he?

"A rut?" she managed at last.

"Yes. We were doing the same things all the time. It's no one's fault. It happens. Between that and the long hours, well, I..."

She stared at him, waiting to hear this excuse. When he was silent she said, "You ran off with your secretary. We were supposed to be engaged and you went away with another woman. That's more than a rut, Grant. That's the entire Grand Canyon."

He shifted on the seat. "I can see this upsets you."

"You bet it does. You took off without warning. You called me from the hotel to tell me what you'd done. You even called collect. You were a coldhearted, selfish bastard and we both know it."

"All right." He rose to his feet and stared down at her. "You're going to be emotional about this. Fine. I can be logical for both of us. I'll admit my behavior was inappropriate. I shouldn't have run off with her. I won't take all the blame, though. She's very young and pretty. She was making a play for me and one day I stopped resisting. That was an error."

He was so calm. Molly didn't know whether to laugh or start throwing furniture in his general direction. "Spare me the details," she said.

He went on to explain how the trip to Mexico had been an impulse. When he started describing the white sandy beaches, she tuned him out. This wasn't getting them anywhere.

"What's your point, Grant?" she asked, cutting him off in midsentence.

He blinked, then motioned to the flowers. "I would have thought that was obvious. We need to reestablish our emotional connection. The intimacy and trust have been battered."

He'd run off with his twenty-two-year-old secretary and he considered their relationship battered. What would it take to seriously cripple it?

She watched him move around the room. He was treating the area like a courtroom. He was the counsel for the defense and she was—actually, she wasn't sure of her role in the whole charade. He was reasonably attractive, but she couldn't imagine loving him. Not anymore. Not ever, maybe. What had it been? A convenience? Another way of settling, of not expecting too much so if she lost she wouldn't hurt too much?

"Do you love me?" she asked.

"Molly, how can you ask that?"

"Because I want to know. Do you love me?"

"You're the woman I want to spent the rest of my life with. We'd talked about having children together."

"That's not an answer. Why aren't you with your secretary right now? What happened in paradise?"

Grant had the good grace to flush. "She's very young."

"And?"

He cleared his throat, then shoved his hands into his slacks pockets. She realized he was in a suit and that it was the middle of the day. He'd actually taken off work to come talk to her. Amazing. Then she glanced at the clock and realized he was here on his lunch hour.

"We didn't have that much to talk about," he admitted.

"I see."

"You should really be happy," he said. "I've gotten all of this nonsense out of my system. Before we were married and there was a chance to do harm."

So he thought no harm had been done. Oddly enough, he was right.

"How did you know I wasn't at work?" she asked. After all, he'd been gone and she hadn't had the chance to tell him about being let go.

"I went by the office Friday. Your boss told me you'd taken a couple of days off. He also mentioned you'd been given a promotion and a big raise. Congratulations."

"Oh, thanks."

"Actually, that dovetails nicely with our plans."

She didn't remember much about their plans. "In what way?"

"Now, after we're married and we sell your condo, we

can go house hunting. I can tell you now I was a little concerned about living here for too long. The address isn't that prestigious. Certainly that's important in my line of work.''

He didn't like her condo. Of course he didn't. She saw that now. She wondered if he'd liked anything about her. Maybe she'd been a convenience, too. Maybe he'd settled. If so, what was Grant hiding from?

She looked at him, at his bland face and the way he rocked back on his heels. There was no point in prolonging this, she thought, and rose to her feet. "I'll be right back," she told him.

Once alone in her bedroom, she crossed to the small jewelry box sitting on her dresser and pulled open the bottom drawer. A large ruby ring sat there. It was the engagement ring Grant had given her. He hadn't bought her a diamond because one of the senior partners' wives had told him she thought they were common. Molly remembered her disappointment because she'd always imagined wearing a pretty, sparkling diamond engagement ring. But she'd never told Grant.

She curled her fingers around the ring and returned to the living room. Grant still stood in the center of the room. She walked back to the sofa and leaned forward until she could rest her forearms on the cushioned top.

"I had a bad few days," she said. "That week you ran off with your secretary was probably the worst time of my life."

"I've told you I'm sorry," he said.

"I know and I accept your apology. But that wasn't all of it. You see, you called me on Tuesday, but first, on Monday, I was let go."

"You were fired?" He sounded incredulous. "But I spoke to your boss yesterday. He didn't say anything."

"They want me back."

"Good. So what's the problem?"

What, indeed? "You weren't here when that happened, Grant. I was alone. I tried to call you that night, but you weren't home. I realize now that you'd already left for Mexico. The very next day you phoned to tell me you'd run off with your secretary."

His shoulders hunched forward slightly. "I can't change what happened, Molly. What do you want me to say?"

"I want you to listen. I don't think you understand the impact all this had on me."

"I see. You're using this as an excuse to explain your behavior. Something *did* happen with that guy on the motorcycle."

"I'm not trying to justify anything, because I don't have to. You ran out on me, not the other way around." She shook her head. "You're not listening, Grant. Please. Hear me out. The day after you left, Wednesday, I found a lump in my breast. I was doing a self-exam in the shower and I—"

"Oh, my God! You have cancer."

Molly looked up in time to see him take a step backward. His expression tightened, as did his body language. He looked as if he were trying not to breathe in too deeply.

The last drop of compassion or duty or whatever she wanted to call it dried up. This man was nothing to her. She was having trouble figuring out what she'd ever seen in him in the first place. She wasn't sorry it was over— better to have learned it now than after they were married. The real sadness, though, was the contrast between his reaction and Dylan's. Dylan, who was only a friend, had been comforting and compassionate. Grant acted as if he'd just come in contact with a contagious disease.

"I don't have cancer," she said quietly as she straightened. "They removed the lump and checked it out. I'm fine."

"You must be relieved." He still looked shell-shocked.

"I am. But it's been over two weeks of complete hell. I didn't known whether I was going to live or die. You were supposed to care about me. You were supposed to be at my side, no matter what. Yet I was forced to go through this without you. I can't trust you and I know I don't love you anymore. I don't think I ever loved you."

She walked forward and held out the ring. Grant stared at her. "You can't mean that. I won't let you break our engagement." He frowned. "They're sure about the lump? It couldn't possibly be something, you know, fatal."

"The doctor got two opinions. They're sure and so am I." She walked to the door and held it open. "Goodbye, Grant."

He moved toward the entrance, then paused. She wondered what he would say to try to convince her not to get rid of him. A lawyer's closing arguments.

"You're making a big mistake," he said. "I'm not going to have any trouble replacing you. Can you say the same?"

She handed him the ring. After all this time, she didn't feel a thing for him. All she wanted was him out of her life.

"I can honestly say I don't give a damn," she told him, and shut the door behind him.

She leaned against the door frame and waited for the crush of emotions to fill her. It had been a difficult day, to say the least. She wasn't sure where she should go next or what she should do. Maybe for now she wasn't going to do anything.

Her lips curved up in a half smile. It wasn't every day that a woman got to toss around two engagement rings, she thought. The smile faded and she sank to the floor. As she pulled her knees up to her chest, the first tears began to fall.

"I don't know what I'm going to do," Molly said three days later. She was stretched out on the sofa, talking on the portable phone. She rolled onto her side. "I've settled two out of three issues in my life. That's worth something."

"I don't want to pressure you—" Janet said.

"Yes, you do," Molly interrupted with a smile.

"Okay." Janet chuckled. "Maybe just a little pressure. You know, enough to keep you motivated. I'm thrilled that you're healthy and I agree with your decision to dump Grant. But you have to make a decision about work. They're not going to hold the job open forever."

"I'm not asking them to. I said I would decide by the end of the month. Look, Janet, they fired me. I'm not going to jump through hoops just because they've changed their mind."

"What if they hire someone else in your place?"

"Then I'll find another job." She drew in a deep breath. "When everything was falling apart and I was waiting to hear from the doctor, I promised myself I wouldn't settle ever again. I want to live my life. I've been so afraid and I've made the safe choices. I'm done with that. Unfortunately, I don't know what that information really means to me, so I'm going to have to take the time to find out."

"I understand," Janet said slowly. "Except for one thing."

"Which is?"

"Why didn't you tell me you'd fallen in love with Dylan?"

Molly sat up. She supposed she shouldn't be surprised. Janet had always been able to read her perfectly. "How'd you guess?"

"When we talked while you were gone, you mentioned him all the time. How nice he was being, how much fun you were having. Then you stopped talking about him. I didn't think he'd stopped being wonderful, so I made the obvious leap. That something had happened between the two of you."

Molly clutched the phone. "It wasn't what you're thinking. We…" Her voice trailed off. "Will you be mad?"

"Oh, Molly. Don't worry about that. Dylan and I were through with each other years ago. I don't think about him and I'm sure he doesn't think about me. I'm very happy in my life."

Molly knew all that was true, but it was nice to hear the words as confirmation. "I didn't plan for anything to happen. It just did. He was so good to me and I'd always had a crush on him. One thing led to another and I realized I loved him."

"How does he feel about you?"

Molly smiled sadly. "He likes me a lot. He thinks I'm special. For reasons I still don't understand, he thinks I'm very pretty."

"That's because you *are* very pretty."

"Uh-huh, sure. You're my sister. You have to say nice stuff about me. But Dylan doesn't, so I guess he's telling the truth. He's so good and kind. I don't know why he agreed to go away with me, but I'll be grateful for that the rest of my life."

"You didn't tell him, did you?"

Molly closed her eyes. Here it was—the truth she'd been trying to hide from. She had told Dylan that she loved him. She supposed that in the back of her mind she'd hoped he would come looking for her. That he would ride up on his motorcycle and carry her away.

But that sort of thing didn't happen in real life. He wasn't a commitment kind of man and he was probably happy to have escaped her.

"I promised myself no regrets," she said. "So yes, I did tell him. He hasn't been in touch with me since. I'm okay with that," she added hastily, then stared out the window at the trees in the courtyard beyond. "He got me through a rough time. I have the memories and the strength. That's enough."

"Is it?" her sister asked.

"It has to be. So for now, I think about what I want to do. In the next week, I'm going to make some decisions. I might take the job offer or I might find something else. I've even been thinking about going back to school and getting my master's degree."

Janet sighed. "You're right about all of it. You have to decide. I'm sorry I bugged you."

"I'm not. It reminds me that you care and I appreciate that."

"Call me in a couple of days and let me know how you're doing, all right?"

"I promise."

They said their goodbyes and hung up. Molly *did* appreciate her sister's concern. She wasn't worried. The answer would come to her soon. She had faith and patience. She also had the satisfaction of knowing there was nothing with Dylan that she could regret. Oh, it would have been nice if he'd wanted to stay around, but she couldn't control that. She'd done her best. She knew the difference between not giving up without a fight and beating her head against a wall. If he wanted her, he knew where to find her. At least for now.

Dylan set the phone back in the receiver and glared at the offending instrument. His attorney was pressing him to make a decision. The offer from the large motorcycle manufacturing firm was more than fair—it was generous. There was no reason to say no. No reason at all, save that it didn't feel right.

Of course, in the past two weeks nothing had felt right. He'd learned how dark and cold the world could be when he didn't have Molly around to provide the warmth and light.

He missed her. He wanted her and he needed her. It was a hell of a state to find himself in. No matter how he tried, he couldn't forget their time together. Memories haunted him, making it impossible to eat, work or sleep. Just yesterday Evie had told him that if he didn't get an attitude adjustment and quick, she would quit. He couldn't even blame her. He'd been snapping at everyone.

It wasn't just because he missed Molly—he also regretted that he'd left her without telling her the truth. That he loved her. He, who had never loved anyone before.

He wasn't sure when it had happened. He still wasn't sure he even believed in love, except there was no other way to describe his feelings for her. She filled his mind until all other thoughts faded. At different times in the day he wondered what she was doing, what she was thinking. He wanted to be with her. He wanted to spend the rest of his life getting to know all of her. He wanted to learn her moods, discover the mysteries that made her such an incredible person. He wanted to touch her and hold her. He wanted to make love with her night after night, until the passion was a familiar friend that kept them warm till the break of dawn.

But—always but. He had no right to drop into her life. She'd made her decisions. She had a job and she had Grant. He couldn't show up and disrupt that. He wouldn't hurt her for the world.

If only he had something to offer her. Something of value. But he was just that kid from the trailer park. He didn't know how to be a husband or a father. He really didn't even know how to love; he just knew that he did. He would rather miss her than upset her in any way. So he didn't contact her, even though he ached to hear her voice and see her smile. He was the one who'd wanted to stay in touch, but he couldn't bring himself to just be friends. He was a coward.

He looked around his office, at all that he'd struggled with. At one time it had been a source of pride, but now he couldn't see the point. Without Molly, he had nothing.

He stood up and grabbed his jacket, then walked to the front of the building. Evie gave him a wary look.

"You going somewhere?" she asked, trying not to sound hopeful. With him out of the building, the mood would return to normal.

He nodded. "I'll be gone the rest of the day." He motioned to the phone. "Call my attorney and tell him I'll sign."

Her dark eyes widened. "You're letting the company go?"

He knew her concern wasn't for her job. He'd discussed the offer with all his employees and they knew their jobs were secure.

"Yeah. Somehow I've lost the drive to do it my way. This will be better for everyone."

With that, he left. His motorcycle was parked in front. He'd been driving it ever since he'd come back from spending those two weeks with Molly.

He started the engine, then headed for the freeway. He might not have the right to contact Molly directly, but that didn't mean he couldn't ask about her.

A little over an hour later he pulled into a west-side

underground parking structure. After locking his bike, he headed up to the twenty-first floor to have a brief conversation with Molly's fiancé.

The receptionist took one look at his black leather jacket and frowned. When he said he didn't have an appointment, her expression got even more wary. Dylan sighed and pulled out a business card. She read it twice, then her face softened into a welcoming smile.

"Mr. Black, it's so nice to meet you. My brother races and he has two of your custom motorcycles. Please, have a seat while I see what I can do about squeezing you in."

He found himself ushered to a plush sofa, plied with coffee and cookies and offered the current issue of everything from sports magazines to a national tabloid. Ah, the price of fame.

The receptionist disappeared to work her magic. Fifteen minutes later he was taken into Grant's office.

The slick attorney didn't bother getting up from behind his huge wood desk, nor did he express any surprise at Dylan's interruption. Instead he leaned back in his oversized leather chair and raised his sandy-colored eyebrows.

"What can I do for you, Mr. Black?"

Dylan hadn't thought far enough ahead to have planned what to say to Molly's soon-to-be husband. If he was to be completely honest with himself, he wanted to put the fear of God into the creep and warn him that if he ever ran out on her again he, Dylan, would make sure his running days were ended permanently.

Normally, he didn't like to show his hand, but in this case, there was no reason not to tell Grant what he was thinking. "Molly is very special. I want to make sure you understand that."

Grant rose to his feet and stared at Dylan as if he'd lost his mind. "Special? Is that what you call it?" Contempt filled his voice and he practically shuddered. "I don't know why you're here, but if she sent you to convince me to give her a second chance, forget it. I gave Molly the chance to come back and she didn't take it."

His words sank in slowly. Dylan played them over in his mind. "Molly didn't forgive you?"

Grant shrugged. "Good riddance, as far as I'm concerned. As I told her, I won't have any trouble replacing her. In fact, I already have dates with two different women this weekend. But she's going to be sorry. Men like me don't come along every day. She's not that pretty to begin with, and now that she's had that issue with the lump..." He shuddered. "I don't know which would have been worse—the cancer or her being disfigured."

Dylan reacted without thinking. Later he would tell himself that physically assaulting an attorney wasn't the least bit smart, but in his heart and his gut, he didn't give a damn. Let the little bastard sue him. It was worth it.

He crossed to where Grant stood, pulled back his arm and punched Grant hard in the face. While the other man was still in shock, he hit him in the stomach, then pushed him back into his chair. Grant collapsed with a loud huff of exhaled air.

Blood poured from his nose. He made choking, whimpering sounds. Dylan glanced at his knuckles, but he hadn't split the skin. Still, his hand tingled and he knew it would be sore for the next couple of days.

"That was for Molly," he said. "Don't you talk about her as if she's damaged goods. She's ten times the person you'll ever be. I'm glad she had the good sense to dump you. Stay away from her. If you bother her again, I'll be back to finish this."

Then he walked out. He passed through the reception area, not bothering to say goodbye to the pretty receptionist.

Nothing mattered to him except the fact that Molly hadn't taken Grant back. The idea gave him hope. Until he remembered she hadn't contacted him to tell him the news. Was she waiting for him to make the first move? After all, he'd been the one to insist that they stay in touch. And he hadn't done a thing about it. *He* knew the reason was he couldn't bear to hear about her reconciliation with Grant, but she didn't.

As he stepped into the elevator, the hope flared again and this time he couldn't deny it. That last day, Molly had told him she loved him. At the time he'd assumed she meant in a fraternal way. She loved him like a brother or a friend. Not romantically. But now he wasn't so sure. And it was starting not to matter.

Molly deserved the best. Someone incredible and courageous. He wasn't that man, but he didn't think he could step aside again. The past two weeks had taught him that his life wasn't worth living without her. There were many men who would be more her match, but there wasn't anyone who would love her more.

The elevator doors opened in the parking garage. He forced himself to step out, but he could barely move. He loved her. He, Dylan Black, the man who had sworn he didn't know if he even believed in love, cared more about Molly than anything in the world. She was all things to him. He loved her and he wanted to be with her. Forever.

He hurried toward his bike. Had he left things too long? She'd never actually said anything about wanting to make their relationship permanent. Could he risk asking? Could he risk letting her get away?

He knew the answer to the last question. He would do anything to be with her. She was the most amazing person he'd ever known. Not just her beauty and strength, but her gentleness, her humor, her compassion all drew him. He could imagine growing old with her. He loved her.

He started the motorcycle and headed for the street. He would go to her now, but first he had to make one stop.

Molly stared at the boxes filling her apartment. "Yes, I'm sure," she said as she secured the phone between her shoulder and head. "Janet, you're going to have to trust me on this. I want to start over somewhere else."

"I can't believe you're doing this," her sister said. "I can accept you're not going back to Grant. I never thought he was good enough for you. I even sort of understand not wanting to go back to your job. I think getting your M.B.A. is a great idea, but why are you putting your condo up for sale?"

"I told you. I want a fresh start. I want to get rid of my old life and begin anew." She thought about telling her sister that she'd already had three offers on the place and would be in escrow at the end of the week but figured Janet had heard about as much as she could handle for now.

"San Diego isn't that much farther south," she continued, and settled on the sofa. "I'll get a job and apply to the state college there. Trust me, Sis. I'm going to be fine."

"Are you sure?" Janet asked.

"Probably for the first time in my life. I'm nervous, but I'm not hiding and that's what's important."

She heard a crash, following by the wail of tears. Janet moaned.

"I've got a crisis. I'll call you later, okay?"

"Sure. Bye."

She hung up the phone, the glanced around at the cartons, some already sealed. She had figured out most of what she was keeping and what she was giving away. Maybe Janet was right and she was being hasty about moving, but

Molly didn't care. She couldn't stay in this place. Even returning to school wouldn't be enough to distract her. She'd promised herself that she would get on with her life no matter what. She'd been given a second chance and had learned an important lesson. She wasn't about to mess up again.

If only she could forget him, but she couldn't. Thoughts of Dylan filled her every waking moment, which was why she'd decided to move. In another city, she could make new memories that didn't include him. She would always love him—she'd come to accept that fact. But at least if she went somewhere else, she would be distracted.

"So that's everything," she said, rising to her feet.

"Not quite."

The voice was blissfully familiar. Every nerve in her body went on alert. For a second she thought she'd imagined the sound, that he was starting to haunt her days with the same regularity that he haunted her dreams.

"Molly?"

He sounded so real that she turned. "Dylan," she breathed when she saw him standing in the doorway, not sure she could believe her own eyes.

He wore jeans and his leather jacket. His hair was too long and he looked as if he hadn't slept in weeks. He was still gorgeous.

"What are you doing here?" she asked.

He stared at her, then smiled. "I prepared this great speech on the way over and now I can't remember a word." He crossed to her and took her hands in his. "So forgive me if this doesn't come out exactly right."

She didn't know what to think. Her heart was pounding so hard she thought it might jump right out of her chest. Her throat was tight; her entire body quivered. She wanted to believe that something wonderful was about to happen, but she was scared. Dear Lord, she still loved him so much.

"I can't let you go," he said. "I've tried and tried, but I keep thinking about you, about how much I want you and need you in my life. You are so incredibly strong and brave and you deserve someone so much better than me. I know that. But I also know no one will ever love you more." He squeezed her fingers tightly in his.

"I love you, Molly. All of you. I love how we laugh together, how smart you are, how you look first thing in the morning. I love how you feel in my arms and my bed. I want to be with you always. I want to marry you and make babies with you. I want my life to be an adventure...with you."

She was too stunned to move or speak. The words slowly filtered through her brain. He loved her. He wanted to marry her. *Her!*

He released one of her hands and reached into his jeans pocket. When he pulled out a ring, the last of the air fled her lungs.

This wasn't the plain gold band he'd offered her sister ten years ago. This was a beautiful round diamond that glinted in the afternoon light. He took her left hand and slid it in place.

"Molly Anderson, will you marry me?"

Then the feeling returned, along with her ability to breathe. Love and need and indescribable happiness flooded her. She flung herself at him and wrapped her arms around him.

"Yes, Dylan. I love you so much. I want to be with you forever."

She felt the tears on her face. Tears of joy. It was so right to be with him.

He kissed her then and they clung to each other. They both murmured words of love and happiness.

"I'm so glad you came back," she told him, wondering if she would ever get close enough to him. She felt as if she wanted to crawl inside him.

"I was going crazy," he admitted. "I figured you'd gone back to Grant and everything was perfect."

She grimaced. "Not a chance."

"I'm glad."

He held her some more, then they moved to the sofa and cuddled. "Tell me about the boxes," he said, indicating the cartons all around.

"I'm selling the condo." She looked into his dark eyes and smiled. "I didn't take the job offer, either. I decided I want to go back to college and get my M.B.A."

"The University of California at Riverside isn't all that far from me."

"Good." She snuggled closer. "I'm willing to confess I really liked your house. I wouldn't mind living there with you."

"How would you feel about working for a small but growing design firm? The boss can be tough at times, but I hear he's fair. He's also looking for a partner."

"You mean that?"

"I would very much like you to be a part of Black Lightning. If you're interested. I hate the business end of things. I want to get back to design."

It was too perfect, she thought, and kissed him. "Yes! I'd love to work with you. I figure I can get my M.B.A. in two years. In the meantime, I can learn about the industry, maybe work part-time."

"Until the babies start arriving."

She touched a hand to her belly. Children. "You're giving me everything I've ever wanted."

"You're my miracle, too," he said. He glanced around the room. "I've got the bike. Want to come home with me now? We can rent a truck later and come get your things."

"That sounds perfect. I want to make love with you in your bed."

He shuddered as his eyes darkened with desire. "Do you know how aroused I'm going to be the whole way there?"

She laughed. She *did* know.

She quickly packed a small bag, then started for the front door. Dylan paused.

"I have to make a fast call," he said.

"Go ahead."

He moved to the phone and dialed. After a minute, he said, "Evie, it's me. Call my lawyer back and tell him to cancel the deal. I'm not selling." He grinned and held the phone away from his ear. "Evie always starts shrieking when she gets excited."

"I'll fill you in when I get back to the office." He glanced at Molly and winked. "Don't expect me for about three days."

Molly felt herself smiling and blushing. The happiness bubbled up inside her. Six weeks ago, her entire world had fallen apart. Now she had all she'd ever dreamed of and more.

She glanced at the diamond ring sparkling on her left hand. It was a perfect symbol of their love. She knew they would survive all that life had to offer. They'd already learned so much, and they'd grown strong together. He was the kind of man she could depend on, just as he could depend on her. They were well matched and in love. There was nothing they couldn't do. Dylan had said she was his miracle. The best part of it all was that he was her miracle, too.

* * * * *

We, the undersigned, having barely survived four years of nursing school, do hereby vow to meet at Granetti's at least once a week, not to do anything drastic to our hair without consulting each other first and never, _ever_—no matter how rich, how cute, how funny, how smart, or how good in bed—marry a doctor.

Dana Rowan, R.N.
Lee Murphy, R.N.
Katie Sheppard, R.N.

Christine Flynn
Susan Mallery
Christine Rimmer

prescribe a massive dose of heart-stopping romance in their scintillating new series, **PRESCRIPTION: MARRIAGE**. Three nurses are determined _not_ to wed doctors— only to discover the men of their dreams come with a medical degree!

Look for this unforgettable series in fall 1998:

October 1998: **FROM HOUSE CALLS TO HUSBAND** by Christine Flynn

November 1998: **PRINCE CHARMING, M.D.** by Susan Mallery

December 1998: **DR. DEVASTATING** by Christine Rimmer

Only from

Silhouette®SPECIAL EDITION®

Available at your favorite retail outlet.

Take 2 bestselling love stories FREE

Plus get a FREE surprise gift!

Special Limited-Time Offer

Mail to Silhouette Reader Service™

P.O. Box 609
Fort Erie, Ontario
L2A 5X3

YES! Please send me 2 free Silhouette Special Edition® novels and my free surprise gift. Then send me 6 brand-new novels every month, which I will receive months before they appear in bookstores. Bill me at the low price of $3.96 each plus 25¢ delivery and GST*. That's the complete price, and a saving of over 10% off the cover prices—quite a bargain! I understand that accepting the books and gift places me under no obligation ever to buy any books. I can always return a shipment and cancel at any time. Even if I never buy another book from Silhouette, the 2 free books and the surprise gift are mine to keep forever.

335 SEN CH7X

Name	(PLEASE PRINT)
Address	Apt. No.
City	Province	Postal Code

This offer is limited to one order per household and not valid to present Silhouette Special Edition® subscribers. *Terms and prices are subject to change without notice.
Canadian residents will be charged applicable provincial taxes and GST.

CSPED-98   ©1990 Harlequin Enterprises Limited

Silhouette ® SPECIAL EDITION ®

Newfound sisters Bliss, Tiffany and Katie
learn more about family and true love
than they *ever* expected.

A new miniseries by
LISA JACKSON

A FAMILY KIND OF GUY (SE#1191) August 1998
Bliss Cawthorne wanted nothing to do with ex-flame
Mason Lafferty, the cowboy who had destroyed her
dreams of being his bride. Could Bliss withstand his irresistible charm—the second time around?

A FAMILY KIND OF GAL (SE#1207) November 1998
How could widowed single mother Tiffany Santini be
attracted to her sexy brother-in-law, J.D.? Especially
since J.D. was hiding something that could destroy the
love she had just found in his arms....

And watch for the conclusion of this series in
early 1999 with Katie Kinkaid's story in
A FAMILY KIND OF WEDDING.

Available at your favorite retail outlet. Only from

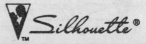

Available September 1998
from Silhouette Books...

World's Most
Eligible Bachelors

THE CATCH
OF CONARD COUNTY
by Rachel Lee

Rancher Jeff Cumberland: long, lean, sexy as sin. He's eluded every marriage-minded female in the county. Until a mysterious woman breezes into town and brings her fierce passion to his bed. Will this steamy Conard County courtship take September's hottest bachelor off of the singles market?

Each month, Silhouette Books brings you an irresistible bachelor in these all-new, original stories. Find out how the sexiest, most sought-after men are finally caught...

Available at your favorite retail outlet.

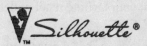

Silhouette®

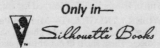

COMING NEXT MONTH

#1195 EVERY COWGIRL'S DREAM—Arlene James
That Special Woman!
Feisty cowgirl Kara Detmeyer could handle just about anything—except the hard-edged stockman escorting her through a dangerous cattle drive. Rye Wagner had stubbornly insisted he'd never settle down again, but a daring Kara had *every* intention of roping in the man of her dreams!

#1196 A HERO FOR SOPHIE JONES—Christine Rimmer
The Jones Gang
Vowing to reclaim his father's lost land, ruthless Sinclair Riker embarked on the heartless seduction of beguiling Sophie B. Jones. But Sophie's sweet, intoxicating kisses had cast a magical spell over him—and he ached to do right by her. Could love transform Sin into Sophie's saint?

#1197 THE MAIL-ORDER MIX-UP—Pamela Toth
Winchester Brides
Travis Winchester fought an irresistible attraction to his missing brother's mail-order bride. Even though he didn't trust Rory Mancini one bit, he married the jilted city gal after taking her under his wing—and into his bed. But he couldn't stop wonderin' if Rory truly loved her *unintended* groom....

#1198 THE COWBOY TAKES A WIFE—Lois Faye Dyer
Sassy CeCe Hawkins was forever bound to her late husband's half brother, Zach Colby. Not only was her unborn baby heir to the Montana ranch Zach desperately coveted—and half-owned—but a forbidden passion for this lonesome, tight-lipped cowboy left her longing for a lifetime of lovin' in his arms.

#1199 STRANDED ON THE RANCH—Pat Warren
When sheltered Kari Sinclair fled her overprotective father, she found herself snowbound with oh-so-sexy rancher Dillon Tracy. Playing house together would be a cinch, right? Wrong! For Kari's fantasies of happily-ever-after could go up in flames if Dillon learned her true identity!

#1200 OLDER, WISER...PREGNANT—Marilyn Pappano
Once upon a time, tempting teenager Laurel Cameron had brought Beau Walker to his knees. Then, she'd lit out of town and left Beau one angry—and bitter—man. Now she was back—pregnant, alone, yearning for a second chance together. Could Beau forgive the past...and learn to love another man's child?